TRUTH AND CONSEQUENCES

"All's fair in love and war," Jerry said softly.

"Is this love or war?" Rachel asked.

"We'll see," Jerry said and held out his hand to her.

Rachel reluctantly allowed him to draw her to her feet. Her body seemed to hum with physical desire—so much so that his hand clasping hers felt like a magnet drawing her to him. How many years had she known him? And his lips had never more than brushed her cheek or her lips. Now he held her against the length of him and warmed her mouth with his.

"Do you want me to stop, Rachel?" Jerry asked in a soft whisper in her ear, even as his hand caressed her breast and her nipple stiffened under the satiny fabric of her gown. "I want to make love to you, but I don't want you to do something you don't really want. Can you tell me the truth?"

But what was the truth? Would Rachel be making the same old mistake if she said yes? Or would she be seizing her one chance at happiness with this man whose words promised so much—and whose touch promised still more. . . .

THE HEALING TOUCH

Elizabeth Neff Walker

A SIGNET BOOK

SIGNET
Published by the Penguin Group
Penguin Books USA Inc., 375 Hudson Street,
New York, New York 10014, U.S.A.
Penguin Books Ltd, 27 Wrights Lane,
London W8 5TZ, England
Penguin Books Australia Ltd, Ringwood,
Victoria, Australia
Penguin Books Canada Ltd, 10 Alcorn Avenue,
Toronto, Ontario, Canada M4V 3B2
Penguin Books (N.Z.) Ltd, 182–190 Wairau Road,
Auckland 10, New Zealand

Penguin Books Ltd, Registered Offices:
Harmondsworth, Middlesex, England

First published by Signet, an imprint of Dutton Signet,
a division of Penguin Books USA Inc.

First Printing, April, 1995
10 9 8 7 6 5 4 3 2 1

 REGISTERED TRADEMARK—MARCA REGISTRADA

Printed in the United States of America

PUBLISHER'S NOTE
This is a work of fiction. Names, characters, places, and incidents either are
the product of the author's imagination, or are used fictitiously, and any resemblance to actual persons, living or dead, events, or locales is entirely coinciden-
tal.

With my sincere thanks to my
special friends Kay Turner and
Berniss Swearingen Benbrook
for their constant encouragement
and support.

Chapter One

S o, do you think they're going to make it?" Rachel Weis whispered. She was watching the bridal couple sip champagne from each other's glasses. Rachel had a glass of champagne of her own, which she raised to the couple, but her gaze had shifted to Jerry Stoner, who stood beside her.

"Hey, I'm a psychiatrist, not a fortune-teller," he protested, laughing. "But, yes, I think they will, given any luck."

"So luck is a part of it, huh?" Rachel mused. "I hadn't really thought of that. Hard work, persistence, love certainly, but luck, well, who would have thought?"

Jerry lifted his shoulders negligently and took a sip of his champagne. "Hey, I'm just trying to disclaim any inside knowledge here. They're both good people. Like you and Dan. Like me and Barbara. But Dan died and Barbara divorced me. Let's call that bad luck."

"I see." Rachel linked arms with him, giving a little arm-hug in the process. "I like the concept, Jerry. You take blame out of the equation. We lawyers have a hard time with that, though."

"The newest concept is personal responsibility,"

Jerry said. "Lawyers are going to have an even harder time with that."

"Thank heaven I don't do personal injury," she said, sighing. "Working for the medical center is tough enough. One of these days everyone's going to go to arbitration."

"And you'll be a great arbitrator."

"Probably. Who's the beauty with Ralph Benninger?"

Jerry shook his head, then cocked it to one side. "Actually, I did hear someone say. A pediatric intern, I think."

"Wow." Rachel considered the statuesque young woman, whose blond hair hung down to the middle of her back. From across the room it was evident that she felt a little uncomfortable in the gathering, probably because she didn't know anyone there. "Maybe we should talk to her. Ralph isn't paying much attention, though heaven knows why."

"That's what I like about you, Rachel. Always ready to jump in and rescue someone, even if she's a gorgeous someone who probably doesn't need rescuing."

Rachel grimaced. "Just because she's beautiful doesn't mean she can't feel uncomfortable at a wedding where she doesn't know very many people. She doesn't even know Cliff and Angel, does she?"

"I doubt it. And they're way too preoccupied to worry about one wedding guest at the moment. We'll pick up the slack, shall we?"

"To the rescue." Rachel gave a toss of her head, whose curly brown hair was slightly graying. "We'll have her shaped up in no time. And you might even warn her about Benninger's reputation."

"Me? You must be kidding. Besides, I don't know what you're talking about."

"Oh, right."

They strolled companionably across the living room toward the windows overlooking downtown San Francisco. The views from Twin Peaks were spectacular; Clifford Lenzini's house made a perfect location for a small, intimate wedding. Jerry hadn't been at all surprised to hear they were holding it there. He'd been astonished, however, that Cliff and Angel had managed to invite just enough people not to overwhelm the spacious room. The bride's family, the groom's family, and no more than two dozen other people were reasonably accommodated for the brief ceremony.

Jerry loved watching the videotaper wander through the group catching people in conversation against the backdrop of the Mediterranean-looking city. Cliff and Angel, well, they made you almost believe in love and marriage again. Not that Jerry was totally cynical about marriage. He'd been divorced for five years, was on perfectly reasonable terms with his former wife, and had two terrific sons from the union. It would be unreasonable to ask for more than that, and a rewarding career, at forty-seven, wouldn't it?

Rachel was already introducing herself to the young woman, who informed them that her name was Erika Amundsen. Jerry was surprised that at close range she was even more attractive than she'd appeared from across the room. She wore very little makeup, and her face had the fetching open look that one associated somehow with

shepherdesses in the Alps. Heidi, he thought irre-
levantly. She should have braids and be wearing a
dirndl or something. Erika was, in fact, wearing
a deep blue dress that shimmered in the light. She
looked wholesome and athletic, yet elegant and
approachable. Quite a combination, Jerry thought.

"You're training at Fielding?" he asked.

"Yes, in pediatrics. I've seen you there," she
admitted with a self-conscious smile. "You're a
psychiatrist, aren't you?"

"Right. Have you heard bad things about psychiatrists?"

"Oh, no." She frowned. "Though people don't
seem to know quite how to act around them, do
they? As if they were going to be able to tell something awful about you just by looking at you."

Very astute, too, Jerry decided. "That's about
right, but we're no more mind readers than anyone else."

"Still, if we say certain things, we can give ourselves away," Erika pursued.

"Give yourself away how?"

"Well, for instance, if I were to say, oh, I don't
know, to say that I hated hurting little children,
you might easily assume that I actually did hurt
little children."

"Do you?" Rachel asked.

Erika sighed. "Yes, actually I do. Not out of cru-
elty, of course, but because medical treatment often hurts the patient. Spinal taps, blood drawings,
all sorts of things. They say I'll get used to it."

Rachel looked at Jerry questioningly. When he
nodded imperceptibly, she said, "Yes, that must be
very difficult," and excused herself to visit the
bathroom. Jerry unobtrusively guided Erika away

from the others toward a corner of the room. "We have a program of intern and resident support," he said. "Do you know about it?"

She nodded but looked down at the glass of champagne that had hardly been touched. "No one else seems to find it so disturbing. I think I have to learn to steel myself."

"Some of us have fewer defenses than others. There's no shame in asking for help. I'm sure you realize that."

Erika met his eyes, but briefly. "There's very little time."

"There has to be enough time to take care of yourself. Otherwise everything else is ultimately unsuccessful." Jerry ran his hand through his graying hair. He wondered if he'd done a presentation to Erika's residency group. "Come by my office next week and we'll talk."

"You're always busy."

His brows rose. "Have you come by when the door's been shut?"

She shrugged. "Once or twice I've noticed it. I hadn't decided whether to talk with you."

Jerry bent toward her, earnest in his empathy. "If you've thought about it, then you should come. If you like, we can make an appointment."

"No, no, I'll just drop by some day." She shook off her seriousness with a twist of her head, a warm, open smile appearing to light her face. "This is no time to trouble you with my problems. It's such a lovely place for a wedding, isn't it? Dr. Lenzini's sister showed me around a little."

"It's a great place," he agreed, and added, "I'll count on seeing you next week."

Erika's date for the occasion, Ralph Benninger,

a pediatric neurosurgeon, appeared at her side, nodded to Jerry, and said, "There's someone I want you to meet, Erika."

Jerry watched them walk away, a thoughtful look in his eyes. Rachel appeared beside him and said, "I trust I was the height of discretion, Jerry. Surely you can help her adjust to the downside of pediatrics. She looked for a minute as though she'd been set on a high wire without a safety net. Poor kid."

"I'm sure we can help. It's just a little disconcerting that her residency adviser hasn't sent her before this. Maybe she's keeping quiet about it."

"And just couldn't resist unburdening herself to you. You have a real touch, Jerry. They're lucky to have you."

"You'd hardly know it," he grumbled. "Associate professor after twenty years."

"If you won't play the game, you can't expect to win."

Jerry had known Rachel for most of those twenty years, not because she'd worked at the medical center all that time, but because they were neighbors. The two couples, Rachel and Dan, Barbara and Jerry, had exchanged dinners several times a year. Not enough to be the closest friends, but to know each other's children, each other's concerns about work and leisure. Nowadays, when he needed a companion to take to some hospital function, he asked Rachel, who would know the participants and who knew him well enough to make it unnecessary for him to try to impress her. Sometimes, though, he was almost sorry she knew as much as she did about him. He couldn't, for instance, get away with bemoaning his fate at Fielding Medical Center as far as promotion went. He hadn't bothered to watch out for whose toes he stepped on over the years, so long as he felt certain there was a cause to be championed, a patient to be protected.

His brown eyes crinkled at the corners now. "There are people who believe I should have been recognized for my intrinsic merit, in spite of any chaos I may have caused over the years."

Rachel snorted. "Who are these people? I've never met any of them."

"Such an unbecoming lack of faith." Before he could taunt her any further, they were accosted by the newly married couple. Jerry kissed the bride, Angel Crawford, and shook hands vigorously with the groom, Clifford Lenzini. "I knew you could do it if you put your minds to it," he said.

Cliff, a giant of a man, general surgeon and all-around male chauvinist, said, "We couldn't have done it without your help, could we, Angel?"

"Probably not." Angel squeezed Jerry's hand. "Actually," she confided, perfectly loud enough for Cliff to hear, "he hasn't the slightest idea how true that is."

Angel was in the last year of a family practice residency and had had her moments of doubt about her prospective husband's sexist attitudes. Jerry knew that his confidence in the relationship had helped her overcome her concerns. He winked playfully. "He's a lot to take on. Just remember we're here if you need us."

Cliff had turned his charm on Rachel. "I'm glad Jerry had the good sense to bring you, Rachel. He's just moldering around in that condo of his, not going out enough to need to polish his good shoes. When we get back from our honeymoon, which is going to last about two days because of Angel's residency, we'll have you both over to dinner. I cook a wicked Cornish game hen."

"He incinerates them," Angel explained. "I've seen him do it with my own two eyes."

Jerry felt a brief exhilaration in their presence. Their youth, their good looks, their energy, their love—it all invigorated him. Though he realized forty-seven wasn't all that old these days, and that he had at least twenty years left of his career, he had begun recently to question just what he'd accomplished in his life. Whether it was enough to be where he was. Had he sat back and let things happen to him? Had he drifted along doing the work he liked and ignored the things that would have obtained more power and prestige and money? Hell, he had a lot to show for his age, he reminded himself. The important things.

Cliff put an arm around Jerry's shoulders. "Thanks for offering the cottage during your month, Jer. But Angel deserves to be waited on hand and foot on her break, and I'm just not the type to do that. Some hotel in Hawaii seemed far more appropriate."

"Then they can wait hand and foot on him, too," Angel explained.

"I did think of that," Cliff admitted. "But it was for my one and only bride that I chose this particular place, Angel being far too busy to look into hotels on Maui. It's not like the old days," he sighed, "when no matter how busy a woman was she did it for her husband. Looked into the travel arrangements, I mean."

"Obviously we haven't shaken it out of him yet,"

Angel said, poking her newly wedded mate in the side with an elbow. "Rachel is not interested in hearing your observations on how women used to behave. She'd probably have a few things to tell *you*."

"I might at that," Rachel agreed. "But I won't."

Jerry looked curious. "Will you tell me?"

"I don't think so."

"Too bad. We psychiatrists can always learn something new. It might be just what I need to help some poor woman who's struggling with the same issues."

Angel lifted her brows. "I suppose all psychiatrists are voyeurs to some extent, don't you, Rachel?"

"Probably. All for a good cause, of course."

"Of course," Jerry said. "We don't call ourselves voyeurs. We call ourselves good listeners."

"Right. Like a surgeon is a magic healer." Cliff grinned down at his wife. "And a family practice doctor is a medicine man . . . um . . . or woman."

"Very good." Angel beamed at him. "He's such a quick learner."

"It's a good thing he's not an older dog like me," Jerry said. "Teaching us new tricks is so time-consuming."

"What's got *you* down?" Cliff demanded. His shaggy brows descended low over his eyes and he cocked his head with amusement. "Feeling sorry for yourself just because it's a wedding?"

"Not at all. I'm delighted for the two of you and it's a very festive occasion."

"He looks very festive, doesn't he?" Cliff asked, of no one in particular. "You probably need a break, too, Jerry. You've been working too hard."

Jerry shrugged. "Maybe I'll go to the cabin myself for a few days. They can get along without me at Fielding."

"Not until you've seen the pediatric intern," Rachel reminded him.

"There's always someone," Jerry grumbled, but he looked more cheerful. "When are you going to start the dancing?" he asked Cliff.

"Right now."

Cliff gave the trio a prearranged signal and swung Angel into his arms. Their guests backed up along the walls of the room and allowed the newlyweds to claim the floor to themselves for a few minutes before they began joining the dancing. Jerry offered a hand to Rachel who accepted it with a reminiscent smile. It was not a reminiscence of dancing with him, Jerry knew, because he had never danced with her before. There weren't, after all, so many occasions he attended where dancing was offered as part of the entertainment. And he wasn't a particularly good dancer, come to that, though he rather liked the activity. Rachel didn't seem to mind. She followed his lead with ease and merely shrugged when he stepped on her foot.

"It takes a minute or two to catch on," she said.

Not that he'd danced much with Barbara. There had seemed plenty of other things to do—raising the kids, his work, her work, camping and hiking and swimming and tennis. He couldn't actually remember if Barbara had liked dancing. If she had, she'd certainly never pushed him to do it more often. Or maybe he just didn't remember that, either.

"What are you thinking about?" Rachel asked. "You look puzzled."

"Oh, nothing much," he admitted, looking down at her head of curls only slightly touched with gray. Barbara had been dyeing her hair even before she left him five years ago. "About dancing and Barbara and matters totally unrelated to being here."

"It's the wedding, don't you think? I've been thinking about Dan, too, off and on all day. And about the day we were married. God, we were young. I look back at pictures of our wedding and I can hardly remember looking like that." She grinned up at him. "We were married on a beach. Did you know that?"

He shook his head. "I had no idea. Hippies, were you?"

"Something like that." She sighed. "Free spirits, we said. Unencumbered by conventions and societal restrictions. His parents were horrified when they found out, and we had to go through a formal family party with them, with about a hundred people. My folks didn't mind so much. They paid for a honeymoon to Mexico for us."

He and Barbara had had a traditional Jewish wedding, followed by a honeymoon in Europe. There was money on both sides. They had been right out of college. Hardly a ceremony on the beach.

Jerry thought he was dancing better now. Maybe it was just that Rachel had caught on to his oddities. And then the trio switched from slow to fast music and he glanced around apprehensively. What kind of fast dancing did people do now? He'd never kept up with that sort of thing.

"Maybe we should wait until they play something slow again," he suggested.

"Coward." Rachel laughed and followed him to the sidelines, where they watched the energetic younger people, and Ralph Benninger, dance every which way, their arms and legs and torsos thrashing about like palsy victims.

"A neurologist would have a field day," Jerry muttered.

"Maybe you're hungry," Rachel suggested sympathetically. "There's a terrific spread in the dining room. I noticed it on my way back from the bathroom."

"What if we're not supposed to eat it yet?" he said, but followed behind with interest.

"Oh, I don't think they'll mind."

There were already a number of guests filling plates with mouthwatering delicacies. Jerry was indeed hungry, only remembering then that he'd skipped lunch to check on a patient before picking Rachel up. "I love all this little stuff," he said, helping himself to the bite-size treats. "I could live on it. What I should do is make an arrangement with a caterer to drop off a barrel a month and I'd never have to try to cook again."

"I thought you only heated TV dinners," Rachel said.

Jerry wrinkled his nose and sighed. "I did, for the first couple of years. But they're as boring as the cafeteria food. It would be a lot simpler if people didn't have to eat."

"Wouldn't it?" Rachel hesitated before the miniature cheesecakes but eventually put one on her plate. "You could go to the Price Club and stock up."

"Don't think I haven't considered it." Jerry finished heaping his plate and motioned toward the small balcony off the side of the room. "I imagine we can sit out there if you don't mind fuchsias in our faces."

Cliff Lenzini had fuchsias of every variety around his house, in pots, in baskets, climbing up trellises, growing as bushes. The view from most windows included pink and white and purple and red hanging blooms, large and small, making the house feel festive, as though in a confetti snowstorm of its own. Jerry, who wasn't as fond of fuchsias as Cliff, climbed with reasonable care over one pot and pushed another basket out of the way so that Rachel could slip past. There was only a slit of view available to them of the city, but the spot was private and quiet.

Rachel leaned back against the house, balancing her plate on the corner of the railing. "I've been meaning to tell you that my career has taken a twist."

Surprised, Jerry looked up from the pasta salad he was inspecting. "Oh? What kind of twist?"

She seemed to hesitate. "I'm a little tired of the law. Sometimes it seems so irrelevant."

"Maybe you liked it better when you worked for the civil liberties groups."

She shrugged. "Better than helping the medical center save its butt, certainly. But that's not it. That doesn't seem to be where the important things are happening. Hell, I'm at a medical center where every day there are life-and-death decisions being made, and being made sometimes without considering all the aspects of the case. I don't mean just medical but social and moral and ethical. For some time now I've been taking medical ethics courses. They intrigue me."

Should he have known that? Jerry helped himself to a bite of egg roll before saying anything. "So how does it work? Do you quit your job at Fielding and set up a practice, or what?"

"Fielding doesn't want to pay legal rates for such nebulous services, but I've politicked and they've agreed to hire me, part-time, at a reduced rate. I'll have a private consulting service as well. Fielding isn't the only place in the area that needs medical ethics services. I've never been able to forget some of the decisions that were made when Dan was dying."

"Hmmm. I remember. But, Rachel, it's a big step to make."

"At my age," she added, since he hadn't.

"At any age," he said, realizing that that indeed was what he had meant. Rachel, too, was in her forties. Changing careers, going to part-time, starting up a consulting service, taking reduced fees—it all sounded pretty shaky to Jerry. He knew Dan hadn't left Rachel a rich woman, what with the medical costs at the end. "So tell me about it."

Her eyes snapped with irritation. "You make me feel like a patient, Jerry. What I want you to say is, That's great, Rachel. Congratulations. I hope you'll really enjoy it."

Obviously he'd blown it. It was not like him to blow it, at least not with patients. He didn't seem to be able to concentrate on anyone else this afternoon. His thoughts kept swirling around himself and his life, instead of outward on the people he was with. "I'm sorry, Rachel. Of course I'm delighted for you. You'll be very good at it. I'm just surprised that your interest in medical ethics was strong enough to make you decide to actually give up your legal position."

She shook her head. "I still hear a lack of enthusiasm, Jerry. But that's all right. I guess I didn't convey my real excitement. This is something special for me. Something that makes me resonate right down to my core. I'm dying to do it."

"Then I'm really happy for you. Not everyone gets a chance to do what they want to do, and I know the last few years haven't really been satisfying for you." He leaned over and kissed her cheek, since his hands were occupied and he couldn't hug her. "Really, Rachel, I think this is great!"

"Thanks." She seemed reasonably content with his eventual response, motioning with her fork to make a point. "Everything hinges on the patient's right to know, when you get down to it. Of course there will always be some patients who don't really want to know, and you have to accommodate for that."

Rachel continued to talk, but Jerry was only half listening. Here was Rachel, he thought, a woman his own age, with no more security than he, willing to take big risks with her life over something that interested her. She had found something that animated her in a way he hadn't seen before—her eyes were sparkling and her face radiated her excitement.

Did anything still excite him that way? Well, he loved his work, it was true. He felt challenged and rewarded by it, as well as frustrated and disappointed at times. His modest position at the medical center was something of an embarrassment, and, though it was where he had landed himself through want of tact or kowtowing to the higher-ups, he wasn't perfectly sure he didn't want to have a better position. He shouldn't have let them postpone a full professorship last time. Maybe he should have given an ultimatum—give me my just deserts or I'll leave.

But would he have? If you threaten to leave, you have to be prepared to follow through. And he couldn't really think of a place he'd prefer practicing psychiatry than Fielding. How could he give up treating truly devastating mental illness and indoctrinating young physicians in the science of psychiatry as well as its art for a practice where he saw the same individuals each week, or examined and evaluated workers' compensation cases?

There was something disturbing about having been passed over, though. He really did believe, despite Rachel's teasing, that he should have been recognized for his efforts, his expertise, even if he had occasionally proved a thorn in someone's side. Where was the fairness in passing him by? Jerry sighed inwardly. Didn't that sound naive? Fairness. As if he thought he should expect fairness from the world. If his boss ever heard him say something like that, he'd think Jerry needed to be locked up with the other crazies on 4 West.

Rachel was regarding him curiously. Blown it again! "I'm sorry," he apologized. "My mind just seems to keep wandering today, Rachel. It's not you, and it's not the wedding. I'm just," he shrugged, "out of it, I guess."

"It's too soon to leave, so maybe we should go back in and dance. That might distract you."

Jerry couldn't tell if she was hurt by his inattention. That was the nice thing about Rachel: she was so practical and easygoing. He followed her back into the living room, where Ralph Benninger was dancing a little too closely with Erika Amundsen and Cliff and Angel were surrounded by a small group, including Angel's former roommate Nan LeBaron, who were determined to get them to cut the wedding cake and be off on their honeymoon.

Just another social occasion. Just another wedding. Just another day. There was nothing to get so distressed about, was there? Jerry was grateful it was a slow dance. He pulled Rachel into his arms and maneuvered her around the other couples. He was better than some of the younger men at slow dancing, probably because of his age.

Chapter Two

The phone was ringing when Jerry brought Rachel to her door. "I won't stay," he said. "Go ahead and get it."

Though the machine was on and she could easily have said so, Rachel smiled and thanked him and hurried in to snatch up the receiver. She watched absently through the living room window as he climbed back into his car. It was her daughter Jennifer, who lived in Boston and often called on weekends because of the lower rates. A very practical child, much like her mother, Rachel supposed.

"How was the wedding?" Jennifer asked.

"Very nice. Small, comfortable, but elegant, too. You remember Cliff Lenzini, I'll bet. He was that big bear of a man, Jerry's friend who's a surgeon. You'd have met him at the hospital."

Jennifer, at twenty-five, had not quite gotten over the trauma of her father's death. Rachel tried to help her by being matter-of-fact about it these days, but Jennifer resisted. "Not the one who made so much trouble, I hope."

"No, that was Dr. Jefferson. Cliff is one of the good guys."

"You have to keep a scorecard," Jennifer complained. "Yeah, actually, I remember Dr. Lenzini. He's hard to forget."

"Well, he and Jerry are good friends, so we were invited, but only half the people were from the medical center. One young girl, though, reminded me a little of Trish."

"How come?"

"Oh, she looked a little like Trish, blond and tall. Only much blonder and much taller. But she was troubled about her residency in pediatrics. I've often thought Trish worries about her capabilities as a teacher, even though she doesn't say so. Maybe she talks about it more with you."

"Are you kidding? She wouldn't give me the satisfaction of seeing her anything but perfect." Jennifer groaned. "That sounded rotten. I didn't mean it like that. She just doesn't like to seem vulnerable."

"No, and she is, I think, more than you are. Heaven knows why."

"Obviously it's because I take after you," Jennifer teased. "Nerves of steel. That's what everyone says, anyhow. Some guy was coming on to me in the supermarket the other day and he asked what I did and when I told him I was a private investigator he nearly dropped his teeth."

"Surely that didn't surprise you." Rachel had tossed her purse on the coffee table and now stretched out on the sofa, kicking off her shoes. "You only tell them that if you want them to leave you alone."

"Not necessarily. It's a kind of test. If they leave me alone, then I know they wouldn't be worth seeing."

Very practical, Rachel thought with a smile. "So

another doctor has been gobbled up, Jennifer, and there you are without a life partner."

Her daughter laughed. "In Boston you stumble over doctors every few feet, and I haven't met one who turns me on yet. Sorry. You may have to wait a long time for this kid to make it to the altar."

"Oh, I can handle that." It was a standing joke between the two of them, the Jewish mother pressing her daughter to marry a doctor. And yet, Rachel knew, she'd feel a little more comfortable if her daughter would indeed find a nice man to settle down with. How trite of me, she thought. Especially with Jennifer, who was independence personified. Now with Tricia it was another matter entirely. Trish would benefit from the steadiness of a solid husband in her life, someone to show her she was appreciated and talented and dear. Jennifer didn't seem to need the same amount of reassurance.

"Actually," Jennifer said, rather slowly, "I did meet someone this morning. A guy, I mean. Only . . ."

"Only what?" Immediate visions of a Boston strangler type jumped to Rachel's mind. After all, Jennifer was likely to run into some strange types in her line of work.

"Only he's much older. Like almost your age."

Funny what that did to Rachel. It made the breath stop in her chest. It made her left hand clench. It made her think again about Dan dying before Jennifer, in a rebellious phase, had completely made her peace with him. "How did you meet him?" she asked.

"Oh," Jennifer's voice sounded like a shrug, "he's Caitlin's uncle, actually. When I went to pick

her up for tennis he was dropping off an old
sofabed for her new apartment. He came along
with us to the tennis courts and made fun of us."

Clever fellow. Well, Rachel reminded herself,
Jennifer was a levelheaded young woman who
knew what she wanted. "Did you tell him you
were a private investigator?"

"Yeah. He was intrigued."

I'll bet. Rachel sighed, but not into the phone.
"What does he do?"

"Some kind of advertising, I think. We didn't really get into it. I don't suppose I'll see him again,
but he was kind of interesting."

You'll see him again, Rachel thought. "He's not
married, is he?"

"Mom! What do you think I am? Of course he's
not married. That's one of the advantages of his
being someone Caitlin is related to—I don't have
to worry about whether he's lying to me or not."

"Do men lie to you a lot?"

"Sure. They think it's some kind of game. Remember my line of work, Mom."

Rachel sighed, this time into the phone. "Yes,
dear, I remember it."

"I lie to them, too, of course, in the line of
duty."

"Of course."

"And sometimes even not in the line of duty, if
it's easier."

Rachel didn't quite know whether she wanted
to pursue that line any further. "I told Jerry about
my ethics consulting service today."

"I'll bet he was excited for you."

The kids had known Jerry most of their lives.
Rachel knew they liked his being around to keep

an eye on her. "Well, he was, after a fashion. But he seemed distracted. Must have had something on his mind."

"Probably some patient who thinks he's Satan and is threatening to kill him," Jennifer suggested, in her most bloodthirsty voice.

Rachel laughed. "I hope not. Weddings—and funerals, too—sometimes remind people of the past. You get to thinking about when you were young and how your life has gone."

"Were you thinking about Dad?"

"A little. I remembered our wedding day. I was telling Jerry how Dan and I got married on the beach."

"I'll bet he did something like that, too."

"Nope. Apparently he had a very traditional wedding. It just goes to show you, doesn't it?"

"It does, when he was the one who ended up with the long hair and Dad in a pin-striped suit."

"Jerry's had his hair cut a little. It's still long, but not as long as it was."

Jennifer whistled. "Wow! Is he bucking for professor or something?"

"I'm not sure. He wasn't talking, just thinking."

"Well, he'll tell you sooner or later. You guys are buddies."

Yes, and it had been great having a buddy these last few years, Rachel realized. She hoped whatever was going on with Jerry wasn't going to spoil that. She was about to say something more when she heard Jennifer's call waiting beep. "Go ahead and get that, honey."

Jennifer was back in a moment, a certain tension in her voice. "It's . . . uh . . . Caitlin's uncle,

Mom. If you don't mind, I think I'd rather not have to call him back."

"Sure. No problem. It was good talking to you. All my love." She hung up the phone with a shiver of trepidation. Caitlin's uncle. Almost as old as me. And Jennifer barely twenty-five. Well, that's the sort of thing that happened these days, Rachel knew. It was just that she had hoped it wouldn't happen to her daughters. Somehow it didn't seem quite fair. But who said life was fair?

Rachel gathered up her shoes and wandered back to her bedroom, where pictures of her family dotted the bureau and hung on the walls. There were pictures of her own parents, and pictures of herself as a child with her brother and sister, and pictures from a variety of ages of her own children. She had often, in the years since Dan's death, stood before a deceptive picture of the two of them at their wedding. Something about the photograph made it look as though they were standing in front of a sparkling waterfall. It was a soft, glowing study of just their faces, staring into each other's eyes. It spoke of love and commitment and romance and youth. Rachel would often turn from it to the last good picture of Dan before his death. He was squinting because of the sun on a vacation in Hawaii and he looked tanned and vital and happy.

Dan had been a hippie carpenter when she met him. He'd dropped out of college to pursue his interests (mostly in obscure musical instruments) but was earning his living working on building sites. But because he was extremely bright, and surprisingly ambitious, eventually he had finished school and gone on to get a master's in business

administration and had ended up owning a construction company in the city. He had liked the
ties he kept with the blue-collar workers. He had
prided himself on never looking down on them, on
respecting their abilities and their contribution.
He had loved going to job sites and talking with
them, even pitching in when some sort of crisis
arose. But he had lost his taste for beer.

And you couldn't very well swill wine on a job
site at the end of the day. Rachel considered one
of the photos of Dan in his hard hat and a suit.
What's wrong with this picture? was always her
first reaction to it. Hard hat and business suit,
bridging two different cultures, really. But Dan
had been good at that because he'd always related
to people who worked with their hands. He was
infinitely patient working with wood himself,
spending hours lovingly sanding shelves for a
bookcase or mitering corners for a picture frame.
It didn't seem right that he should have died so
young.

Rachel stepped out of the skirt of her green silk
suit and hung it in the closet. The jacket would
need to be pressed before she wore it again, but
she put it back in as well, and then the blouse.
Standing there in her slip she realized she had intended to invite Jerry in for dinner if they hadn't
eaten enough at the wedding, and then maybe
they would have gone out later to a movie. Instead
she was alone, with thoughts of Dan making her
feel sad and lonely.

Not that Jerry would have been great company
tonight. She hadn't seen him distracted this way
before, but it would have been a struggle to keep
his thoughts on matters at hand. He was better

off, she supposed, being by himself to think things through. And she to don a pair of lounging pajamas and fix herself a pot of tea and watch something on the VCR that she'd taped during the week for later viewing. She grimaced at herself in the full-length mirror. A truly exciting evening.

Jerry had been relieved to hear Rachel's phone ringing. He really wasn't up to spending the evening with someone, especially not someone who expected him to be enthusiastic for her. He much preferred going home where he could soak in his hot tub and try to investigate his own frame of mind.

When he pulled into the parking garage under his condo he realized, perhaps for the first time, that the hot tub was the only reason he'd bought it. Not that he was stuck in the Marin-County-peacock-feather-and-hot-tub syndrome. Hot tubs struck him as more relaxing than sexually stimulating. He had in fact seldom been in his own hot tub with anyone other than his grown sons, who were far from shy about their bodies, due to his own casual approach to nudity and life in general.

So why, he wondered as he let himself into the nondescript, beige-colored condo, did he feel so churned up today? It was more than Cliff's wedding. He had been feeling like this for several weeks, when he looked back. Ordinarily he was easygoing, flowing with the work and the patients and his friends and his family. His divorce was old news. He'd had two relatively long-lasting relationships in the time since then, but hadn't wished to make either of them permanent. Permanence didn't seem quite permanent anymore.

Jerry went first to the balcony, where he checked the thermometer on the hot tub, turned the heat up, and removed the plastic bubble cover. Then he returned to the bedroom where he stripped naked, tossing his clothes on a chair and wrapping himself in a kimonolike robe. He wandered into the kitchen and poured himself a glass of bottled water over ice. The champagne had given him a slight headache.

When he lowered himself into the water it hadn't quite reached the temperature he wanted, but it was easier to warm up along with the water than to lower oneself into an already hot tub. Sitting on the redwood shelf he could stretch his feet across to the bench opposite and turn on the jet with his toes. He took a sip of the cold water and rested his head back against the wooden deck. Nothing felt quite as luxurious as soaking in his private spa, with the bubbles stirring past him like champagne. Given the bland nature of his condo unit, given the boring neighborhood in which his building was located, he would still have chosen this place just because of the hot tub.

He supposed he could have found a house with a hot tub, or added one to a place he bought, but at the time that had seemed like too great an effort. Certainly he hadn't wanted to stay in his old house once Barbara left. Here he could at least look out over a limited view of the ocean from the hot tub.

His legs and arms began to relax. The water floated up and down on the black hair of his belly as he shifted farther down on the seat. He closed his eyes against the late afternoon sun gleaming off the ocean. Maybe it was the fall days that were depressing him, the difference in the light, the coming of winter. But autumn was usually a favorite time, mellow and intriguing. Jerry didn't really think the season had anything to do with his restlessness.

He had left the sliding door into the bedroom open and heard the phone ring. Usually he brought the portable phone with him to the hot tub, but today the answering machine was still on from earlier in the afternoon, so he listened as the caller left him a message.

"Dr. Stoner, this is Pam on the psych floor. I know you're not on call this afternoon, but if you have a chance, I'd like to talk with you about Brad Green. He's behaving strangely and it feels like something is going wrong. Thanks."

Jerry sat staring out at the slice of ocean he could see. Brad Green had arrived on the floor five days ago. At first he was diagnosed to be suffering from a brief psychotic episode brought on by work conflict, with bizarre ideation and paranoid thoughts as well as some homicidal ideation about his boss. He'd been placed on Haldol for his aggression. More recently he was becoming withdrawn and apathetic, with increased body rigidity. Today he'd had some fever when Jerry visited, and he'd looked almost like a Parkinson's patient. Jerry frowned. This was beginning to look like a drug reaction, possibly a very dangerous drug reaction. He suspected, from Pam's message, that she was picking up the same signals.

Moving quickly now, he pulled himself from the hot tub. He did some of his best thinking there. Whether Brad Green's puzzle was solved or not, something needed to be done, and soon, so he

would go to the medical center and call a meeting
on Brad, requesting immediate input from a variety of specialists other than psychiatric. Jerry
readily admitted that he didn't know everything,
even after so many years of practicing. This was a
case where he needed help. Probably before the
day was out he would have learned something
new, a possibility which reassured him.

His body steamed in the cooling air and he
stood for just a moment naked in the privacy of
the redwood enclosure, wondering why all this
didn't seem enough: the challenge of his work, the
pleasure of his hot tub, his enjoyment of his sons,
his friendships and collegial relationships. Something was missing, and he couldn't put his finger
on what it was. He sighed and wrapped himself in
a towel before heading into the bedroom to dress.

Both the internist and the pharmacologist
agreed it was NMS, Neuroleptic Malignant Syndrome. Brad Green's response hadn't been perfectly typical, but the pharmacologist had seen a
similar reaction when doing a fellowship at a mid-
western university. In the intensive care unit, with
a regimen of Dantrolene, a muscle relaxer, and
bromocriptine, a dopamine helper, Brad would be
brought back to health.

Jerry could relax as he left the floor later that
evening and made his way to the cafeteria for a
snack before returning home. The cafeteria was
mostly empty, with a few pockets of people scattered around. He almost overlooked the lone
woman in scrubs seated back in the shadows at
the rear of the room. It was the pediatric intern
he'd met earlier in the day, Erika something. The

one who was having trouble. Jerry made his way to the back, where she only looked up from a textbook when he stood beside her.

"Mind if I join you?" he asked.

"Oh, please do." She cleared a spot at the table for him, shoving the book down into a backpack on the floor at her feet.

"I thought you probably weren't working today," he said as he settled his tray across from hers. "Since you were at the wedding, I mean."

A flush rose to her cheeks. After a moment's hesitation, she confided, "Actually, I wasn't supposed to. But Dr. Benninger was so . . . so overwhelming that I wanted to get away. So I had a friend page me."

"Rachel told me I should warn you about Benninger's reputation." Jerry felt irritated that Rachel had been right and that Benninger had once again given the profession a bad name. "I hope he didn't upset you."

Erika shrugged. "Oh, I knew his reputation. I thought I could handle him. I did handle him. But I wouldn't have gone with him in the first place if he hadn't been so insistent. It wasn't *exactly* as if I felt pressured into it. I mean, that's like saying I was afraid not to because he'd make things difficult for me or something. And I don't think that's true."

"But you wouldn't have gone with him if he hadn't been so insistent?" Jerry took a bite of the sandwich he'd chosen, and wished he'd gotten the chili. "Isn't that pressure?"

"Let's put it this way," she suggested, biting her lip in an unconscious way that fascinated him. "I might have gone with any man, a lawyer or a store owner or a garbage man, who was that insistent just to have done it and be able to say the next time that I knew what I was talking about when I said I wasn't interested in going out with him. They always say, 'How can you know you wouldn't like going out with me if you've never done it?' So, sometimes I go, just to shut them up."

"I see. So you won't be going out with Benninger again."

"Nope." She laughed. It made her eyes crinkle. "And besides, I used him in a way, too. I thought it would be fun going to a wedding where there would be people from Fielding whom I'd see on a more personal level. But I got a little shy when I realized there wasn't anyone there who I knew. He'd made it sound like everyone from the whole place would be there."

"Just like Ralph. Was there someone in particular you were hoping to see?"

She bit her lip again. "You won't take this wrong? I kind of hoped I'd see you there. You know, someone I could talk to. Well, not talk to right there but . . ." She sighed and gave a tsk of frustration. "It was stupid of me, but I guess I thought if you were there I'd get up the courage to talk to you about . . . you know, my trouble with pediatrics."

"And you did."

"Yeah." Her mouth twisted ruefully. "But I expected magic, Dr. Stoner. I thought you would say, 'Erika, you haven't a thing to worry about. This is normal and tomorrow you'll go back to work and everything will have fallen in place and you won't have any more trouble.' See what I mean?"

"You're telling me that didn't happen?" he demanded, feigning disappointment. "What a charlatan I am!"

"You did just what you should. You told me to come and see you. You couldn't solve all my problems at a wedding."

"Well, on my best days I might have," he teased. "But today I was a little off. Even Rachel had a hard time getting me to pay attention."

"Is Rachel your wife?"

Surprised, Jerry blinked and said, "Oh, no, just a friend from way back. Her husband died a few years ago and she's had a rough time adjusting. They had a good, solid marriage and I guess they were best friends, too. She works here at Fielding, and she's about to make a change in the direction of her career."

"She seemed like a nice woman."

"Very nice." Which just about dismissed poor Rachel, didn't it? Jerry considered adding something to his remark but decided it was more important to get the discussion back to Erika and her problems. "Tell me what it is about pediatrics that bothers you."

"I think what I hate most," she said, frowning down at her hands, "is that they accept it, you know? The little kids who are dying. As if they don't have any right to grow up and have a real life like the rest of us. I know it's good in a way that they accept being sick. It's realistic and it helps them adjust and all that. But, God, it's so unfair. And I feel like an imposter pretending that I can help them, when I know there's no more to be done. And when I know that very likely I'll live to be eighty and their parents and siblings may, too. Sometimes that really gets me down."

Jerry nodded. "What else?"

"Procedures like spinal taps, drawing blood. They're so frightening and so painful to the kids. And sometimes we do them for no real purpose other than to prolong their misery." She met his eyes. "With adults it's different. They pretty much know what to expect and they can refuse treatment. Did you ever hear a kid try to refuse treatment? Nobody pays the least attention. Well, I suppose they can't decide for themselves but we treat them like . . . like they're our pets or something, a dog you've taken to the vet's office."

"I see what you're saying. How should it be handled?"

Erika made a helpless gesture with her hands. "I don't know. Somehow you have to let the kids know you understand their frustration and impotence. But what we say is just words. It's okay, sweetie. It won't hurt but a minute. This is going to help you, believe me. Why should they believe me? Actually, sometimes it doesn't help them, and sometimes they're in pain a lot longer than we expect. Dr. Stevens says I'll get used to it. Do you think I will?"

Jerry took a sip of his coffee before answering. "Probably. The trick is always learning some detachment without disconnecting. That's what makes becoming a doctor so difficult. Being a good doctor means maintaining a real empathy with patients. Which is hard to do because they hurt, and they're afraid, and they expect too much of us."

"Sometimes I can't do a procedure, when I know I'm inexperienced and I'm going to cause them pain. How can I justify that? Just because I need to learn doesn't mean I should practice on some helpless child, does it?" An agony of indecision seemed to blaze from her eyes. "And yet I have to do it and I have to learn, mostly because it's expected of me and I expect it of myself. I practiced intubation on a dead baby. That sounds so ghoulish, you know? But it was good experience. I did it until I felt comfortable with the procedure. On a dead baby." Her eyes filled with moisture, which she didn't allow to spill over. "A baby I had tried so hard to save, a tiny little thing, just 500 grams. We can sometimes save 500 grammers."

"Yes."

"The other interns take it out on the parents."

"I'm sorry. I don't understand."

"Well, they seem to blame the parents for what's happening. I don't mean in abuse cases. Just as a general rule they think parents are dumb and overconcerned and interfering. As if they wouldn't do the same thing if it was their kid. They like parents who are meek and obedient and don't get in their way."

"What kind of parents do you like?" he asked, curious.

"Oh, the ones who demand everything—to know what's going on, to have the doctor's attention when their kid is in trouble, to take up the nurse's time for some extra help. The meek ones scare me. Like, we had a woman the other day who just went along with everything Dr. Stevens suggested, nodding her head and saying, 'Yes, doctor,' and I thought what if she knew he was making a mistake because her kid was allergic to penicillin or something, and she couldn't bring herself to speak up. We run roughshod over people like that because it's so convenient for us not to have to deal with them."

"What you're saying is that you don't really want to be changed by the system, because the system is wrong."

Erika's eyes widened. "Is that what I'm saying? Yes, maybe it is. Maybe I'm afraid I'll get all this empathy trampled out of me. That someday I'll be like the older residents who don't give a damn if a kid is scared of a lumbar puncture or get annoyed if a parent questions them too closely about a treatment. I don't want that to happen." She leaned toward him, her brow knit. "But, Dr. Stoner, I'm sure they all thought that, at first. And now look at them."

"They become technically competent doctors."

"That's not enough!"

"Everyone else in the medical center looks at the pediatric residents and remarks on how they're the nicest of the residents in the hospital, the most sympathetic, the most concerned. Yet that doesn't square with what you're seeing."

"You think I'm wrong."

Jerry shook his head. "No, no, Dr. Amundsen. But it *is* a matter of perspective. And one's perspective *does* change over time. Take the way you felt about medicine in college compared with the way you felt about it in medical school. There's a progression there that has to do with knowledge but also with perspective. The more you become an insider, the more you identify with the problems of the insider."

"Like knowing about the long hours and the sleeplessness and the huge amount of material we have to learn and resenting lay people for thinking doctors don't deserve their salaries and their respect?"

"Something like that, yes."

Erika's pager went off and she glanced at the number. "I'm not on call but I asked Bill to page me when he was about to do a chest puncture. I want to learn. But I don't have to go."

"Go. We can talk more later. I still hope you'll drop by my office. And call me Jerry, okay?"

"Okay, Jerry." She rose to her statuesque height, which brought her to the same place as Jerry, who rose along with her. "If you'll call me Erika."

"Sure."

After shouldering her backpack she released the long blond hair that was trapped under the strap. A charming smile warmed her wholesome features. "It *has* helped me, talking with you. Just the fact that you don't seem to judge me or anything I say. Everyone else is so eager for me to fall in line. Thanks."

"Anytime."

Jerry watched her cross the room with a confident stride and disappear through the door. An interesting woman. A very attractive woman. And, beneath all the confidence, still a troubled woman. He felt sure he would see her again.

Chapter Three

Rachel's first day on her new schedule was nerve-racking. There was only one call for an ethics consultation and her advice was largely ignored when she gave it. The doctors weren't used to approaching decisions the way she advocated, and there was a certain amount of grumbling at her rehashing of the situation. Her insistence that the patient and his family required full, and she did mean *full*, disclosure was disturbing to them, even though they would have considered themselves complying with the spirit of the law.

"You can't just make these decisions on your own," she had said, at least half a dozen times.

"But we've informed the patient about the general state of affairs. He's a hysterical type. If we get into particulars, he'll just lose it," Dr. Whittaker said.

And yet one of the younger doctors had called for the ethics consult, clearly feeling uncomfortable with the way things were going. Rachel had addressed her next remarks to him. "Dr. Bhutto, how do you think this situation would be best resolved?"

"Obviously he has to know the full diagnosis and the consequences of treatment," Dr. Bhutto said, scratching his right ear nervously. "I would tell him, but everyone else insists that he will scream and carry on and do himself an injury. They say he's done it before."

So Rachel had listened patiently to the other doctors and nurses describe the patient's previous behavior, and then she'd closed her file. "Dr. Bhutto is ready and willing to tell Mr. Walton the exact nature of his situation. I suggest that you let him do so, and cope with the hysteria if it develops."

There had been grumbling and a general denial of the need to follow her advice, so Rachel had smiled pleasantly at them and said, "My recommendations are, of course, only that. Let me know if I can be of any further help." And she'd left the room with five of the six medical people glaring after her. In the hall she'd shaken her head. This was going to take time, getting the respect of this group, or any other at the medical center. She'd been well trained, and she was accustomed to dealing with people, as well as being very familiar with the law, so Rachel knew that eventually things would shake down more to her liking.

But doctors were often difficult to deal with. Too many people were trying to tell them how to conduct their business now—the risk managers, the DRG (Diagnostic Related Groups) system that paid hospitals, utilization review teams, discharge planners, even the occasional judge—and doctors were feeling imposed on in a major way. They hadn't gotten beyond a kind of rebellious stage Rachel remembered from when her children were younger: If you won't let me play my way I'm going to pick up my toys and go home. Doctors, who had for so long been in complete control, were no longer in that enviable position, and they were pissed about it. Rachel understood that, and she knew she'd have to tread a very fine line in dealing with them if she was going to be of use to both the patients and the staff at Fielding Medical Center.

She did paperwork in her small office for a while, and made some phone calls, but when nothing further arose, she decided to leave for the day. Her nerves were on edge, so she dug in the metal cabinet that lined the side wall of the room until she found the swimming bag she always kept with her. Nothing was as relaxing as swimming a few dozen laps, and the pool was just in the next building. Rachel put on her answering machine and attached her pager to her belt. Not that she was likely to be called for anything urgent at this point in her new career.

As she pushed open the outside door of the building, Jerry was coming in. He smiled, looking almost apologetic. "I wasn't much of a companion the other day," he said. "You leaving? Let me buy you a cup of coffee."

"Thanks, but I'm headed to the pool."

"God, that sounds good. I wonder if I still have a suit in the locker with my racquetball stuff." He considered this for a moment, his brown eyes narrowed thoughtfully, then said, "I might. Tell you what. I'll walk over with you and join you if I do."

"Swimming isn't really a companionable sport, Jerry. You can't talk like you do playing racquetball."

They had started to walk toward the recreation

building but he stopped. "Don't you want me to join you?"

"You can if you like." Rachel felt slightly annoyed with him. She liked the anonymity of the pool environment. People in their swimming caps and goggles were hardly recognizable and she liked it that way. But she also felt revealed somehow in a bathing suit when there was someone there who knew her. After all, a swimming suit was little more than a camisole, especially the sleek, form-fitting ones she liked to swim in.

Oh, what did it matter? He probably ran around naked all the time at home and wouldn't think a thing of it. Unfortunately she wasn't so comfortable with nudity. "Sure, come along. This is the perfect time of day to get a lane to yourself."

"Or share one with you," he suggested.

"Yeah." Maybe he'd find he didn't have his suit in his locker after all. Rachel started walking again, following the concrete trail past liquid amber trees beginning to flame into color. "I did my first ethics consult this morning."

"How did it go?"

She laughed. "About like you'd expect. But it will get better."

"Who called for it?"

"An internal medicine resident. It was rather brave of him, actually, since he knew how his group felt. Everyone else was very uncomfortable with the idea of the patient having hysterics, but he just seemed to accept that as part of the game."

"Which it is. You know, Rachel," he said, pushing open the door for them to enter the recreation center, "I was a little hurt that you hadn't told me you were preparing for this career change. I've seen you any number of times in the last year and you never mentioned it."

"I kind of liked keeping it to myself. I didn't really tell anyone I didn't have to, except my daughters." Rachel paused in front of the women's locker room door. "I'm not as open a person as you are, Jerry."

He frowned. "No, I suppose not. And I guess I'm used to having people tell me all kinds of stuff. There wasn't any reason you should have told me."

"No. Look, I'll see you at the pool if you find you suit."

"Right."

Rachel found the locker room, as usual, full of women who were changing to work out on the various machines as well as to swim. The recreation center was relatively new and lacked the dinginess that city facilities so often had. Younger women walked around with no more than a towel around their waists, and Rachel wondered if even at their age she'd been so unself-conscious about her body. She stripped now, quickly, and donned the navy suit with its small gold anchor appliquéd at about the level of her appendix. Her routine was to slide her clothes into a locker, latch the combination lock, shoulder her towel and put on her cap in front of the mirror, before briefly showering and pushing through the door into the pool area.

There were two lanes with only one person in them, and one entirely empty. She sat on the side of the pool, slipped on her goggles, and slid into the empty lane. Without hesitating even a moment to see if Jerry was anywhere around, she began to do a crawl across the pool. Only on that first lap could she breathe every four strokes. Then she did a pattern of a lap of breast stroke or side stroke or back stroke alternating with a lap of crawl. She was on her fourth lap when someone joined her in the lane. Since Jerry had neither a cap nor goggles to disguise himself, it was quite obvious who he was. Plus, he waved at her, an energetic wave very in keeping, she found, with his method of swimming.

Rachel prided herself on the gracefulness of her swimming, but she also found herself to be competitive, often swimming faster just to keep up with someone in another lane. She was just exploring the aerobic possibilities of the exercise, she told herself. Today, with Jerry there, and making no secret of his interest in her method of swimming, she attempted to keep her pace steady and only slightly stretched for effort. He himself did not swim particularly fast. Usually men could outdistance her with ease, and she wasn't sure that Jerry couldn't, too, but he swam along, keeping pace with her, much as if they were out walking together. Rachel wished he'd cut it out.

He copied each stroke she did and he wasn't particularly talented at the breast stroke or the back stroke or the left-sided side stroke. In fact, he looked a little like a puppy who had landed in the water by mistake and was doing a modified doggy paddle. Rachel realized, after a while, that he was teasing her. She shook her head and laughed and splashed water at him. He grinned in return and took off at great speed doing a crawl to die for. Rachel didn't try to keep up with him.

It was only when he was half a length ahead of her that she realized that he wasn't actually in a bathing suit at all, but in his racquetball shorts, which floated around his athletic legs in a casual way that left a great deal of flesh exposed. Like his buttocks. Rachel hadn't, of course, ever seen Jerry naked. She averted her eyes, after a while. It was just like him, she thought, to swim in any old thing that left him naked as a jaybird. If he hadn't had racquetball shorts he'd probably have jumped in in his underpants, which would have been perfectly transparent. And he wouldn't have cared one bit, though the rec center people probably would have.

Rachel found herself a little, just a very little, turned on by Jerry's nudity. And by the way his body cut through the water easily, the black hair on his arms and legs, stomach and chest perfectly visible in the clear water. He looked good in the water, almost more at home than he did in his usual casual sport jacket and slacks. Jerry refused to wear a tie for almost any occasion, which had driven more than one head of his department quite distracted. "What the hell does it matter what I wear?" Jerry always demanded. "I wear a name tag. They know I work here. So what's the big deal?" Trust Jerry to do things his own way.

And not to be promoted. Doing things your own way often had a cost, Rachel knew. She had herself toed the line very carefully for most of her life. This newest venture of hers did not fall cleanly into that category, which frightened her sometimes. And she felt certain she shouldn't, at her age, feel frightened about such a mundane thing. It was about time she showed a little spirit, wasn't it?

She'd lost track of the number of laps she'd done, but she continued to swim for some time longer. Maybe Jerry would give up and leave. Probably he had a patient or a meeting. But she never once saw him glance at the clock on the wall and, when she finally grew a little tired, she stopped and indicated to him that she was leaving. He followed her over to the side of the pool and watched with interest as she drew herself out of the pool. "You're very good," she said.

"Thanks. Now don't wander off. How about having a cup of coffee with me up there," he said, motioning his head toward the little cafe that overlooked the pool.

"Why not? But it'll take me about ten minutes to dress and dry my hair."

"No problem."

Rachel could feel him watching her as she gathered up her towel and walked to the shower room. She felt skittish and embarrassed walking on the hard tile, unlike her comfort in the water. He had seen her in the pool, so what difference did it make? But she was a moving target then, splashing and twisting and gliding through water. Now she was a five-foot-five woman in a skimpy suit crossing a wide expanse of floor to disappear at last through a door. She breathed a sigh of relief as she twisted the shower control and a spray of warm water splashed over her. Swimming was definitely a solitary activity, as far as Rachel was concerned.

* * *

Jerry felt differently. He liked doing just about everything with other people. Sometimes, in fact, he was surprised by his own lack of need for personal time. But he had plenty of it anyhow, living alone the way he did. When Barbara had left him he'd found gaping holes in his life, holes that she had filled, and filled joyfully, for so many years. He had tried not to just fill in the holes with anything and anyone, and had grown to enjoy a certain amount of time alone. But not too much. And seldom if he could talk someone else into doing something with him.

He arrived at the cafe before Rachel. After all, he did little more than towel his hair after dressing and she would have to blow that thick though short curly hair dry under one of the hand dryers set high on the wall. Jerry hadn't realized how compact her figure was. She tended to wear large sweaters over split skirts to work, which he appreciated a great deal more than business suits. But he'd thought she was hiding what women called "figure flaws" under the loose sweaters, and that had turned out not to be the case at all. Which was perfectly evident in the suit she chose to wear. Jerry wasn't at all sure about the suit.

It didn't seem to be the sort of thing she'd feel comfortable in, so revealing in its simplicity. Rachel, being given to hiding her body, had taken him by surprise in the tank-type suit. Even her nipples had been visible through the thin material. But she'd seemed very dubious about his paying any attention to this exposure. She was like an ostrich with its head in the sand, sure that no one could see the rest of her because she wouldn't look at anyone else. He'd seen people in the hot tub like that, too: if I don't look at you, you won't look at me. As an attitude it mystified Jerry, since he found nudity perfectly acceptable.

When Rachel arrived her cheeks were flushed from her exertion and her sweater was hiked up slightly in back. Jerry tugged it down as she stood beside him at the counter. "That's what I get for trying to dress quickly," she said.

"You didn't have to hurry for me."

"That's what they all say."

"Do they?" Jerry was eyeing the bulletin board with the list of coffees and muffins. "The men you date?"

Rachel said, "I'll have a cappuccino and a blueberry muffin."

Jerry added his own order for the young woman serving them and turned to lean backward against the counter, facing her. "Not going to answer my question?"

She shrugged. "I was just making small talk. Teasing, really. Men seem to think that women take forever dressing, but they're often patronizingly polite about it."

"I hope I wasn't."

"Oh, Jerry, you know you weren't. How did we get into this discussion?"

They were in this discussion, Jerry knew, because he wanted to be in it. Rachel has just told him several things about herself that he was curious about. She'd told him that she was trying to please him, and that she felt men made unnecessary demands on her and were often patronizing to her. And she would hate his making those kinds of interpretations about her. So he said, "Damned if I know. Have you talked with your kids recently?"

This was generally a safe topic of conversation, but today he watched her brow draw down. "It was Jennifer calling when you dropped me off the other day. She seemed in good spirits. She asked about you. But, I don't know, she mentioned something that bothered me. She was thinking of seeing a friend's uncle, a man a great deal older than she is."

"What's the problem with that?" Jerry took the cappuccinos from the server and let Rachel pick up their muffins. They walked over to a table overlooking the medical center campus. "Jennifer isn't likely to be intimidated by someone older."

Rachel seated herself and pushed the bran muffin toward him. "It's not that. And I know it happens all the time. But think about it. He's probably been married before. He has a *past*. He may have children, he's from a different generation. Everything isn't going to be shiny and new for him, the way it is for her, if they fall in love. I find that sad for Jennifer. She deserves more."

"But the men of her generation may not seem up to her weight," he suggested. "They may seem young and inexperienced and awkward."

"Yes, I suppose." Rachel didn't sound convinced. "But why can't they be? Shouldn't there be men as strong and independent and exciting as she is?"

"There probably are. She just hasn't run into them."

"Maybe."

Jerry watched as she spread butter sparingly on the muffin. Her hands always looked so capable. He remembered watching her prepare dinner for them one night, her fingers instinctively reaching for herbs or retreating from an advancing chopping motion of her knife. Sometimes he had wanted her capable fingers to touch him, but he'd always been smart enough not to say so. She was the type of woman who took sex very seriously, he guessed. The type of woman who wouldn't be able to go back to a friendship if a sexual liaison didn't turn into a lasting relationship. Jerry liked to remain friends with the women involved in his life.

"What do you hear from Harris and Sam?" she asked, changing the subject.

His sons were well known to her; the four children had been close in age. Now they were scattered around the globe—Harris at twenty-five was in a graduate physics program in Michigan and Sam, just twenty-three, was with the Peace Corps in Africa. Her Jennifer was in Boston, and Trish lived closest in Palo Alto. Jerry jumped into a detailed account of his last letter from Sam, but mostly he was monitoring Rachel's reactions. She smiled and nodded and injected a question here and there, especially when he moved from Harris to Sam.

"Are you going to visit him there?"

Jerry had been considering it, but had made no firm plans. "Africa has always been one of those places I longed to see, but they don't have any photo safari trips where Sam is. I suppose I could do both things, but it's a huge continent."

"It would be a shame to miss the opportunity. He comes back next summer, doesn't he?"

"Yeah." Jerry let his gaze wander across to the ambulatory care building. "Maybe I'll go over at Christmas."

"Do you worry about him?"

"Surprisingly little. Barbara always said I wasn't a worrier and I think it's largely true. I tend to worry only about things I can do something about. And I can't do a thing about Sam in Africa."

Rachel sighed. "No. Or me about Jennifer in Boston, really. I like her having her own life and making her own decisions. It's just that I want her to be happy."

"She will be. What other woman her age would have graduated from college with honors and decided to become a private investigator?"

"I ask myself," Rachel muttered. "No, really, I know she'll do fine. Jerry, if I needed a psych consult for my ethics business at another hospital, could you do it?"

"I'd have to have privileges there, probably, but you could always ask." He covered her hand with his, something he'd been wanting to do since she joined him. "Thanks for thinking of me, Rachel, but you'll find good people at all the hospitals in the area. I'd always be happy to recommend someone." He gave her hand a squeeze and released it, feeling marginally closer to her.

She didn't seem to notice the moment particularly. They were friends and from time to time he touched her arm or her hand in an encouraging way, a thankful way. She smiled at him and gathered up her purse and swimming bag. "I'd better let you go," she said. "Thanks for the coffee."

"Thank you for the swim." He rose along with her. Her brown eyes swept over the table to make sure she wasn't forgetting anything and then she bent toward him, lifting her face to kiss his cheek. She'd never done that before and he was moved.

Maybe she had noticed his touch after all. Or been unconsciously affected by it. Jerry knew that could happen. Sometimes he planned for it to happen, when words seemed too bald or crude a way of expressing his affection. "Good luck with the ethics business."

As he had with Erika the other night, he watched her walk away from him. Rachel's walk didn't have the same confident insouciance as the younger woman's, but there was mature energy there and a certain mystery as well. Rachel was a more secretive person than Erika, probably. After all these years he really didn't know her that well. She kept more to herself and regarded herself in a different way than the open pediatric intern. God, Jerry thought as Rachel waved and disappeared from sight, women were fascinating. Much more so than men, in his opinion, and he was a decidedly opinionated man—psychiatrically speaking.

Chapter Four

Jerry had been working at his office computer for half an hour when he felt that someone was looking at him. He swung around and found Erika Amundsen standing hesitantly in the doorway. "Come on in," he said.

"You're busy."

"Not particularly. This report isn't due until next week." He pushed his swivel chair away from the terminal and maneuvered it beside the visitor's chair, which he patted with insistence. "You wouldn't have come if you didn't have something to talk about."

"It's been a hard day. I'm post call." She moved to the chair and gracefully, gratefully lowered herself. "One of my patients died today, but it was expected. I think I'm more upset over another one, a little boy who has just been diagnosed with leukemia. I have the strangest feeling about him. Even though they can save so many of them now, I don't think he's going to be one of them. Isn't that awful? Why would I think that?"

"Maybe he reminds you of some other child who died of leukemia."

"Hmmm." She thought for a moment and then nodded. "Yes, he does. When I did my first pediatric rotation as a medical student there was a boy who looked like him, but more than that, he had the same kind of almost angelic quality to him. I suppose that's it."

"Does it make you feel like a bad doctor, as though you might do less for him because you think he might not survive?"

"Not exactly. It's a kind of superstitious thing, I think. As if I might hex him."

Jerry nodded. "But you're a scientist and you know you can't hex him and you know you'll do as much for him as for any other patient."

"Yes." She sighed. "And I'm probably wrong, anyway. I don't have any crystal ball, to know which of them is going to survive."

But the way she said this, almost as if she didn't quite believe it, alerted Jerry to her problem. "Have you come to think that maybe you *can* tell which of them is going to die?"

Erika looked suspicious. "How do you know that? I've never told anyone."

"You just sort of told me."

Though it was obvious she didn't understand him, she explained, "It's happened several times, you know. I've known when I've first examined a child that he or she was very, very sick. And I've suspected that they would die. And they have. It's kind of eerie. And probably very unprofessional of me."

"More likely it's a particular sensitivity you have. You're picking up clues that the final process has begun and can't be reversed. Is that possible?"

"Why wouldn't other people pick up the same clues?"

"Maybe they do. Maybe they just don't want to

say anything, the way you didn't. Or maybe they've trained themselves to believe that every child is salvageable until proved otherwise." Jerry leaned slightly toward her. "I don't think you need to believe there's something supernatural or unprofessional about your feelings. They're just what they are, Erika. Someday one of the kids you thought would die is going to live, and out of the blue a kid you thought was getting well is going to die. Probably it will happen when you're even more experienced than you are now."

She cocked her head at him, the blond hair falling away from her face. "Do other people feel this way?"

"Sure. So many things are out of your control when you're an intern. Maybe this is a way to feel like you have some control over what happens. Not consciously, of course. But a sort of ultimate fatalism. Or it may have something to do with protecting yourself. You may not invest as much emotionally in someone you believe is going to die. Or you may choose to spend your emotions precisely there, where they may be most needed."

Erika laughed. "Well, obviously I'm a very straightforward person."

"Hardly anyone is," Jerry assured her. "We all find our own ways of coping with the stresses in our lives. Not all of the ways are equally efficacious or benign."

She looked suddenly exhausted. Her hand came up to stifle a yawn. "Sorry. I'd better get home." She rose and extended her hand to shake his. "Thanks. I'll think about what you've said. I'm not sure whether I'm adapting usefully or not but it helps to talk about it."

"Good. Come in anytime."

She had turned to go, but swung back now with a frown. "Do you have to report my visits to my department head?"

"I usually do. Does that bother you?"

"It's just that they don't really encourage us to go for help."

"Well, they should. I'll make a point of stressing that to your boss. Insinuating that house staff should tough it out is just plain bad policy."

"Am I the only pediatric intern who's talked with you?"

"No, but I'd hope you wouldn't let that influence you, Erika. What the others do or don't do for themselves can't really be relevant to you."

"I suppose not," she said doubtfully. "Hell, I'm exhausted. I've got to get out of here. This hospital is starting to feel like a prison."

Even in her fatigued condition she looked like a model, Jerry thought. Though her step was a little slower than the other night, it was still confident. On her the white coat looked like a designer jacket over her green print dress. As she walked down the hall, male heads turned to observe her, but she didn't seem to notice. Naturally, he realized, she was used to the effect she had on men. Even on him.

The news from Boston, in Rachel's opinion, was all bad. Of course, that wasn't how her daughter saw it. Jennifer was intrigued and becoming captivated by her friend's uncle. The man's name was Fred.

"He's a lot of fun, Mom," Jennifer insisted, probably suspecting her mother's true state of

mind even in the face of Rachel's determined
cheerfulness on the phone. "He took me to a beer
festival in one of the old industrial towns near
here. You know, oom pah pah bands, and German
beer steins, and people singing and pork roast
with sauerkraut. And all kinds of silly games. It
was terrific fun. He doesn't mind doing things
that would embarrass the guys I know. That's really an advantage of his being older."

Oh, there would be advantages, Rachel knew.
He would probably be an exquisitely experienced
lover. He would be self-assured and financially
stable. "What does he do, dear?"

Jennifer laughed. "I knew you'd want to know
that. He's in advertising, television advertising.
Actually, he's kind of a big shot where he works."

"Does he like his work?"

"Sounds like it. One afternoon, though, he took
off—playing hooky he called it. Isn't that quaint?
Anyhow, I was on an incredibly boring stakeout
and he came to sit with me. We talked for hours."

"I hope he didn't distract you from your work."

"Oh, Mother. I suppose you have to say that.
No, he didn't distract me. It was just fun having
him there. He's going to take me out to dinner to
meet some of his friends from work next week."

Things were moving right along, then. Rachel
didn't dare ask exactly how old he was. "I'm glad
you're having fun, honey. He sounds like a nice
guy." Lie through your teeth, Rachel, she told herself.

There was a soft sigh. "Yeah. I haven't met
anyone like him in years. Maybe ever."

Rachel wanted to ask other things: is he divorced, is he Jewish, does he have kids, how old

are they, does he have them some of the time, all of the time? Maybe he'd never married. What would *that* mean? Maybe he didn't have kids. That would certainly make things easier. She was acting, Rachel told herself, as though things were already at a no-stopping point with her daughter and this Fred.

Rachel brought her attention back to their conversation. Jennifer was describing a new comforter cover that she'd found at a discount store. "I'll send you a picture when I have my film developed. And maybe one of Fred, too, since I took this roll at the beer festival. He's kind of nice looking, you know? Tallish, and with dark wavy hair. Sort of athletic. He runs almost every day. We're talking about trying to run together if we can make our schedules mesh."

"It's nice having things in common." Would Jennifer take offense at that? She hadn't meant it about anything but the running—like age. But Jennifer apparently didn't notice.

"We're going down to the Cape this weekend, so don't worry if I'm not around. The weather's been holding and I'd like to walk along the beach before winter really gets here." There was a brief pause. "Fred has a friend whose summer house there we can stay in. It sounds perfect."

Rachel felt suddenly as though she wanted to cry. Things really *were* moving fast. And there was no use warning Jennifer. She'd just sound like an overprotective mother, and possibly dampen Jennifer's enthusiasm. Which she was certainly entitled to. There was nothing quite like falling in love, after all. It made the world sparkle with unending potential. "I hope you'll have a terrific time, Jen."

Though they talked for several more minutes, Rachel didn't give her full attention to the call. Things were changing again. Maybe important things. It was easy for Rachel's mind to leap ahead to the time when Jennifer would marry, or at least have a relationship with a man that would forever change her relationship to her mother. Not in a bad way, necessarily. But another stage of Jennifer's, and Rachel's, life would be reached. It was what she wanted for Jennifer; it wasn't exactly what she wanted for herself. Rachel had trouble adjusting to change, even when she initiated it herself.

Like her job. She knew, theoretically and practically, that she'd made a good move. She was a little worried about the money, but with both daughters supporting themselves, she could manage on less income. Still, Rachel knew there would be blocks of time when she wasn't working, had no work to do in fact, that she would need to fill with something else. Take up gardening, or stained glass or pottery, so that as her new work responsibilities grew, she could drop the leisure activities to concentrate on them.

And she would have to face people at the medical center in a different way. As an attorney and risk manager, she had defined responsibilities, and her approach to personnel reflected them. Now she faced doctors and nurses and ancillary personnel as well as patients and family in a different role—that of ethical arbiter. Ultimate decisions were not hers, but her recommendations would carry a definite weight and status, as long as she did her work well. And her persuasive abilities might become the most important aspect of her work. Most everyone had a vested interest in some position, and they were hard to leverage from the stance without the proper authority. For the first time in her life, Rachel had determined to not represent an authority, but to be an authority herself. It was a frightening, and potentially exhilarating, proposition.

The phone hadn't been in its cradle for more than a minute when it rang again. Absently Rachel picked it up to find her other daughter on the line. "Trish! How nice to hear from you." Did that sound critical? As though Trish hadn't called in a while? You had to be careful with Trish, who had a prickly side to her that made Jennifer talk about walking on eggshells in her presence.

"It's been a rough semester," Trish replied. "I think teaching middle school is even more challenging than high school. One of the mothers told me this is the age when the kids are either their best or their worst. And she should know, having eight of them ranging from twenty-five to eight. Three marriages."

"Wow. Which one do you have?"

"The seventh, a girl in seventh grade. But that's not why I called. I wanted to hear about your new medical ethics career. How's it going?"

Rachel wasn't sure Trish approved of her changing careers. Trish had an even stronger thing than Rachel did about security and change. And yet Rachel suspected that Trish had ideas of her own about wanting to make changes in her life. "So far so good," she said. "They haven't called me in on too much yet, and they haven't just lapped up what I have to say, but things are going about the way I expected. It takes time to make this kind of change in their thinking. And of course anything that makes doctors feel they're giving up even more power isn't going to be readily embraced."

"I suppose not. Do you worry that it won't work out?"

"Not particularly. I can always go back to doing some kind of law."

"But maybe not at the hospital. They'll have hired someone for your job."

"True. But somewhere else."

"Well, you know, Mom, it's harder to get a job when you're older. Everyone says they like to hire younger people and bring them along."

Rachel laughed. "I'm sure that's true, but I'm going to be okay, hon. You're not to worry about me."

Tricia sighed. "No, I suppose if worse came to worst you could always sell the house and live off that."

In San Francisco it was a definite possibility, Rachel knew. But that wasn't what she had in mind. "If things got a little tight, I think I'd rent out a room or two to make ends meet."

"My room?" Tricia asked, sounding distressed. "Where would I stay when I came to visit?"

"Trish, I haven't decided to do it, and I don't think I'm ever going to have to, but if I did we'd manage somehow. It's a big house."

"You could have sold it and bought something smaller."

"I could have. I just didn't want to. I like the idea of you and Jennifer having the house you grew up in to come home to."

"I do, too. And I come up more often than Jen, of course, so maybe you should think about her room first, if you have to rent one of them out."

Rachel shook her head with dismay. "Honey, I'd probably think of the den first." She wished she hadn't brought the subject up at all; she'd just been trying to alleviate Tricia's fears about her possible financial difficulties. "I'll let you know well in advance if I do anything at all about it."

"It would give you company," Tricia said, obviously trying to see the positive side of such a move. "You'd have someone to talk to."

And someone to stumble over, or be annoyed by. It was hard living with other people, whether you were related to them or not. Sure, she was often lonely. She missed Dan, and she missed the girls. Sometimes the house seemed too quiet. But then she'd turn on the radio or the stereo and get down to work. There had been an awful lot of years when she was constantly at someone's beck and call.

Guiltily, she relished a lot of the time when no family made demands on her. Life seemed so uncomplicated, somehow, when you didn't have to make dinner for three other people, when there wasn't always a stack of dishes that everyone else was too busy to help with, a hamper of laundry no one else remembered to take to the basement and put in the washing machine. Now she ate when and what she chose, she did the dishes only if she felt like it, she sometimes took her laundry out. Rachel felt pampered in a way she never had when she had a full family around her.

She supposed it was her own fault. If she'd insisted, she could have made them all do their share of the work. But it had been a grueling task, and the others always had heavy schedules that didn't easily accommodate housework and regular hours. How could you ask them to turn their lives around just to fit in some stupid task like doing dishes? "Why don't you get some household help, Mom?" the girls always asked when she attempted to "impose" on them. "We can afford it" seemed to be the justification for this. And sometimes she did have household help, but she didn't really like a regular cleaning person coming in the house, being there when she wasn't around, scratching copper and streaking windows and forgetting to clean behind the couch.

Rachel had wandered off into her own thoughts and was only brought back by Tricia demanding, "Well, aren't you?"

"I'm sorry, dear. I didn't catch what you said." And please don't take offense. I'm not in the mood to smooth ruffled feathers.

"Really! I asked if you weren't afraid of getting some kook in there with you. There was a movie about that."

"I'd just ask them to move out again, Trish. In your own house you get to do pretty much what you want."

"I suppose. Some day I'd like to have a place of my own but real estate is so expensive around here."

"I know." Rachel wondered if Tricia was asking for her help but decided this wasn't the time to go into such a discussion. "Tell me about you. What's going on in your life?"

Finally given an opportunity, Tricia recounted the latest crises in her life. They were seldom big ones, but the stuff of which life is made. Still, Tricia took them very seriously because it was her nature to do so. And Rachel listened with patience and encouragement. On a good day Tricia could make her howl with laughter over a school episode, or almost weep with the heartbreak of a child's story of neglect. Tricia felt things with an intensity, which she easily conveyed to others, an ability Rachel felt might lead her daughter to some other career eventually—something in communications or journalism. But Tricia would have to come to that on her own. It wasn't the sort of thing Rachel could suggest to her. She would discover her strengths in her own time, with any luck.

Rachel was startled by her pager going off. The number it indicated was unfamiliar to her. She hated to interrupt her daughter and fortunately Tricia asked, "What's that, Mom?"

When Rachel explained, Tricia said, "Oh, boy, you get to be just like the doctors, huh? Nobody will leave you alone."

"I'm hardly in that great a demand, but I should call in."

"Sure. Well, good luck, Mom. Maybe I'll come up next weekend."

"That would be great."

The information Rachel got when she responded to her page made her leave immediately for the hospital. Not that she precisely had an ethics consult. What she learned from the nurse who called her was that nurses weren't allowed to call for an ethics consultation. Somehow the hospital administration had neglected to tell Rachel this, and it made her mad as a hornet. That was treating nurses as if they weren't an important and integral part of the care team at the hospital. Well, *that* would certainly have to change, Rachel decided as she climbed into her minivan. Obviously there was more work for her to do than she'd anticipated.

Deciding that she'd need a little weight on her side, and because the case involved a psychiatric problem, Rachel stopped by Jerry's office. She was disappointed not to find him there, since it was her impression that he worked day and night. Fortunately the unit secretary was able to track him down on the ward, and he joined her before she met with the nurse who'd called.

"What's up?" he asked, falling into step with her.

"Did you know that nurses aren't allowed to call for ethics consults?"

"Sure. It's been policy at Fielding as long as I've worked here."

Rachel stared at him. "For what possible reason? These people know the patients better than anyone else."

"True. But all they have to do is tell a doctor and the doctor calls the consult."

Rachel felt exasperated with him. "What if the doctor doesn't agree?"

"Then you don't get a call from us," he said, grinning at her.

"Jerry, this is serious business. And no way to run a medical center, for God's sake. If a nurse thinks a situation is desperate enough to call for an ethics consult, and if you value your nurses, why wouldn't they be allowed to call a consult themselves?"

He scratched his head. "I suppose the idea was that they'd do it all the time, Rachel. They get more emotionally involved than the doctors do."

"Heaven help me!" she said, feeling the greatest urge to stamp her foot. "Nurses deserve to be able to call an ethics consult. They are not hysterical women, like too many doctors want to see them. They're professional and they work closely with patients and if they call a few ethics consults that are in a doctor's view unnecessary, the hell with it. Better to have one that isn't needed than not have one that is."

Rachel was furious, not only with the situation, but increasingly with Jerry, who had always seemed sympathetic to a reasonably feminist view of the world. Sometimes even good-hearted people were blinded by habit or tradition, but she hadn't expected it of him. "Well, if you can't see a need for nurses to call ethics consults, I won't need your help," she snapped. "I'll manage this on my own."

He regarded her with skepticism. "Well, actually, Rachel, if you want to be able to hold an ethics consult you'd better tell me about the situation and let me call for one."

"I don't know the whole situation yet. I was just going to see"—she consulted a note she'd written—"Janice Conroy on the second ward."

"Janice?" Jerry frowned. "She's a very capable nurse; not someone who'd go off half cocked. Let me come with you. Pretty please."

He said this with a mock wheedling tone of voice that somewhat eased the tension Rachel had felt building in herself toward him. Was this new job going to pit her against her friends? God, she hoped not. She knew enough about the politics of the medical center to step gingerly around the pitfalls that were obviously there.

"She said she'd meet me in the patient lounge on 4 West since this wasn't official. Don't give her a hard time, okay? It never occurred to me that you wouldn't be in favor of her being able to call a consult. Stupid of me."

"Not at all. I'm not in charge of policy here. Maybe if I were that particular policy wouldn't be in place."

"And maybe it would, huh?" She swung alongside him, walking more quickly because of the pace he set. "I know you like to pick your own battles, Jerry. You can hear her out and give me a little help, but I'm not going to ask you to fight for something I believe in and you don't. I'll find a way to get policies changed by myself."

"Oh, don't be such a martyr," he grumbled. "I haven't said I won't help you. It sounds like a reasonable battle. Just let me think it through, okay? It used to just be a matter of having the ethics committee talk about the situation when they met. There was no one like you on call to help the staff work through issues."

"Sorry." Rachel stopped him with a hand on his sleeve just as he was about to push open the door to the lounge. "It just made me so mad when she told me about the nurses. Angry that such a rule exists, but also that administration didn't tell me about it. I'm sorry if I took my anger out on you."

Jerry squeezed her hand. "Hey, no problem. I don't think I've ever seen you mad before, and I certainly don't want you to be mad at me."

There was a smile lurking at the corners of his

lips but Rachel thought he was serious, too. He didn't want to lose her friendship any more than she wanted to lose his. She liked the way he was straightforward about his impressions, and the way he held her hand as if it meant something, not just a doctorly handshake. Together they walked into the room, where they found Janice Conroy curled up on an uncomfortable-looking plastic couch reading the daily paper.

Jerry waved her back to her seat when she, in her surprise at seeing him there, attempted to rise. "I brought Dr. Stoner," Rachel explained, "because I thought he might be the quickest answer to our problem."

Janice nodded and tucked the paper under the couch as Jerry and Rachel pulled chairs up to talk. The nurse looked almost too fragile to work in a hospital. She had straight, short hair of an indeterminate brown and eyes that blinked behind large wire-frame glasses. Yet there was a steel to her that Rachel could sense from the moment she walked in the room.

"What we have is an elderly man who is refusing treatment. Mr. Paras is perfectly articulate but decidedly confused. The resident called in a psychiatric fellow who said Mr. Paras isn't capable of giving informed consent. And the resident thinks that means he can go ahead with the tests he's ordered. There doesn't seem to be any family here in the city, though they talked of a son in Chicago," Janice explained. "I didn't think of calling Dr. Stoner, but I remember the time he helped me with the Kazinski girl last year. This is different, though. I don't think Mr. Paras wants treatment, and even though he may not be legally competent he does seem to be expressing a strong hatred of hospitals and surgery."

"What kind of tests does the resident want?" Jerry asked, and listened intently as Janice detailed them.

Rachel asked what she considered the most pertinent question about the tests. "Do they have any purpose other than determining if surgery is necessary?"

"No," Jerry and Janice replied together. Jerry added, "They're also invasive and painful."

"So if he doesn't want surgery, there's no use subjecting him to the tests?"

"Right." Janice leaned toward her, eager to emphasize this point. "That's why I called. No one would listen to my objections, which I think are very reasonable. They believe since this man is confused they have the right to do whatever they think is best for him."

Jerry turned to Rachel to ask, "So what's your suggestion, Rachel?"

"Obviously there should be a full ethics consultation, with the med/surg people, the psychiatry people, and a telephone hookup to the son in Chicago, as well as the patient himself. What we're going to have to determine is what Mr. Paras's personal values have been during his lifetime with regard to this kind of situation. His son should be able to help with that, even if Mr. Paras is too confused to be perfectly clear on the issue. One of the things medical ethicists stress is that elders' wishes are too often ignored. We don't want to see that happen here."

"Right." Jerry stood up and said, "Let's round up the troops."

Easier said than done, of course, but within the hour a full conference had taken place, much to the gratification of Janice Conroy and the relief of the patient. Mr. Paras's son had verified that his father had abhorred hospitals all his life, and believed that his father was old enough at eighty-eight to accept his inevitable death from what was obviously an abdominal cancer. The son promised to fly to San Francisco the next day and take his father home with him.

"Nice work, Ms. Weis," the attending surgeon commented as he rose from the table. "I was afraid these ethics consults would wander all over the place. You did a great job of keeping it to the point and reaching a conclusion everyone could accept. My congratulations."

"Thank you, Doctor. I appreciated your help in airing the issues so thoroughly." Rachel shook hands with him, and winked at Jerry as the surgeon disappeared through the conference room door.

"Let's go have a drink," Jerry suggested. "We need to talk."

Chapter Five

J erry had been very impressed with Rachel's handling of the ethics consultation. She had used
all the strength she'd learned as an attorney to
weigh in with her right to guide the discussion
and point out the aspects that each side of the issue was forgetting. As though she'd been conducting this type of meeting for years, she gathered
together the necessary information, made sure everyone agreed to it, and, with consummate skill,
led the participants to the best solution such a situation offered. Yes, he was impressed with her.

And he seemed to be seeing her with new eyes.
First, her irritation at him, which had surprised
him. He had always known her as an even-
tempered woman and in fact had sometimes wondered if she wasn't just a little *too* even-tempered.
The fire he'd seen in her eyes tonight had been
missing before, or perhaps he hadn't paid suffi-
cient attention in the past. And then her ability to
compromise, to apologize, to accept his own apol-
ogy. He had been in the midst of too many power
struggles not to appreciate the grace with which
she conceded some of her personal power for the
sake of the situation.

The participants in the conference had been

handled carefully, not allowed to place themselves in a position from which they could not retreat. That was perhaps the most impressive feat of all. Half a dozen egos the size of California seated at one table and she'd managed to keep them all balanced. A truly remarkable accomplishment. No wonder the attending had complimented her. Jerry felt very much like hugging her.

As they walked side by side through the hospital, Jerry saw her smile to herself and asked, "What's that about? What are you thinking?"

Her eyes flashed with excitement. "God, wasn't that fantastic! I've never had quite that kind of experience before—where everything worked. Everything! It was like magic. I felt like I was pulling the strings, you know? Not in a bad way, but as if I could do no wrong. Oh, I know it won't always be like that, but, hell, if it happened even once a month I'd probably expire from euphoria!"

"You'll get a reputation for being high as a kite," he teased. But he found her excitement moved him both emotionally and sensually. "We could have a drink at my place in the hot tub."

"I'm not as comfortable with my body as you are with yours, Jerry," she protested. "I know people sit around in hot tubs naked without thinking a thing of it, but I'm not like that."

"We could find you a suit."

"Oh, great! Then I could sit there covered and try not to look at you."

"I wouldn't mind you looking at me. Remember, I'm comfortable with my body." He held the outside door open for her and they walked out into the cold November night. "The hot tub is especially invigorating at this time of year. The outside air is cold and the water is hot and your body just tingles with the difference. Steam rises off your flesh like you were cooking. Come on, Rachel. There's never going to be a better time for me to convince you to try something different."

"I know," she admitted, stopping beside her car, an older minivan from when the children were younger. "I'm almost high enough to agree."

"Live dangerously. I'm never going to hold it against you."

"I know you wouldn't." She unlocked the car and hesitated, but her eyes were still echoing the excitement she felt, and probably her need to talk about it. "All right. Just be a little patient with me."

"Promise." He closed her door behind her and patted the side of the car as though it were a horse's flank. "See you there in five minutes."

He could understand her hesitation. She was a woman, and a woman he might be working with more frequently at the hospital. Not every woman was comfortable with nudity, and certainly not Rachel. But they'd been friends forever and he felt sure he could help her, and indeed himself, maintain the proper distance in their personal and professional lives. Jerry was not being completely honest with himself, perhaps. He was refusing to acknowledge that recently he had twice felt quite sexually drawn to Rachel—during the swimming episode and this evening. As a naturally potent man he frequently felt sexual stirrings for the women who passed through his life.

But Rachel wasn't passing through his life, and that made the situation different. Jerry had no doubt, however, that he would be able to behave in an entirely appropriate manner no matter what his feelings were. He was, after all, a psychiatrist, and he knew how reasonably well-adjusted and so-cialized people were supposed to act. He imitated them whenever he felt in the mood.

Rachel was parking her car on the street out-side his building when he pulled into the garage. He met her in the foyer and could tell she'd lost a little of her enthusiasm for the projected adven-ture. "Don't flake on me now," he urged. "You're going to love how relaxing this is. You'll probably order a hot tub for your house the minute you get home."

"No doubt," she said dryly, but she followed him into the elevator.

Jerry never precisely apologized for his condo, but he had a way of looking at it each time he en-tered that gave any visitor some idea of how he felt about the amorphous unit. "Let me turn the heat up in the tub and I'll be right back," he said, leaving Rachel in the living room. On the way back from the balcony through the bedroom he checked in several drawers and the closet in hopes that someone would have left a woman's swim-ming suit. He didn't really expect to find one, but it was possible. Barbara might have left one here when she visited with her new husband (whom Jerry found infinitely boring), or one of his sons' various women friends might have left one, mightn't they?

He returned to the living room with a kimono and a towel. "I'm afraid you'll have to make do with this," he said, indicating the blue towel. "You can just wrap it around you and get into the hot tub with it."

Rachel regarded him skeptically but accepted the two items. Jerry felt it was time to remind her of her excitement from the meeting. "I almost laughed when that surgery resident tried to question Mr. Paras about his medical condition," he said, his eyes dancing.

Rachel grinned. "There was a certain justice to it. Mr. Paras has one of the finer baseball reminiscences I've heard and the 1961 World Series scores sounded a little like Mr. Paras's lab values. And you have to admit the surgery fellow is so full of himself he deserved to be taken down a notch or two."

"Really, Rachel, I never knew you had it in you. You've always seemed such a 'good' woman. It's shocking to find out that you harbor all sorts of vengeful fantasies."

"Hardly." But her eyes shone. "Still, didn't you think it was particularly subtle, the way I handled him? He left there thinking I found him a very skillful diagnostician."

"Well, didn't you?"

"I suppose so, but so stuffy. It was great to see him loosen up a bit."

"And all because of you."

She grimaced at him. "You're trying to flatter me so I'll go in your stupid hot tub." But she couldn't be distracted for long. "Imagine. Every one of them was ready to have me walk them through the process and not be defensive or dawdling. That's not going to happen all the time, you know. It was like being an actress or something. Like I was just doing something that had already been written down. Like everybody followed their parts, and they were just what I would have wanted them to be."

"That's because you were the director," he said, shepherding her toward the kitchen. "Tell me what you'd like to drink. I have wine and beer and hard liquor and mineral water." He opened the refrigerator and pointed to a row of bottles on the door. Rachel chose one and he took it from her to screw off the top. "Now go undress in the spare bedroom and wrap the towel around you and I'll let you keep talking about your triumph."

"Smartass."

"Hey, I'm just trying to be helpful."

When she had disappeared he carried their drinks through to the balcony and set them beside the tub. Since he felt certain she'd be more comfortable if he was already in the water, he returned to his bedroom and stripped quickly. For his exit from the water he brought along the kimono robe he usually used and laid it on the redwood boards. Naked, he climbed into the hot tub and turned on the jets. The water was still not as hot as he liked it, but it would continue to heat even with the bubbles going. It was several minutes before Rachel appeared at the sliding glass doors from his bedroom.

She looked adorable in her blue towel, tucked in modestly over her breasts. It turned out not to be the best place to tuck it in, however, because when she sat down on the underwater seat, the towel had a tendency to spread apart. Rachel kept tugging it together with her hands, looking a little chagrined. She studiously kept her eyes off Jerry's naked body—or at least the most significant parts of it.

Jerry reached over to check the thermometer. "Good. It's just about there now. Doesn't it feel great?"

"Yes," she admitted. "It's heavenly."

"It's even better if you're naked."

She gave him a quizzical look. "I'm sure it is."

"I suppose not all doctors are comfortable with nudity, either. They see naked bodies all the time, but often bits and pieces—identifying the surgical abdomen or doing a breast examination. It's just a body, after all. Nakedness comes to be associated with a lack of power in some way. The caregivers are clothed and the ones taken care of are unclothed. Sometimes I think that's why I like shedding my clothes. It's like dropping out of that phony power game."

"Only doctors see nakedness like that."

"Hmmm. Is that really true? Certainly most people view nakedness as vulnerability. You, for instance. You'd feel vulnerable if you were naked. Now why do you suppose that is?"

"I haven't the slightest idea," she muttered, once again drawing the towel back over her stomach.

"Do you think I would see you as a sexual object? Or that I would take your nakedness to mean that you were sexually available? You know neither of those things is true. Not with me."

"Oh, you're a saint," she grumbled, twisting sideways so that she could let go of the lower end of the towel and still be mostly out of his line of vision.

"Not at all. I'm like every other man, except that I'm used to nudity, professionally and personally. I could easily be a nudist, you know."

"Yes, I'm sure you could."

"Clothes have always seemed constricting to me, especially suits and ties. I mean, what's the point? It's such a rigid, uncomfortable form of dress. I imagine if we all went around naked it would be a little distracting at first, but people would get used to it, like they do at nudist camps, and think nothing of it."

"Have you ever been to a nudist camp?"

"No."

"Then you're just talking through your hat."

He winked at her. "You know very well I'm right. If everyone were naked, it wouldn't be any big deal."

"Well, everyone isn't naked. Some people are modest."

"What's to be modest about? I've seen naked women, Rachel. Hundreds of them. Probably thousands of them, even though it's not as common with psychiatric patients. Do you think I'll judge your body?"

"Of course you'd judge my body."

"No, I wouldn't. I'm not a judgmental type."

"It doesn't matter. You're human. You'd think to yourself, well, her breasts aren't very big and her hips are a little wide and her legs aren't very shapely."

Jerry shook his head. "Nope. I'd say to myself: how great she was able to let her hair down and enjoy herself. *That's* the sort of thing I'm likely to make a comment about, not whether your legs are crooked."

"Not crooked," she protested. "Shapely. Like model legs. Everyone expects model legs."

"I don't."

"Of course you do. And besides, it's not even that, really. My body feels private. I don't share it with other people. I don't walk around my house naked and I never have. You probably do."

"Sure."

"See? It's just a difference of viewpoint. You don't need for your body to be private and I do."

"Why do you suppose that is?"

Rachel, perhaps unwisely, snapped, "I suppose it's because all too often women don't have a *real* choice about what to do with their bodies."

"Ah. Now we're getting somewhere. Give me an example of what you mean."

"I don't feel like giving you an example."

"I see." Jerry closed his eyes, resting his head back against the redwood decking. Without opening his eyes, he began to speculate. "Choice. When I think about choice I think about freely making a decision. That would mean that I didn't feel coercion of any sort. Not by someone else expecting something of me, or even me expecting something more of myself than I wanted to give. For instance, if I were married and my wife wanted to make love, I might not feel, on every occasion, that I had a free choice of saying no."

"Yes, but that probably seldom happens with men."

"I wouldn't say seldom. Men do seem, all hype aside, to take a greater interest in sex than women do. Sex meaning sexual intercourse. Women on the other hand probably take a greater interest in physical affection, cuddling, hugging, that sort of thing."

He had continued to keep his eyes closed. Rachel asked, "Do you know that from your patients?"

"You mean anecdotal experience? Mmm, partly. And partly from reading and partly from personal experience."

"In what way, personal experience?"

"I've known women to give themselves unwillingly because they thought it was expected of them."

"But you let them do it."

Jerry opened his eyes and studied her in the dim light. "Well, it's hard to know all the time why someone is doing something, Rachel. Sometimes they're giving you a gift, and it would be unkind not to accept it."

"I suppose."

"It's not an easy thing to unravel, the relationship between a man and a woman. There are all sorts of factors at play all the time. There are men who do the same thing: have intercourse because they think it's expected of them, though I think it's far less likely for a man than a woman. It's not a subject people can be very open about."

"You're pretty open about it."

"I don't know whether that's my training or my personality, but, yes, I think I'm a little more able to talk about it than most people. It's not always comfortable for the other person, though."

"No."

"My openness sometimes can seem like an invasion of privacy."

"Yes."

"It's not meant to be. Like my urging you to just enjoy the hot tub naked. That's not for me; that's for you. But if it doesn't feel right to you . . ." He shrugged his bare shoulders and smiled at her. "You have to do what you feel comfortable doing, Rachel. If you do something because you feel intimidated or rushed into it, you're going to be resentful."

"Tell me about it," she muttered, letting her legs float in the stream of bubbles. "Can we get back to talking about how brilliant I was tonight?"

He laughed. "Sure. You were smashing. You were powerful and capable and clever and charming. Tom Washburn is probably going to call you in on all his cases now."

"You certainly know how to flatter a woman," Rachel retorted.

But she went on to ask his opinion on a number of questions and to share some exciting thoughts she'd had about the evening and the prospects for her career. Jerry willingly fell in with her enthusiasm and introspection. Her animation was more than a little stimulating. When she at length fell silent he felt so close to her that he wanted very much to hug her, or kiss her. But the hot tub was not the appropriate place. Especially when he'd been assuring her that there was nothing *personal* in his wish to have her naked. Jerry found at this juncture that he was quite mistaken about that. He would very much have liked to be there with her naked, and to see if anything sexual developed between them.

That, of course, would be the height of folly, after what she'd said. And because they'd been friends for so long. Any sexual relationship between them could ruin that friendship for good, and Jerry valued her friendship. Rachel was a mainstay in his life and had been since Barbara left him. When Dan died, he had been there to comfort her and she had been infinitely grateful for his help. Their closeness had been platonic all these years, which had not previously bothered him very much. When he looked at her now, though, relaxed yet vibrant, he wanted there to be something more between them. Obviously it was time to call it a night.

"You're exhausted," he suggested, realizing that indeed she was. "I'll go in to change and you can dry yourself here with the towel and put on the robe."

"Thanks, Jerry."

Surprisingly, she didn't turn her head away as he climbed out of the tub but regarded him with an unreadable expression on her flushed face. He stood there for a moment toweling himself off before donning his kimono robe. Even when he walked back to the sliding glass doors he could feel her gaze on him, and he was tempted to look back. But then she'd suspect that he was going to watch her while she left the hot tub and he didn't want her to think anything of the sort. It was hard for him, though, to obey his conscience and not try to catch a glimpse of her naked body, since he could so easily have done it.

After a while he heard her pass quietly through the room and out into the hall. His own body, turned away from her, was even more aroused than he had suspected. He forced himself to relax. Where was all this disinterested enjoyment he'd been talking about? No wonder she thought he was full of it. She could probably feel his arousal two rooms away. Jerry dragged on a pair of blue jeans and a sweatshirt from Yale. He ran his fingers through his hair to tame it, not bothering to go to the bathroom for a comb. That seemed, at this point, just a little too studied.

On the redwood deck he found her blue towel, wrung out and hung over the railing. He gathered it up along with their bottles and took them inside, wanting to be seated in the living room when she came out of the second bedroom. He drew the beige curtains and turned on a standing lamp whose light on the ceiling threw the rest of the room into weary shadows. Why hadn't he spent more time making the place look presentable? The only real touch of color was a bright red pillow on the floor that he used when he watched TV on his back there. One black wood sculpture of a tall, slender hunter that his son had sent him from Africa stood on an end table, almost invisible in the poor light. Jerry was about to pick it up when Rachel returned to the living room.

She looked sleepy now, and her skirt was just slightly off center. She smiled and sighed. "Back to the real world now, eh? That was great, Jerry. I could fall asleep on my feet."

"You look like you're about to. Do you think I'd better drive you home?"

"No, no. I'll be fine. It's just a bit soporific, your hot tub."

"Mmm." He walked with her to the door, where she hesitated, looking around. "Forget something?"

"Probably not. I've got my purse. It just seems like there should be something else."

No wonder, he thought. "Well, if I find anything, I'll bring it in tomorrow."

They stood in the descending elevator in companionable silence. Jerry walked her out to her minivan, still half aroused by her presence. When she had unlocked the car door he placed a chaste kiss on her cheek and gave her a friendly hug. "This has been a great start for your new career, Rachel. Best of luck with it."

"Thanks, Jerry." She climbed into the vehicle and rolled down the window. "I'm still steaming. I'll probably have the windows fogged up before I get home."

"Sure you don't want me to drive you?"

"I'll be fine." She started the engine and gave a little wave as she pulled out from the curb. Jerry stood there until her car was out of sight.

Chapter Six

Rachel was called to the neonatal intensive care unit for an ethics consultation early the next morning. She had known these cases would be the most difficult for her, but when she looked down at the poor infant, whose features were distorted and placed in strange positions, she felt tears well in her eyes.

"This is Jacob," the resident explained. "He has several problems, some of which are reversible and some of which are not. Let me emphasize that there's no question about that, Ms. Weis. We could, at great effort and with great pain to him, accomplish several procedures that would reverse problems—like an operation for his gastroschisis. That would close his abdomen so that his organs would no longer be exposed as they are now. But he has trisomy-thirteen, which is invariably fatal."

Rachel realized that several other people had gathered around the child's plastic bed and she nodded in acknowledgment of them. "Let's move to the conference room down the hall," she suggested, taking one last look at the child before she turned away. As the group left the nursery, one more medical person joined the group and Rachel recognized her as the young woman from Cliff and Angel's wedding, a pediatric intern. "Hi, Erika. Is Jacob one of your patients?"

"Yes," the young woman said. "And I guess I'm one of your problems."

Rachel regarded her questioningly but they had all arrived at the conference room and Rachel indicated that they should take seats so the discussion could begin. The chief resident introduced a series of doctors and nurses, as well as Jacob's parents and their minister. She shook hands with each of them and took the place they'd left her at the head of the table. "We're here to discuss the situation with Jacob. The important thing is that everyone be able to express their view of the situation and that we try to sort out any problems or misunderstandings. The meeting is for guidance only. No one is bound by our recommendations, but we'll do our best to reach a consensus so that everyone will be comfortable with whatever steps are taken."

The chief resident, Dr. Larimer, was the first to speak, presenting the case with succinct detachment. Probably these things had been told to the parents before, but Rachel watched them as Dr. Larimer detailed the baby's defects—he was blind and had a severe cleft palate, his ears were oddly shaped and placed, he was profoundly retarded because of severe brain structure abnormalities, and there was the gastroschisis.

Next the pediatric surgeon spoke, explaining that since the operation would only prolong the child's suffering he could not in good conscience consider operating on him. He felt he had to honor his obligation to do no harm, and there was no real medical benefit to be achieved to offset the pain he would be inflicting.

The parents then had an opportunity to talk. The mother, in a hospital gown and robe, sobbed quietly while her husband explained that they'd tried to have children for the past ten years. This was the first time she'd been able to carry a pregnancy to term. They didn't care if the child was disabled, they just wanted to have a baby to take home and love. Their minister supported their desire by insisting that they had a right to speak for their child, to insist on necessary care for Jacob.

"Well," Rachel said softly when he was finished, "ordinarily that's quite true. But our medical staff, under the guidelines for infant bioethics, have a right to refuse care where they feel it's inappropriate. Not many doctors will treat aggressively where their treatment only causes pain and suffering with no promise of benefit in terms of longer survival or potential for pleasure for the baby. Ethically the medical community has reached an understanding that no one has the right to prolong the suffering of an incurably ill patient."

Erika had sat silently through this whole exchange but now she moistened her lips and spoke. "We do have the capability of keeping most patients out of pain by medicating them. Couldn't we do that for Jacob so that his parents would at least have a chance to take him home and show him how much they love him?"

Her chief resident had an impatient edge to his voice when he answered. "Erika, we're dealing with an infant. We don't know how much pain he feels, and if we medicate him to the point of oblivion, he certainly isn't going to be able to understand that his parents wanted him kept alive so they could love him."

"I understand your dilemma, Dr. Amundsen," Rachel said, determined to neutralize the situation. The other doctors were irritated with Erika for not falling in line with them, which she obviously would in most instances, since she felt so strongly about causing children pain. Rachel suspected the younger woman had been deeply affected by the parents' grief and was trying to offer them the only assistance she could. Rachel tried to phrase her concept of the situation carefully.

"Dr. Amundsen recognizes how desperately these parents wanted Jacob, and since he's alive she would like to see them have the opportunity to share their love with him, even if only for a brief time. And generally the medical community respects parents' wishes whenever possible. If there were uncertainty about the outcome, I would urge the doctors in this case to respect the parents' wishes, too. But there seems to be no doubt that any medical or surgical intervention in Jacob's case would be useless."

Rachel turned from addressing Erika to facing the parents directly. "Our concern here is, as it must be, with our patient. The doctors believe intervention would only prolong the child's suffering. We're all terribly sorry that that's the situation. Maybe we haven't been able to convey our regret and sympathy to you because of the desperate nature of your baby's illness. Sometimes we aren't able to express our sorrow in the press of technical duties and time pressures. And frankly, sometimes we can't face the emotional burden. But each of the doctors, in their own way, is trying to do what is best for you and your child."

The minister, ignoring her plea for understanding, said forcefully, "We can take the matter to court. We can get other physicians to agree to treat the child."

Jacob's mother put a hand on his sleeve to silence him. "No," she said, her voice catching. "We'll let him go, won't we, Bob? We don't want him to suffer anymore. I didn't know things were so desperate. I'm sorry, Dr. Amundsen. I know you explained but I couldn't understand. It's all right. We can let him go, can't we, Bob?"

Her husband, tears in his eyes, nodded and put his arm around her shoulders. Dr. Larimer, the chief resident, sighed his relief and a nurse who had entered the room late and stood back against the wall came forward to offer support to the grieving parents. The pediatric surgeon and the neonatal intensive care attending spoke quietly and before leaving the room the attending approached the couple to shake hands with them. "We'll keep Jacob warm and comfortable," he said. "You'll want to hold him."

Eventually everyone had left the room except Rachel and Erika. There was no feeling of exhilaration this time for Rachel. The meeting had gone well, certainly, but it had been so very sad and draining that Rachel found it hard to finish packing up her briefcase. Erika started to rise, hesitated, and remained in her chair.

"Mrs. Godfrey begged me to help her," she explained. "She was sure that we were wrong

about how awful little Jacob's condition was. She
wanted to believe that he would be all right. I
mean, how could I not try to help her? And now
I've gotten myself in more trouble."

"With your chief resident?"

Erika sighed. "Yeah, and the attending, too,
probably, and the pediatric surgeon. They'll all say
I'm a soft touch or something, I suppose. They already think I'm nuts about not wanting to hurt the
children any more than necessary."

"They're trying to harden you up, huh?"

"Mmm-hmm." She tossed back the strand of
blond hair that had fallen forward on her face.
"Maybe I wasn't cut out for this."

"On the other hand, maybe you're going to
make a terrific, sympathetic pediatrician. Have
you talked with Dr. Stoner?"

Erika brightened. "Actually I did. He was a big
help. He's a really nice guy, isn't he?"

Rachel agreed. The younger woman sounded
slightly bemused by Jerry, which Rachel found
charming. How nice to be young and believe in
someone's power to make you better. Of course,
Jerry believed in his own powers, too. Witness last
night. Rachel still wasn't quite sure what he had
hoped would happen. Could there really be a man
who would allow her to sit naked with him in the
hot tub and not try to seduce her? Very unlikely, in
her experience. Men who hadn't the least interest
in her, or who had made almost no effort to
ingratiate themselves into her good graces, un-
blushingly attempted to seduce her at the first opportunity. Was Jerry somehow different than they?
Rachel very much doubted it.

"Maybe you should talk with Dr. Stoner again,"

she suggested now. "He's seen half the residents who've come through the Fielding training programs. Well, maybe not half, but a lot."

"Yeah." Erika stuffed her stethoscope more securely in the pocket of her white coat as she stood. "But he sort of reports to your program chief and I don't know if that's good for my record."

"I imagine he knows how to do it so it won't damage your standing. Heaven knows it shouldn't." Rachel stood, too, and placed an encouraging hand on Erika's forearm. "You do what's best for your peace of mind, Erika. You'll never have a harder year than this internship one and any help you can get, you should grab."

The younger woman smiled, an expression that made her look strikingly like the old Breck golden-haired, fresh-faced model on bottles of shampoo Rachel had used years ago. "I'll see him again. And, Ms. Weis . . ."

"Rachel."

"Rachel. Thanks for your help. You made me sound almost legitimate when you were conducting the meeting."

"You *are* legitimate, Erika. Maybe Dr. Stoner can convince you of that."

"I hope so." Erika glanced at her watch and grimaced. "I better get a move on. See you later."

"Good luck."

Rachel took off in the opposite direction, resisting the impulse to make her farewell to the infant Jacob. His parents would be with him now and she didn't want to intrude. Or maybe she needed to keep her own distance, like the doctors did. God, medical issues were fraught with emotion.

But she had known that when she started in this direction, and it was probably one of the reasons she'd chosen to go into the medical ethics field. Patients needed to be treated with dignity and to have a voice in the process. And doctors sometimes needed to be reminded of that. Having gone through a very traumatic time when Dan was ill, Rachel remembered all too well the feelings of fear and frustration she'd known as the wife of a critically ill patient. If at all possible, she intended to spare other people as much of that pain as possible.

Thinking of Dan reminded her of Tricia, which brought her thoughts full circle to Erika, who looked so much like her younger daughter. Erika had the same doubts as Tricia about her capabilities, and yet she had a personal self-confidence that was far more similar to Jennifer's. Rachel was in awe of anyone that age with so much self-confidence. It had taken her years of experience as a woman and an attorney to even presume to such assurance. And in her new job it was taking every bit of her hard-won assurance to exert her authority as an expert in the ethics business. She had been well trained, and she burned with determination and eagerness but she had yet to pay her dues as far as long-term experience went. So she felt like something of a fake when she presented herself as an authority. Authorities were people who had practiced a calling for a long time, who had years of experience to rely on for each new situation they faced. Rachel felt she was flying by the seat of her pants—it was both exhilarating and a humbling experience.

Wrapped in her thoughts, Rachel forgot to get

off the elevator on the second floor where her new ethics office was located. The medical center administration had managed to find an empty closet for her use. Really, the space wasn't much more than that, but Rachel was grateful for the window. She hated offices without windows. So she wasn't going to complain about the size.

People poured out of the elevator and a new group poured in. Rachel stayed where she was and rode back up to the second floor, where she had to work her way through the group to the doors and out into the poorly lit corridor. It was not until she stood before her door that she realized someone had been there to put up the brass strip spelling out her name.

"Looks great, doesn't it?" she heard Jerry ask from behind her.

"I'm tickled," she admitted, turning to smile at him. "It makes me feel very official."

"Well, after your triumph last night you *should* feel official."

"This morning's case was harder," she said, sliding the key in the lock and pushing open her door. "Did you come to see me, or were you passing by?"

"I came to see you." He followed her into the tiny office and glanced around. "I didn't think they made them smaller than mine. This was probably a supply closet when there were labs on this floor."

"That's what I figure. Have a seat." Rachel gestured to the two chairs that faced her desk. They were modern metal ones with caned seats that bounced a little when you sat in them, giving the impression of a larger, more comfortable chair.

She tossed her briefcase on the shelf beside the desk and took her own chair, an outsize secretarial one that barely fit in the space between the desk and the wall. An image of Jerry naked flashed through her mind but she refused to dwell on it. She concentrated on his casual attire of sports shirt, pants, and docker shoes. Rachel was surprised by the return of the physical attraction she'd felt the previous evening and she sternly repressed any sign of it. "What's up?"

"I thought maybe I'd better apologize for last night."

"Why?"

"Well, because it was a lot of bullshit about my not being sexually turned on by a naked woman in my hot tub. Oh, I thought I was telling the truth," he hastened to add with a rueful grin. "But I could hardly get to sleep last night for thinking about you."

Rachel wasn't sure how to handle this but it seemed wisest to treat the whole matter as a joke. "And here I thought you were different from other men, Jerry, because you were a psychiatrist or an M.D. or something. All that talk about seeing naked women all the time. But you know as well as I do that we'd ruin our friendship if we let it get sexual. And I'd hate to lose our friendship, Jerry. I count on you."

"Some people can manage both," he suggested, but not with a great deal of conviction.

"Not me. And I'm not interested in sex. I'm sure that sounds very suspicious to a psychiatrist, but I mean it." Rachel hadn't meant to tell him that, but since she had she added, "It's too dangerous, and too complicated, and too . . ." She shrugged. "I don't know. Something."

"Personal."

"Maybe. Intimate. I'm just not interested. I don't know what else I can say."

"You don't need to say anything at all. We'll stick to our friendship. It's important to me, too, Rachel. I didn't come here to proposition you. I just wanted to try to be honest with you." Jerry rose and extended a hand to her. "Shake?"

"Sure." She gripped his hand firmly, feeling that same weak-kneed sensation, which she again chose to ignore. "You were great last night," she teased him. "Which reminds me. The ethics consult I just did was about a severely compromised infant. Our friend Erika Amundsen was there and stuck up for the parents, which could bring her a little grief with her department. She said you'd been helpful to her and I think she'll come to talk again."

"Good. She'll do fine but she needs a little support."

"She still sees things from many points of view. I imagine in time her training will whittle that down so her medical view is a lot more prominent than her empathy with parents or patients." Rachel frowned. "We have a hell of a training system for doctors."

"Yeah, but some of it's necessary. If they'd give me a crack at all the residents, I could teach them some things that would help them get through without so much stress and confusion."

"So lobby for it, Jerry. Make it a priority."

He grimaced. "I have a lot to do already, Rachel. Maybe it isn't a priority. Certainly none of the training programs think it is."

She gave him a look of faint disapproval. "You're the one who's looking for a little more meaning in your life."

"Why do you think that?" he asked, as if it weren't true.

"Because I know the signs. That's the way I was feeling a while back. Restless. Drifting. Wanting to do something useful. Not that you aren't. Most of the work you do is useful. But you want something new, something different." She shrugged. "At least that's how I felt. I thought I could sense it in you."

"Mmm. Maybe." He regarded her with interest for a moment before squeezing her shoulder and turning to go. "I've got an appointment with Carl at ten. He doesn't like people to be late, and he resents it when we call him anal retentive."

The chairman of the psychiatry department, Carl Norridge, was a short, bespectacled man whom most everyone at the medical center considered meticulous, if not compulsive, but who was brilliant for all that. His sway toward pharmacology in psychiatry had disturbed some of the staff and Jerry had continually pressed for a balance between medication and talk therapy that had irritated the chairman but also managed to achieve some of Jerry's goals.

"Maybe I'll tell him I need to be a full professor. That should make his day."

"Tell him you're willing to work on this new project of training all the residents in some psychiatric concepts, to define a program and get it up to speed, if he's willing to make you a full professor. It would be a real credit to Fielding; he'll be able to see that."

"I like the way you think." Jerry hesitated in the doorway. "You may even be right about what's going on with me. I *have* been restless, haven't I? I'll think about it."

Rachel's phone rang and he waved goodbye without waiting for her to respond. She watched him pull the door closed behind him—and felt a surprising sense of physical relief. Until then she hadn't realized how tense her body was. She gave her head and arms a shake before picking up the phone.

What did she mean, she wasn't interested in sex? Jerry pondered this as he hiked through the hospital to the far wing where the department chairman's office was located. Did she mean she wasn't interested in sex with him? Or that she wasn't interested in sex in general? And, if the latter, was this something of recent origin or something that went back a long way? Rachel, in Jerry's opinion, was a very sexy woman. Not overtly, as some women were, women who wanted to make sure you noticed they were sexy.

Rachel wasn't like that. She didn't dress in a way that called attention to her body, or move in a way that emphasized her figure. In fact he'd realized recently that she dressed to detract attention from herself, and she moved with a business-like gait that said she was too busy and too serious to be sidetracked by sexual matters.

So why did he think she was sexy? Damned if he knew. Her eyes, of course. Her eyes talked to you, and smiled a lot, and seemed to brim with vitality. Was that sexy? Maybe not to some people, but it was to Jerry. And her enthusiasm, the way she threw herself into her projects and gave her best effort and struggled with important issues. And it was sexy that she'd kept a secret from him, that she hadn't wanted him to know everything about her, like when she was studying for the medical ethics career and never said a thing. Why had she done that? They were close friends. It would have been natural for her to tell him.

And something else. Last night, when she'd been in the hot tub, her shoulders had looked so vulnerable. Any trace of summer tan was gone so that her skin had gleamed whitely in the evening light. Her clavicle had looked so incredibly inviting. He had wanted to kiss her right there, in that hollow. And lower, of course. He would have liked to follow the medial end to the manubrium sterni with his kisses. Well, enough of that, he brought himself up sternly. Ms. Weis was not interested in sex. More was the pity.

Jerry found himself in front of Carl's office, though he didn't remember precisely how he'd gotten there, since it was on a different floor. He supposed he'd taken the stairs, since he usually did, but he didn't have a clear recollection of it. So much for concentrating on Rachel's clavicle.

Carl's secretary glanced conspicuously at the clock on the wall behind her desk and waved him into the chairman's office. Hell, he was only two minutes late, and if he'd been earlier, Carl would have made him wait. Still, he felt a little guilty as he tapped on the door and let himself in.

"Hi, Carl. Nice tie."

They all teased Carl about his ties, which his wife was purported to choose. Barbara had insisted Jane Norridge got them at Goodwill, but Jerry had it on good authority that they were Carl's father's ties, and the only items he'd kept after the older man's death. Something very psychological about that, no doubt.

"I wish you'd wear one," Carl retorted, since he was apparently not going to say anything about Jerry's marginal tardiness.

"I don't know, Carl. It's like on the pediatric floor, you know. They dress so as not to stress the kids, and I do the same thing for my patients. You'd be surprised how many people are stressed by doctors."

"No, I wouldn't."

"No, I suppose not." Jerry took a seat opposite Carl's desk and cocked his head inquiringly. "What's on the agenda?"

Carl pushed a patient chart away from him and rolled his chair back a few inches. He locked his fingers together as he studied Jerry in silence for a full minute. "I thought I'd explain to you why I'm proposing Robert Lum for Haroon's position."

"Haroon's leaving?"

Carl gave a tsk of annoyance. "Everyone knows Haroon's leaving, Jerry. He was offered the chairmanship at Yarnell last week. He'll start there next semester." Carl took a swipe at his mustache, a gesture of irritation with which Jerry was familiar. "Because Robert is already a full professor he would automatically be considered for vice-chairman. I realize your longevity and your experience might be considered as compelling a reason as that, but I'm inclined to believe the department needs someone a little more formal than you as my second-in-command."

"I don't actually see it that way myself," Jerry said. "In fact, I distinctly remember your telling me three years ago when you opted for Haroon over me that the next time an opening occurred, I would be the prime candidate."

"Well, I had expected Haroon to stay in the position a great deal longer. I had no idea he was looking for a chairmanship elsewhere."

"You didn't actually put a time limit on your offer. I think there are two points you should consider, Carl. One is that you gave me your word on this. And the other is that you can't pass me over forever, because out of sheer embarrassment I would have to leave. I don't play games. You know that. But the whole department will expect me to be offered the assistant chair position, and if I'm not, they're going to feel very awkward, and that's going to make it difficult for me. To say nothing of the fact that I deserve the position."

"I'm not saying you haven't achieved a great deal at Fielding, Jerry. That's not always why and how one is appointed to a position, however. You don't, as you say, play games. Which simply means that you can't be bothered to do what's politically expedient for yourself." He tapped with one finger on a sheet of paper close to him on his desk. "I'm prepared, in lieu of the vice-chair position, to push forward a raise for you."

Jerry hadn't seen this coming. The offer to increase his salary was insulting. He should have had a professor slot years ago, and he should, by rights, be getting the vice-chairmanship now, but the thought of working that closely with Carl made his skin crawl. There was, however, one thing that he wanted: Rachel was right; he wanted a special training program for the residents. And this seemed as good a time as any to go for it.

"Well, that's very generous of you, Carl," he said, allowing just the slightest touch of sarcasm to taint his words. "But hardly fair. As vice-chairman I would be guaranteed a professorship as well as have a certain amount of influence over the direction of the department. When you think about it, that's probably why Haroon is leaving. He wants to set the direction of a department of his own, and who can blame him? I would have fought for slightly different things than he did in that position."

"Such as?"

Jerry ticked off three items on his fingers, all matters with which Carl was already familiar. "But mainly, I think, I would have pushed for a new program, one that would benefit every resident coming through Fielding, and one that would have an impact on medical training far beyond Fielding."

Carl pushed his glasses farther up his nose, though they hadn't slipped any that Jerry could see. "What kind of program? Every resident spends some time in psychiatry now. They don't have room in their schedules for anything else, heaven knows. And any new program would cost a fortune, just when the medical center is trying to cut back."

Regardless of this discouraging introduction, Jerry relaxed into his chair and said, "Let me explain."

Chapter Seven

Norridge had been no more receptive when Jerry had finished, but Jerry had learned something valuable from the meeting. This *was* a project he wanted to carry through. In discussing it he found that he had formulated it further in his mind than he'd suspected, that he had whole portions of a program worked out already. He knew precisely how he'd approach the subject with each new group of residents, how he would present it to them so that they understood and felt in their guts what he was talking about.

He knew exactly how he would convince them that with a little effort they could master psychiatric techniques that would make them more efficient at their jobs, more in control of their emotional status with regard to themselves and the people around them, and more insightful about patient behavior over a wide range of situations. Hell, it was practically a crime that Fielding (and every other medical center) wasn't already offering such a program.

Surely this was worth a fight. Jerry wasn't sure it was worth a fight over the vice-chairmanship, since he'd undoubtedly lose. Fighting for the professorship was a wholly personal matter and he'd do it, but without the enthusiasm he'd invest in a fight for a useful and innovative program. It wouldn't bother him one bit, either, to be opposing Norridge. Until Carl had taken over as chairman there hadn't been so much fuss made about Jerry's iconoclastic style. And the man couldn't see other points of view for being so sure he was right—about the supremacy of drugs, about who were the best people to lead the department, about what was important for psychiatric patients.

Because he wasn't paying any attention to where he was going, he didn't notice Roger Janek until he'd bumped into him. Roger, an anesthesiologist, was wearing blue scrubs and a colorful flowered scrub cap. "Good thing you aren't Cliff's size," Roger remarked as he steadied Jerry. "Have you heard from the honeymooners?"

"No. I hope they won't waste their time sending me a card," Jerry said. "I was sorry you didn't come to the wedding, Rog, but I suppose it would have been hard on you."

Roger, who had recently married a terminally ill patient and lost her shortly after, ducked his head. "I would have felt like a wet blanket, Jerry. They deserved to have everyone there happy and up. I just . . ."

"Well, of course." Jerry put a hand on Roger's shoulder. "You'd call me if you needed help, wouldn't you? I know Angel's been a comfort to you, but with her away I want you to remember that I'm around. And if you need a break, why not use the cabin? It's my month but I don't have any plans to go up. Or we could go together. That might be a good idea. How about this weekend?"

"Jesus, Jerry, you really do move right along,

don't you?" But it was obvious Roger was considering it. He ran a hand absently through his mass of curly brown hair. The youthfulness of his face had altered subtly in the last few weeks. He toyed with the drawstrings of his scrubs, which hid a wiry build in their ample folds. "It'd be nice to go there with someone else the first time after Kerri's death. We'd planned to go, but then ... Well, we'd better take a lot of frozen food. I've eaten your cooking before."

"Hey, it's only for two days. We can eat sandwiches the whole time."

"Good idea. So shall we meet up there or go together?"

"When can you be free?"

"By seven Friday."

"That should be perfect. I'll drive."

"Why does everyone find my driving so offensive?" Roger grumbled as he turned away. "I've hardly ever had an accident."

"You're just lucky, I guess," Jerry unwisely remarked.

Roger hesitated. "I don't feel lucky."

"No, of course not. I'm sorry." Jerry fell into step beside the younger man. "It takes time, Roger. Give yourself plenty of time."

"Yeah, I try to." At the stairwell he turned to push open the door. "I've got a case now. See you Friday."

Jerry continued thoughtfully on to his office. He hadn't been as much help to Roger since Kerri's death as he should have been, considering that the three of them, Cliff and Roger and Jerry, owned the cottage in the mountains together and thought of themselves as "good friends." Of course, Angel had been helping Roger, and Roger had gone to visit his family for a while, but still . . .

Jerry sighed as he unlocked the ward door. He had not been paying as much attention to what was going on around him as he usually did. Which meant, he supposed, that he had become intolerably self-absorbed. Even Rachel had hinted at it, hadn't she? She'd said he had seemed restless and drifting. Well, he would have to do better. Which could start right now, he decided as he watched Mr. Lever of the borderline personality disorder continue his earnest endeavor to disrupt the whole floor. Jerry was very good with borderline personality types. He appreciated the convoluted reasoning needed to follow their machinations. So he moved quickly onto the ward and into the fray.

Rachel was in the process of collecting her papers to take home for the evening when her phone rang. Jerry asked if he could pop over to discuss something with her and she agreed, though she felt a little tired and edgy and would have preferred postponing a chat until some other time. It would only take a minute, he'd said. She leaned back in the secretarial chair and closed her eyes, trying to practice a relaxation technique she'd been taught at a seminar the previous year.

Who would have thought it was so difficult to empty your mind of everything? For a split second Rachel could picture a blank wall, but then thought after thought scurried by. Should she plan to cook something special for Tricia over the weekend? Would Jennifer move quickly into a relationship with the older man in Boston? Was this possibly the time to allow herself a dog, now that she seemed to be feeling a little needy? Should she have the tiles in the bathroom replaced?

When Jerry arrived he took the same chair he'd occupied earlier in the day and said, "It's sort of a personal ethical question I have."

"Hey, I'm a medical ethicist, Jerry. That doesn't make me a moral arbiter to the world."

"Well, I'm sure you'll have an opinion on this." He slumped down in the chair and considered where to start. "First I ran into Roger in the hall and we decided to go to the cottage together for the weekend."

"That sounds like a great plan. Roger could use some company."

"Especially since he hasn't been there since Kerri's death. But that's not the problem." He frowned and rubbed his chin, which was beginning to bristle slightly. "After I'd attempted to straighten out a mess on the ward and had met with the residents for our daily planning session, along comes Erika Amundsen. She wasn't in very good shape."

Rachel cocked her head. "What was the problem? About her support of the parents this morning?"

He nodded. "Mostly. Her department gave her a lot of grief over that. Stand united and all that bull. I don't think they'd do that with a male intern, but then a male intern probably wouldn't have had any patience with the parents' stand." His brows drew down in a frown. "Did you understand where she was coming from?"

"Yes, but it was a difficult position. I wouldn't necessarily expect her attending to understand.

On the other hand, her support of the parents was the one thing they had to hold on to that kept them from flying apart. Frankly, I think Erika's championing of them made it possible to resolve the matter so quickly. They knew someone understood them and was willing to go to bat for their wishes. Without that, they would probably have felt as belligerent as their minister did. Would you like me to sort of discuss that viewpoint with the attending?"

Jerry smiled. "You're so wonderfully competent and sharp, Rachel. Yes, I think it would be helpful for you to do that, for Erika's sake. But that isn't where the problem comes in."

"No? Goodness. What else could have gone wrong?"

"Well, I sort of stuck my foot in it. Erika was there and she was really down, exhausted and frustrated and depressed and worried. And so I invited her to come to the cabin with us."

"With you and Roger?" She sounded incredulous.

He grimaced. "I know. It was stupid and impulsive of me. I just felt so sorry for her. She's so young and vulnerable."

"And pretty."

"Now, Rachel, that isn't what made me do it."

"Yeah, I know. You can sit in a hot tub with a naked woman and not think a thing of it."

"We're not going to be sitting naked in a hot tub. There's Cliff's room, which she can have, and both Roger and me to keep her company."

Rachel groaned. "Oh, God. Roger's going to think you have some bizarre idea of fixing him up with someone, so soon after Kerri's death. Honestly, Jerry, you should have your head examined."

"See? I knew you'd have an opinion." He rose to pace around her minuscule office. "I'd just been castigating myself for not paying enough attention to Roger and . . ." He shrugged. "It just slipped out. At first she said no, thinking you wouldn't like it."

"Me?"

"Yes, she thought I was going up there with you. When I told her I was going up with Roger and he needed someone to cheer him up, she got fairly enthusiastic about the project. Really, it was all meant for the best."

"Have you spoken with Roger?"

"He's in surgery. I will. I promise. I'll make it very clear that there's no idea of fixing him up with Erika, that she just needed a break and she could arrange to get the weekend off. Maybe you'd like to come, too, to sort of defuse the situation?" he asked hopefully.

"Tricia's coming up for the weekend." Rachel tossed her head with aggravation and the beginnings of something else. She could, suddenly, picture Jerry up in the mountains with a young, beautiful girl who needed his attention and his support. Well, that was his problem. The record showed that men were incredibly susceptible to just that kind of situation and doubtless Jerry was no different from other men, as he'd admitted this morning. At least he was unattached and so was Erika. If they got involved . . . well, that was their own business. Rachel felt like she had a rock in her stomach and she very much wanted to be left alone right then.

"You'll work it out," she said, a note of hearty—and forced—encouragement in her voice. "It's just a weekend, after all."

"You don't think it will get me in trouble with my department?"

"Jerry, how should I know? And why would you care at this late date? She's a pediatric, not a psychiatric, intern, and she's not your patient. It *shouldn't* be a problem, but who's to say? Norridge could make something of it if he wanted to, I suppose."

"I had sort of a run-in with him today."

Rachel knew he wanted her to ask about it but she'd heard all she could manage for the time being. She looked at her watch and frowned. "I'm sorry, Jerry. I've got to get out of here. Maybe we could talk later."

He looked puzzled and hurt, but he rose to leave. "No big deal. I can take care of everything. I just thought you might be interested in helping."

"Don't try to make me feel guilty, Jerry. That's not fair. What you did, you did on purpose, whether you want to believe that or not." Rachel turned to pick up her purse and shrug it over her shoulder. "You want my blessing? I'm sure you don't need my advice."

"Something is going on here that I don't understand," he protested. "You're angry with me and I'm not quite sure why. I don't *think* it has anything to do with our relationship, because I don't *think* you think we have one, of anything other than friendship. But you think I'm aimed for one with Erika and you don't approve of that? Is that what you're trying to tell me?"

"If I were trying to tell you that, I'd just say it."

Rachel got a good grip on her briefcase and used it to nudge Jerry toward the door. "Or maybe I wouldn't. Look, Jerry, I don't want to be your confidante in this situation. It just makes me uncomfortable, okay? Next week if you want to talk about Norridge and what's going on in the department, I'll be all ears. I just need to get out of here now." And don't ask me why, her fulminating look insisted, because I'm not going to tell you.

"Have a nice weekend—with your daughter," he said.

"You, too." Since he had turned toward the psych floor, she turned the other way, even though it would be farther for her to leave the building that way. "Bye."

"It's always better to talk things out," he called, even though he was at the time passing a nurse who looked curiously at them.

"So they say," Rachel muttered. "I've never found it's true."

"Me, either," the nurse said, with a wink at Rachel. Rachel laughed, and gave Jerry a "You see?" wave as she disappeared around the corner.

As a psychiatrist Jerry would not have described his emotions as being "miffed" at Rachel Weis. She had every right to behave as she wished toward him. Never mind that he had helped her celebrate her victorious session the other night, or that he had tried to be completely honest with her about his reaction to her in his hot tub. Never mind that he had brought his tale of trouble to her for her advice. Certainly not for her blessing. How could she have imagined that? And he had invited her to go along with them, hadn't he?

Even now, as he drove out of the city across the Bay Bridge, with Roger seated beside him and Erika already fast asleep in the backseat, he was not reconciled to Rachel's attitude. They had been friends far too long for him to be miffed with her. She was, in her own way, a difficult woman—prickly where relationships were concerned and with a tendency to be secretive about certain things. Why hadn't she, for instance, told him about her plans to change her career until she'd already made them?

And now that he looked back on their friendship since Dan had died and Barbara had left him, he could see that Rachel had kept a definite distance between them, especially if it had seemed that they were getting a little too close. Perhaps her problem was with intimacy, Jerry thought. Not just sexual intimacy, but the natural intimacy between two people who cared about each other. He remembered the time when his younger son had called to say that he would be going to Africa with the Peace Corps for two years and Rachel had been there to ease his worries about the situation. But she hadn't let him lean on her, and she hadn't let him bring anything touchy-feely into the relationship. And what the hell did she mean she wasn't interested in sex? he wondered for the hundredth time.

Roger had been staring at the passing traffic, quiet but not morose, probably tired from a long day in the operating room. When he spoke it was softly so as not to wake their sleeping passenger. "Do you think Cliff and Angel will really move back to Wisconsin when she finishes her residency?"

"Yes. It's part of their bargain. But they'll possibly come back here in time. And actually I think it won't do Cliff a bit of harm to practice out in the boonies." Jerry passed a semi and settled into the right-hand lane at a good speed. "He probably wouldn't have chosen academic medicine if it hadn't been for his father's expectations."

"Or his attempt to beat the old man at his own game," Roger retorted. "Cliff told me once that his father had wanted him to be a neurosurgeon. Funny how some parents think they have to manage their kids' lives for them."

"Do yours?" Jerry asked.

"Nope. They're real worried about me, though. That's why I didn't tell them I had married Kerri until after she . . . died. You know, Jer, it's still hard to say that."

"A lot of people never say it. They say someone is gone or has passed away, because that seems to soften it. You're trying to make yourself come to terms with her death, which is the best thing you could do."

Roger was silent for a minute. His hand clenched in his lap when he said, "It just doesn't seem fair. She was so special. Special people shouldn't die like that."

"No, they shouldn't. But life isn't fair. I suppose a lot of people have said that to you over the last month or two."

"Yeah." Roger was quiet again for a while. When he finally spoke it was with a nod toward the sleeping Erika. "What kind of trouble did she get into with her department?"

"Nothing too serious, I don't think." Jerry explained the situation and added, "Apparently Rachel talked with Erika's attending, and helped sort things out. God, do you remember being an intern and being so tired you could fall asleep standing up?"

"Yes, and now I have trouble falling asleep at all."

Jerry glanced over at him, alerted by Roger's tone of voice. "Do you? That doesn't sound good. Maybe the fresh air in the mountains will help. But maybe you should see someone."

"A shrink?" Roger asked, amused. "Not all of us are crazy, Jerry."

"You don't have to be crazy to see a psychiatrist. You're going through an emotionally demanding period. Sometimes it helps to talk things through." He seemed to be telling that to everyone lately, Jerry thought grumpily. "And to get a handle on it if you're getting depressed.'

"Who wouldn't be depressed when their wife died? Look, no doctor can do anything for me that I can't do for myself. And I've got you and Cliff and Angel for support. I'm doing all right."

Jerry had thought so, too, before this conversation. Now he had his doubts, but this was not the time to press them. Instead he changed the conversation to a discussion of hospital politics, which Roger easily joined in, being as irate as Jerry could have wished over Norridge's attempt to shut Jerry out of the vice-chairmanship. The Volvo was already climbing well into the mountains when their sleeping companion awoke for the first time, saying, "God, it smells good. Where are we?"

"In the mountains already," Jerry said. "In fact, only about twenty minutes from the cabin. Have a good sleep?"

"Yeah, sorry."

Roger laughed. "We were just remembering what it was like being an intern. No need to apologize."

Erika leaned forward to look out the front window. In the headlights the minimal road was apparent, with trees overhanging it and lining the route for as far as one could see. "Will it get cold here tonight?"

"Probably," Jerry said. "But the heating in the cabin is good. You'll have Cliff and Angel's room. And we keep extra blankets in the hall closet—those light new things that look like they couldn't warm a slice of toast. I miss the old Hudson Bay blankets. They *looked* like they'd keep you warm."

"Jerry's old-fashioned," Roger explained. "He likes things like metal juice squeezers where you crank the handle, and ice cream makers where you use rock salt."

"So what's wrong with that?" Jerry waved toward the wilderness around them. "When you're going back to nature it seems like you should be doing things without electricity. You know, roughing it. Though I'm grateful for the heat. I don't think the fireplace in the cabin would heat the upstairs rooms worth diddly squat."

Erika shivered. "I don't know why I didn't realize it would be this cold. I guess I've gotten used to San Francisco."

"Here." Roger stripped off his jacket and handed it back to her. "Jer can turn up the heat in the car. I'm used to things on the cool side."

"Thanks." Erika shrugged into the jacket, which was not all that large on her since Roger's build was slight and Erika was a tall, slender woman.

She flipped her hair out from under the collar and sat back against the seat. "Much better. My body temperature always seems to drop a lot when I sleep. In my apartment I have a waterbed and a down comforter. It's the perfect combination for me, but some people find it too warm."

Some people who sleep in her bed, or some people who have the same combination? Jerry wondered, but of course said nothing. There was not that teasing edge to her voice of a woman conveying sexual information she intended to titillate. But then Erika's matter-of-factness might very well encompass a vigorous sexual life which she accepted as so perfectly natural that it was neither the subject of secrecy nor of salaciousness. In Jerry's experience that kind of true matter-of-factness didn't happen frequently, but he had known other women of Scandinavian background who had a healthier attitude about sex than many of their American counterparts. Like Rachel, for instance, who wasn't interested in sex.

Roger and Erika had taken off on a discussion of pediatric anesthesiology, which Jerry listened to only marginally. He didn't have anything to contribute to the discussion, which immediately became rather technical. Erika had moved to a position behind him where she could more easily face Roger, who had turned halfway around in his seat. Both Roger's teaching abilities and Erika's eager intelligence were obvious. Jerry liked hearing the animation in their voices, both being in need of some relief from their problems. But Jerry had to remind himself that it wouldn't be wise, even if it were possible, to push the two of them at each other. It was too soon for Roger to have another woman in his life.

That moment when they reached the cabin and stepped out into the pine-scented air was always a reminiscent one for Jerry. The rich smell evoked memories of his childhood and the cottage he had gone to with his parents after his father got off work on Fridays. His own life didn't lend itself to such a regular getaway, but he'd been delighted to buy the cabin with Cliff and Roger and have his share of the year there. Every third month he cleared a block of time to spend in the mountains, usually alone. He'd decorated his room in a simple, meditative Japanese style that smoothed whatever ruffled feathers he'd developed in the weeks between.

And, alone, he did live more simply—building fires in the fireplace to warm the living room, and chopping wood out near the shed. Of course the phone was always there, reminding him of his city life and his obligations, but when it didn't ring he could fancy himself far away from the world, at some degree of peace with nature and his fellow man. Funny how easy it was to be at peace with one's fellow man when one's fellow man wasn't around.

Jerry unlocked the cabin while Roger and Erika unloaded the trunk of his Volvo. The cabin was cold and smelled slightly musty, and he immediately bumped up the thermostat to produce some heat. His companions banged through the screen door and deposited suitcases and grocery bags on the hall floor. Jerry tried not to regret not being alone. Or having Rachel there with him. Why hadn't he ever invited her to come along? Being together would give them a chance to know each other even better. Of course, maybe she didn't want that.

And what was this thing he had about being alone at the cabin, anyhow? It was hardly as if he lived with a lot of people who infringed on his space in San Francisco. Since his sons were grown and lived elsewhere, they visited only rarely. And he'd never actually gotten used to living alone in the city. But the cabin was a refuge from his work, a rare opportunity to commune with nature, to explore his own soul—or something like that. Jerry grimaced at himself as he carried the groceries into the kitchen. God, he hated cooking.

Erika joined him in the kitchen to help put away supplies. As Jerry plugged in the refrigerator she filled it with vegetables, beer, and eggs she unloaded from a paper sack. "This is a great old bread box," she remarked as she stuffed in a loaf of seven-grain bread. "Someday I'm going to get myself a bread box."

"Why haven't you already gotten one?" he asked, curious.

"Oh, my life seems so transient right now. Why buy a heavy old bread box to have to lug around to the next apartment, you know? I have as little stuff as possible. Does that say something about me?"

"Probably, but I have no idea what. Come on, I'll show you Cliff's room."

She insisted on carrying her own suitcase and followed him energetically up the stairs. "This one's Roger's," he said, unnecessarily, since Roger was in the room, standing transfixed in front of several framed photographs on the bureau. Jerry silently drew the door closed to give him privacy and continued on down the hall to his own room. He flung the door open and switched on the light, but didn't enter. "This is mine. A bit ascetic, I suppose. But Cliff doesn't believe in any of this deprivation stuff. You'll have everything you need."

Erika stood for a moment in the doorway of Cliff's room, surveying the corner full of sporting equipment, the bookshelves scattered with magazines, and the watercolors on the walls. The navy and maroon bedspread and curtains were tailored and masculine-looking. "I take it Angel hasn't gotten her hands on this yet," she said, laughing as she pushed her suitcase in onto the blue carpet.

"No, and since they'll be going to Wisconsin next summer, they're going to leave it as it is." Jerry pointed to the bed. "A surprise for you. It's a waterbed. Cliff leaves it heated the whole time, so we make him pay the whole PG&E bill."

"I'll feel right at home." Erika stuck her hand in under the comforter to feel the water temperature. "Perfect."

"Cliff keeps a TV and a CD player in the cabinet there, with a great CD collection. There's only the one bathroom next door. I think the clean sheets are in the cabinet, too. The rule is that we leave beds with clean sheets, so those will be fresh and you can change them before we leave."

Erika had already stripped off Roger's jacket and hung it over a chair back. She sat on the edge of the bed now, removing her shoes, her hair falling down over her face. Her full breasts strained against her shirt. "You won't mind if I just go straight to bed, will you?"

"You do whatever you like. This is a vacation."

Jerry backed out of the room, drawing the door closed behind him. "Sleep well, Erika."

He heard her drowsy "I will" as he retreated back down the hall.

Chapter Eight

The mountain morning was sunny but chill, with wisps of fog gradually disappearing from the forest above the cabin. Jerry had long been up, finding errands to do that brought him back to the cabin from time to time to check if his guest needed anything. He had heard Roger take off at dawn, running on the path by the creek. Erika slept until almost noon.

Jerry was fixing himself a toasted cheese sandwich when Erika wandered down the stairs and into the kitchen. She wore a sweatshirt so large that a pair of shorts barely peeked out below. Her hair was tousled and there were lines on her rosy cheeks from the bedclothes. She smiled at him, then yawned and stretched. "God, you probably thought I'd never get up. I don't even sleep this late when I'm at home. It must be the fresh air."

"Probably. Or the change in altitude." Jerry motioned to the griddle. "Want something I can fix? Pancakes? Bacon? A toasted cheese sandwich?"

Erika wrinkled her nose. "No, thanks. I have yogurt with me, and some fruit. If there isn't a toaster, I could use the griddle, though."

"There's a toaster." Jerry looked around and didn't see it. He wondered briefly who had destroyed it this time. Then he remembered that they'd decided to keep it in a plastic bag in the cupboard to discourage tiny crawling things from congregating around the crumbs. He started opening and closing cupboard doors, finally locating it on his sixth try. "Here it is. You can plug it in by the stove."

Erika removed the plastic wrapping and bent down to stuff the wrapping in a container of similar items. She had incredibly long legs, Jerry noticed. He returned his gaze to the griddle. His sandwich was smoking slightly and he flipped it with a tsk of annoyance.

"Something the matter?" she asked.

"Nope. I'm just waiting for the cheese to melt enough."

Erika busied herself taking the yogurt container from the refrigerator and finding herself a bowl and utensils while her seven-grain toast heated. She scooped the rich, slithery golden flesh from a persimmon, commenting, "This is about the end of the season for these. I miss them when they're gone."

"I've never had one. At least not since I was a kid. I remember how bitter they could be."

"Oh, only when they're not ripe," she protested, offering him a bite with her fingers. "Try this."

The fruit was too slippery to take from her so she slipped it into his mouth and stood with questioning eyebrows as he chewed and swallowed it. Jerry wondered if something was going on here that he wasn't in control of. "Delicious," he pronounced. "I'd forgotten."

"People ignore a lot of the strange-looking

fruits," she said, turning back to the preparation of her breakfast—or lunch.

Jerry used a spatula to transfer his sandwich from the griddle to a small plate. He had already poured himself a glass of beer that he picked up now along with his sandwich. "I'm going to eat outside. Why don't you bring yours out when you're ready?"

"Sure."

She didn't even glance at him. Jerry told himself that she was not being deliberately provocative. She was, in all likelihood, behaving exactly as she always behaved, with friends and lovers alike. Unfortunately, the way she behaved was tantalizing for the men around her. She was a very sexy woman. Jerry wondered if she'd ever been warned about that. If she had, she would probably have said, "That's not really my problem, is it?" And maybe it wasn't. Why should she have to behave differently just to discourage male attention? But the sexy ones did—usually—if they didn't want to run into problems.

Jerry was halfway through his sandwich when she appeared, letting the screen door shut behind her. Her sweatshirt said University of Washington, where he imagined she'd gone as an undergraduate, perhaps to medical school as well. She blinked in the sunlight and her face brightened. "Gorgeous." Unself-consciously she then sniffed the air and shook her head in amazement. "Just as good as last night. This is fantastic."

"Glad you like it."

She sat down across the weathered redwood table from him and took a bite of the unbuttered toast, her gaze wandering over the scenery. Behind them was a rising mountain, in front of them a sort of valley. To the right a creek could be heard chattering downstream. And to the left was the dirt road they'd driven in on the previous evening. "Where's the best place to start exploring?"

"Probably the path by the creek. It wanders along for a couple of miles in either direction."

"Do you run?" she asked hopefully.

"No, but Roger does. He took off at dawn and I haven't seen him since."

"Well, he'd probably rather be alone."

Smart girl, woman, he corrected himself, as he nodded. "But you can't get lost, if you go alone. I do a lot of walking but jogging plays havoc with my left knee. Sorry."

"Hey, no problem. I just love to run. I feel so free." She took a bite of the vanilla yogurt into which she'd apparently deposited the persimmon. "Ah, heavenly. Eating is one of the great pleasures of life, isn't it?"

Which only served to remind Jerry what one of the other great pleasures was. She looked so young and appealing, so full of enthusiasm, so charged with energy. He knew exactly how she would approach sex: with an electric excitement and a generosity of her body that few women, he suspected, could match. Oh, there were women who professed to adore sex, but their adoration was more pathological than real. Their need was for reassurance of their own sexuality more than a delight in sharing the experience with a man. Most women enjoyed the physical sensations but they would have treasured a good hug almost as much. These musings on sex brought him once again to the question about Rachel's sexuality that had been in the forefront of his mind lately.

Jerry didn't remember whether he'd answered Erika's question, but it was probably rhetorical in any case and she was studying the view toward the creek when his attention returned to her. "There are stepping-stones across the creek, but they get washed away sometimes. The path on the other side leads past an old octagonal church up on the hill, long since abandoned."

"Why octagonal?" she asked, her head cocked toward him.

He frowned. "I don't remember what the saying was, exactly. Something about the devil not being able to corner you, or an idea of that sort."

"Maybe we could walk up there later. I thought I'd run for a while now."

"Sounds good." Jerry's sandwich had grown cold, the cheese congealed unappealingly, but he finished it anyhow. "I'm going to take a rest in the hammock."

"There's a hammock! What fun. I'll try it later."

You could try it with me, he thought, not even bothering to scold himself for the licentious thought. What was the use? She was a sexy young woman and he was in close proximity with her and absolutely nothing was going to come of it, except these loose thoughts. Pretending he wasn't having them wasn't going to do a bit of good. He just had to be sure they stayed in his mind and not on his lips, even in jest. Because Erika would know that a jest held a real invitation. She was too experienced and too bright not to.

When she went into the cabin to change he moved to the hammock he'd hung earlier. It wasn't as if she was a patient, because she most definitely wasn't. He had given her some support psychologically when she'd needed it, but he not only wasn't her therapist, he held no authoritative position above her. There would be nothing *wrong*, from an ethical standpoint, with his becoming involved with her. Except that he wasn't going to do it. She was scarcely older than his son, for God's sake. She was especially vulnerable right now, too. And he was restless. Not a good combination, he thought ruefully.

He heard the screen door slam and he tried to keep his eyes closed, but found it impossible. She'd tucked her hair back into one of those brightly colored fabric elastics. Her shorts were skimpy and her T-shirt clung to her chest like a second skin, though he could see a sports bra outlined there. She gave a friendly wave as she took off down the path. Jerry told himself to shape up.

Rachel's house in the Forest Hills section of San Francisco was a two-story beige stucco building from the 1930s that Dan had brought up to every modern standard—copper plumbing, 220 wiring, remodeled kitchen and bathrooms. The oak floors gleamed under scattered rugs of bright colors and interesting designs. In the dining room there was dark wood paneling and a coffered ceiling. Dan had retained the casement windows with their small panes because they added charm to the sunny rooms. Only the rear windows were shaded by the large eucalyptus trees in the backyard. Unlike large sections of the residential areas of the city, Forest Hills was laid out on winding streets that drifted up and down at will. The area was generously sprinkled with enough trees to make it feel as if you weren't in a city at all.

Tricia had decided to stay with Rachel for the weekend, which was all to the good because Rachel had had no intention of accompanying Jerry and Erika and Roger to the mountains. Let Jerry extricate himself from the situation he'd created. He would not really have thanked her for being there. Whether he realized it or not, he wanted the opportunity to spend time alone with Erika. Roger's presence made things respectable, but he wasn't likely to spend much time with his companions. Rachel knew Roger would try to be by himself as much as possible, if only to avoid inflicting his sadness on the others.

Saturday morning Rachel was working on some papers in the den when she heard Tricia let herself into the house and call out a greeting. She hurried out through the hallway past the living room and hugged her daughter tightly against her. "I'm so glad you've come. You look great."

Actually, Tricia looked a little peaked but it would never do to tell her so, even if one only meant to be sympathetic. She always read such comments as criticism, no matter how carefully Rachel explained her meaning. And Tricia did look good in many ways—her blond hair shining, her runner's body clad in a bright fuchsia sweatsuit. "I decided to run on my way here, at Crystal Springs," she explained, dropping her gym bag full of the weekend's clothes.

Rachel picked up the bag to carry it up to her daughter's room, but Tricia removed it from her grip. "None of that, Mom. I'm a grown woman now. You should hear what my friends say about how Jen and I took advantage of you when we were younger."

"How do they know?"

"You're supposed to say, 'But you never took advantage of me, dear.' " Tricia laughed. "Well, when they are talking about washing the dishes, or doing the laundry, or making meals when they were in high school, I always tell them I never did that stuff. They're horrified."

"No wonder," Rachel said dryly. "Your father thought I should insist, but I just couldn't do it."

"It hasn't done us any harm. Not me, at least. I'm getting pretty good at cooking, and I keep my place reasonably clean. I don't know about Jen." She had gotten halfway up the stairs now, with Rachel following. "Have you heard from her recently?"

"Just the other day. She was going to the Cape with a friend for the weekend."

Tricia paused at the head of the stairs. "A man friend?"

"Yes."

"Wow. She hadn't met anyone interesting the last time I talked to her. Did she tell you about him?"

There was a trace of envy in Tricia's voice that she tried hard to disguise as curiosity, but Rachel was her mother. "She's told me a little. He's a friend's uncle, and quite a bit older. She sounds pretty interested."

Tricia dropped her bag on the bed and looked around her room. "You sound like you don't approve."

"Do I? I'm just a little worried. I guess I think it would have been nicer for her to find someone her own age. This man may have another family, an ex-wife, all sorts of things to bring to a relationship that just complicate it."

"Hey, who can be choosy? You take what you find."

"You don't mean that."

Tricia wrinkled her nose. "I don't know, maybe I do. Hell, it's so hard to meet a decent man. All the good ones are already married. Or they're not ready to settle down yet. What does that mean, Mom? Not ready to settle down?"

Rachel shook her head. "You tell me."

Tricia took an agitated turn around the room, then dropped onto the bed, waving her mother into the rocking chair by the window. "It means they want to keep on screwing around. It means they want to keep looking for the perfect woman: someone who has a great career, is beautiful, and wants to cater to them for the rest of their lives. Men are so selfish! At least the ones I meet. And they don't want to take any responsibility for anything."

"Like what?"

"Oh," Tricia said, blushing, "even about sex. They expect the woman to supply the condom. Really! They're so immature. And they whine at you about how you expect too much of them." Tricia had a remarkable facility for imitating people that she put to good use now. *"Hey, baby, you can't expect me to show up right on the dot. I've got a heavy schedule.* Like you don't," she scoffed. "Or, *I'm not into talking about my feelings, lady. They're a private matter.* Actually, Mom, they don't have any feelings. They're just façades for lust machines or little boys who never grew up and learned how to take care of themselves."

"Maybe that's why Jennifer is interested in an older man," Rachel mused. "He probably seems more mature than the guys she knows her own age."

"Probably." Tricia laid flat on the bed and stared up at the ceiling. "But then, it's probably all my fault. Maybe there's something about me that leaves them cold or something. Or makes them not want to take me out. I'm probably too needy or too desperate. Hell, I'm only twenty-four and already I feel like my chances of meeting the right guy are pretty well shot. And why do I need a guy anyway? Jennifer has a perfectly satisfying life whether she's in a relationship or not. Why can't I be like that?"

"Everyone's different. Why do you think you need a relationship? What do you get out of them?"

Tricia shrugged. "What everyone else gets, I guess. A companion, someone who thinks I'm special. And someone I can lavish a little affection on." She grinned over at her mother. "It's not all one-sided. I like doing things for a man, just not everything. With Steve I loved to write him little notes and buy him little things to show him I cared about him. And I liked fixing him meals and doing his laundry with mine. It made me feel like a couple, you know? And somehow that's really important to me. Maybe it shouldn't be, but it is."

"I don't see why it shouldn't be."

"Well, it isn't for you, is it? You've never remarried."

"No one's asked me."

Tricia frowned at her mother. "That's because you never see anyone for very long. Except Jerry."

"Jerry and I are friends."

"Yeah, I know. And it's probably better that way."

"How come?"

"Because he's a psychiatrist. I don't think it would be very comfortable to be married to a psychiatrist. But I bet you could have married someone else."

"Maybe. It didn't seem worth the effort."

"Now that's what I mean," Tricia agreed. "For a klutz like Ray Mittermeister, why would you bother? You're so much more . . . everything than he is. Sometimes I feel like that, too. Not very modest of me, is it? But sometimes I think I'm smarter and more attractive and less neurotic than any of the men I meet and why would I bother to try to interest them in marrying me? Who wants a jerk for a husband?"

"No one."

Suddenly Tricia's eyes filled. "I miss Steve something awful sometimes."

Rachel reached out and clasped Tricia's hand. "I know you do."

"I shouldn't have done it, you know? I should never have given him an ultimatum. But it had been two years. Two years!" Tricia's voice rose to a wail. "How much time did he need to decide if he wanted to spend his life with me? I needed to get on with my life. I want to marry and have a family. I don't want to be old when I have my kids. I want to be young so I can enjoy them. Is that so wrong?"

"Of course not, sweetie. You were very brave to

make a decision and stick by it." Rachel wasn't sure it had been the right decision, seeing Tricia's pain, but it had been a decision she'd supported Tricia in making because it was what her daughter had wanted. "There will be someone else. I promise."

As if she could promise something like that. But it seemed such a sure thing, given Tricia's age and desire. "Maybe it's better if it doesn't happen for a while. You need time to get over Steve. And you will, honey. Time heals your wounds, even when you don't think it ever will."

Tricia rubbed at her eyes and sat up. "Yeah, so I hear. Jen and I used to worry about you after Dad died. But you seem okay these days, you know? You seem to be happy now you've found something you like better than the law."

"Yes. It's made a difference." Rachel noticed a hummingbird hovering near the window. Hummingbirds always made her smile. "Medical ethics is the kind of challenge I've needed. Not another man in my life."

"Well, you've *had* a man in your life, a good man. He'd have been hard to replace." Tricia untied the band around her hair. "I need to take a shower. Then I'll help you fix lunch."

"Great. I'll be downstairs." Rachel rose and brushed the top of her daughter's golden head with hummingbird-light lips. "See you in a bit."

Jerry had fallen asleep in the hammock but woke abruptly when he heard the screen door slam. Roger was coming out with a sandwich in one hand and a beer in the other. "Sorry," Roger groaned. "I didn't mean to let it bang like that."

Jerry blinked and rubbed his eyes. "No, it's okay. I didn't mean to fall asleep at all. Is Erika back?"

"I haven't seen her." Roger swung one leg over the bench by the wooden table. "I only got back a few minutes ago."

"Have a good run?"

"Yeah." Roger stared off toward the creek. "I had really wanted to get her up here one last time. She loved it here."

"I remember." Jerry hauled himself out of the hammock and walked over to sit opposite Roger. "You were up awfully early."

Roger shrugged. "I couldn't sleep. I've been waking around five and can't ever get back to sleep. It's too late to take a pill so I just read or get up and have breakfast."

"Do you take something at night?"

"Sometimes. I have some Halcion."

"Do you think you're clinically depressed?"

"Of *course* I'm depressed." Roger took a long swallow of the beer and thumped the bottle irritably back on the table. "Who wouldn't be depressed, Jerry? I wanted Kerri to live forever, or at least to outlive me, like most women do. Yes, I knew she was dying when I married her. And it doesn't make the least bit of difference. There just doesn't seem to be as much to live for as there was a couple of months ago. And, yes, I find that depressing."

"Clinical depression is a specific condition, Roger." Jerry screwed up his face and recited from the diagnostic bible of therapists. " 'Dysphoric mood or loss of interest or pleasure in all or almost all usual activities and pastimes.' And then you have to have four of the following symptoms nearly every day for at least two weeks: poor appetite or significant weight loss or increased appetite or significant weight gain."

Roger looked down at his sandwich. "Tastes like sawdust."

"That's one. Insomnia is two. Psychomotor agitation or retardation we'd never be able to figure out for you. You're always fiddling with something."

"I am not," Roger protested, even as he tore strips off the beer bottle label.

"Loss of interest or pleasure in usual activities, or decreased sex drive. That seems to apply."

"Who in the hell am I supposed to want to have sex with?" Roger demanded. "That's not a fair one."

"It was the decreased interest in usual activities I was referring to. How about loss of energy or fatigue?"

"Well, how can you have as much energy if you can't get a good night's sleep? That's not fair, either."

"Hmm. Feelings of worthlessness, self-reproach or excessive or inappropriate guilt." Jerry cocked his head questioningly.

"You mean like I feel guilty that I'm alive and Kerry isn't? Yeah, I've got that. Not big time, though. I mean I'm not going to beat myself up about it. Doesn't everyone feel that way?"

"I'm sure a lot of people do. How about your ability to concentrate?"

Roger sighed. "I'm okay at work, because I have to be. You can't be giving people anesthesia when you're not really there. I've called in sick once or twice because I was too upset to do my job right. But I can handle it the rest of the time."

"Hmm. Number eight is about suicidal ideation."

"I don't think about committing suicide, ever." Roger propped his elbows on the table, his chin in his hands. "Sometimes I think about the state I put people into in the operating room, you know? I think about the blankness of being under anesthesia, where there's no pain and you don't even miss the time you're gone. That seems like an ideal state right about now. Where you're not responsible and you don't feel anything, and later on when you wake up you can get on with your life." He shrugged. "But that's just because of my work."

"And because you feel a little numb right now?"

"I suppose so. Look, Jerry, I'm okay. I can handle this."

"I know you can, Roger. I just don't like to see you doing it the hard way." A breeze lifted the long hair over Jerry's ears and twisted it up around his forehead. He paid no attention to the tangle. "I'm not suggesting you won't come through this without professional help. But you might make things easier for yourself if you'd see a therapist for a few weeks. You do have several of the signs of clinical depression."

"Yeah, and so does everyone else whose wife dies. They don't all go to psychiatrists."

"Well, most of them have support of some kind, family, friends. And you do, too, of course, but Angel and Cliff have been away and they both have rough schedules. You may be reluctant to use me just *because* I'm a psychiatrist. Just think about it, okay?"

Roger drank down the last of his beer. "Okay, Jerry."

But it sounded to Jerry as though he was just trying to placate him. Never mind, he'd try again another time. Roger had taken a big step in even agreeing to come to the cabin this weekend to face his ghosts here. It wouldn't do to pressure him.

Jerry was about to suggest that they try a few shots at the rusted basketball hoop when Roger surprised him by asking, "Did you see a therapist when Barbara left you?"

It was a perfectly legitimate question, given the way Jerry had been probing him, but Jerry was stunned into silence for a moment. They weren't the same thing at all, divorce and death. At least, not to most people. Carefully, Jerry picked through the things in his mind that he was willing to tell Roger.

"Actually, we went to a marriage counselor for a few sessions. Mostly for me, I guess. It was Barbara's decision to leave."

"She'd fallen in love with someone else."

Wow, let's be blunt, Jerry thought, and wondered whether Roger was trying to pay him back for prying. "Yes. There was never any question in her mind about continuing the marriage."

"But there was in yours?"

"I was . . . hopeful." He cleared his throat. "It's kind of hard to believe someone you love could fall out of love with you."

"I think about that," Roger admitted. "I think about whether Kerri would have loved me forever if she'd lived. And that's the one thing I'm grateful for, I guess. Because I couldn't have borne her not loving me anymore. Is that sick or what?"

"It's an understandable thought to run through your mind. I wouldn't worry about whether it's normal. It's just there and probably the only thing your mind can dredge up to give you comfort."

Erika appeared around the side of the building. Jerry combed back his hair with his fingers as he rose.

"How was the run?" he asked.

Erika's face was lightly flushed and her shirt soaked with patches of perspiration. "Great! It feels so incredibly healthful to be running where you aren't breathing in all those car fumes."

"I know what you mean," Roger said. "It's almost like getting your lungs cleaned out."

"I hadn't been out of the city since July when I started at Fielding." Erika plopped down on the bench where Jerry had been sitting. "And of course I'm not going to be able to get home for Thanksgiving, so this is the perfect break."

Jerry sat down a few feet from her and contemplated the wisdom of inviting her to share Thanksgiving with him, but he didn't even know what he planned to do for Thanksgiving. Besides which, it really didn't sound appropriate. He had kind of thought he might spend Thanksgiving with Rachel; they sometimes did, at her house with her younger daughter there. But she hadn't said anything yet and it was only a few weeks away. Maybe Rachel had other plans. But shouldn't she have told him?

Jerry brought his attention back to the present situation. What fascinated him was how at ease

Erika was, being off in the mountains with two men. She wiped away the sweat from her forehead with a sweatbanded wrist and plunged into a story about taking a trail past a deserted campsite where a groundhog had wandered across her path.

"I used to go camping a lot," she explained, "when I was in medical school in Seattle. A bunch of us would just take off for the weekend. It didn't matter what the weather was like, or how many of us packed into Ted's van. We just had to get away for a while. We'd always bring our books, and some of the others would wander off to study, but Ted and I rarely did. It was like a pact we had. We'd play cards and stuff and come back to school feeling like we'd had a real break. I think that's how I got through medical school."

Jerry wondered if "and stuff" included making love with her friend Ted. He could very easily picture Erika and Ted left to the van by their companions who would know they wanted some time alone. And he thought about all the pressure of medical school and the relief it had been for him to come home to Barbara and lock the bedroom door against a curious toddler. How they'd tried to be quiet but would eventually erupt into laughter, merely making the experience all the more enjoyable.

Sex. It was different when you were young. More exciting, perhaps. More fevered. But there was something to be said for a leisurely approach. A savoring of sensations, the suspense of a slow build-up, the reward of waiting and anticipating. Jerry wasn't sure he'd trade mature lovemaking for an impassioned mating. But he didn't mind thinking about it, and wondering if it was for a chance to relive those younger days that men his age had affairs with women Erika's age. Women who had young, desirable bodies and who had been raised to take a healthy interest in sex. Unlike some older women, who weren't interested in sex.

Jerry decided it was time for him to go inside the cabin and call Rachel.

Chapter Nine

Tricia answered the phone when it rang and called to Rachel, who was in the garden working on a bed of chrysanthemums, which were still blooming heartily. With her hand over the receiver, Tricia said, "I think it's Jerry, but he didn't say."

Rachel's eyebrows rose. She hadn't expected to hear from him this weekend. Though Jerry had bought the cabin with the other two doctors almost four years ago (when the house from his marriage had been sold to divide up their property), she'd never been to the mountains with him. But here he was taking Erika. Rachel drew off only one of her dirty gardening gloves to accept the receiver. "Hello."

"Hi, Rachel. It's Jerry. There was something I wanted to check with you."

"Shoot." But don't make it some ethical question about whether you should sleep with a beautiful pediatric intern because I have no intention of answering questions like that, Rachel advised him through mental telepathy.

"We haven't talked about Thanksgiving and it's getting kind of close. Have you made other plans?"

"Thanksgiving? No, I hadn't thought about it this year. I'm not sure I want to go to all that work, what with the new job and everything." But Tricia probably expected it, Rachel thought. And why was Jerry asking about it, anyhow? Did he want to make plans with Erika? The idea made her suddenly sad. Well, let him. She and Tricia could eat out somewhere.

"I wondered if we were, you know, planning to have it together," Jerry said.

"We hadn't made any plans, Jerry. You should do whatever you like."

There was a moment's pause, as though he were trying to figure out what to say. "Well, I'd like to have Thanksgiving with you, Rachel, but I don't want to invite myself. I know it's a lot of work, and I'm no help at all."

"I was just thinking Trish and I might go out to eat."

"Could I take the two of you out? We could go to one of those places that serve a traditional meal, turkey and all the trimmings."

"Let me discuss it with Tricia, okay? She's such a traditionalist, and she's sort of down now. I don't want to upset her. Either way, you could spend the day with us—but you don't have to, just because we've done it before."

"No, I want to. Really. It was just that someone mentioned Thanksgiving and I realized we hadn't really settled about it and so I thought I'd call."

Right. "Someone" had mentioned it. Obviously Erika, but in what context? Rachel wondered. No, she was jumping to conclusions. It could as easily have been Roger, with no place to go and feeling lonely. I'm such a shit, Rachel castigated herself.

"If Roger or Erika doesn't have a place to go for Thanksgiving they could share it with us. In fact, if there were going to be a number of people, I guess I could do it here."

"I wasn't angling for that kind of invitation," Jerry protested. "We'll just do it the two or three of us, you and Tricia and me."

Rachel was torn. She didn't want to be a shrew but she suspected there was a subtext here that she wasn't getting and which might be significant. *Maybe he had called up hoping that she already had plans and he would be free to do what he wished.* Oh, the hell with it. How could she know what he really wanted? They had been honest with each other when there wasn't any reason not to be. Like when neither of them was seeing someone else. Did that change when he showed an interest in a woman young enough to be his daughter? Rachel told herself it was none of her business what he did. She couldn't think of a thing to say to him.

"Rachel?" he said, after she had left a long silence. "Are you there?"

"Yes, I'm here. I'm thinking, trying to figure out what you want, Jerry. And what I want. All of a sudden it seems confused."

"But it's not. Rachel, I don't think either Roger or Erika would be free on Thanksgiving, anyhow. Probably both of them are working, Roger so he'll be busy and Erika because she's bottom of the heap. This doesn't concern them. Just you and me."

Rachel removed her second glove and rubbed a fist against her forehead. "Okay. Then we'll plan to spend the day together, and we'll eat out. Okay?"

"Fine."

"How are things going in the mountains?"

"These two are a barrel of laughs," Jerry teased. "No, they're okay. Roger is depressed and probably should see someone. Erika slept until noon, she was so exhausted. They've both been out running. Not together. You don't run, do you, Rachel?"

"You know I don't."

"Well, there have been some things recently that you haven't told me, so I wasn't sure."

"You mean about the change to medical ethics?"

"Yeah. Stuff like that."

"I don't think there's been anything else, Jerry."

"No, well that was a rather big one."

Rachel hooked a stool with her foot and drew it close so she could sit down on it. Out the kitchen window she could see chrysanthemums bobbing in the breeze. "I can't explain why I didn't tell you, Jerry. It wasn't that my decision wasn't important. I guess mostly I didn't want it influenced by anyone—not the kids, not you."

"But you told your kids."

"After I'd started the classes, yes. They asked."

"And I didn't?"

Rachel sighed. "It wasn't that. I wouldn't have told you if you had. Your opinion would have carried too much weight, Jerry. Like Dan's would have, in a way. You'd have been like a substitute for him, telling me your impression of whether I should do it, whether I *could* do it. I didn't want that. I wanted it to be my decision."

"But you could have ignored my opinion."

"Maybe. This way I didn't have to find out, you see?"

"No, not really." Jerry suddenly changed directions. "There's something else I wanted to ask you, Rachel."

"What?"

"What did you mean when you said you weren't interested in sex?"

Rachel chewed thoughtfully on her lip. "Are you asking as a psychiatrist, Jerry? Are you worried about my mental health?"

"No, I'm asking as a man, as me. Just wondering how personally I should take your remark."

"Like, whether I meant I wasn't interested in sex with you or in general?"

"Right."

"In general."

There was a long pause. "That's all you're going to say? Just that you're not interested in general?"

"Yep. That's about the long and short of it. I don't think it's anything physical and I don't care if it's something psychological. It doesn't bother me one bit."

"Oh, sure."

"Is that your comment as a man or as a psychiatrist?"

"Both. I find that hard to believe."

"Well, believe me. Life is much less complicated without sex."

"It may be less complicated but it's hardly a simple matter to drop it out of your life."

"Wrong. It's been perfectly simple and wonderfully relieving. Make of that what you will." Rachel rose from the stool, ready to end the conversation. "If there's nothing else . . ."

"Hmm. Maybe we could discuss this more the next time I see you."

"Maybe."

"You're not being very helpful, Rachel."

"It's not something I want to be helpful about. I've finished being helpful about sex. I'm sorry if that bothers you. There are lots of women who are perfectly happy about sex and I'm sure you run into them every day." Like today, and yesterday. Like Erika with her healthy young body and her equally healthy attitude about sex, Rachel imagined. "You don't need me to be lusting after you, Jerry. You probably wouldn't *want* me to be lusting after you, if you thought about it. Let's be friends, okay? That works well for both of us."

"Grumble, grumble, grumble," Jerry said. "We'll talk. In person."

"Mmm. Have a nice weekend."

"I am. You, too. See you when I get back."

"Right." He'd forget. He'd get busy. But if he forced her into a discussion of her sexuality, she'd be honest with him. Rachel hung up the phone with a self-conscious shrug. It was, indeed, rather alarming that he was a psychiatrist and supposedly knew what it meant if you weren't interested in sex. That there was something seriously wrong with your psyche, no doubt. Well, the hell with psychiatrists and everyone who wanted to pin labels on women like her. There was nothing wrong with her mental health and she wasn't going to let anyone talk her into believing that there was. With an abrupt gesture she drew on her gardening gloves and returned to the backyard.

* * *

Disgruntled, Jerry hung up the phone and stared out the window toward where Roger and Erika were talking desultorily at the redwood table. Roger seemed more relaxed than he had in a while. Though he fidgeted with the band of his wristwatch, there was nothing new in that. Jerry had watched him over the years tug at his earlobes, pull on the drawstring of his scrubs, tap his heel to an unheard beat—the regular gamut of nervous habits that even a relatively laid-back young man might have. Roger had a lot of physical energy that was belied by the stillness he kept when he was administering anesthesia. Or maybe the energy just exerted itself when he had a chance to be away from a calling that kept him relatively motionless for such long periods of time.

Erika sat with her arms around her legs, which were bent at the knee up on the bench. She had beautiful long legs but seemed genuinely unconscious of her body at the moment. Her brow was drawn down into a thoughtful frown over strikingly blue eyes. She said something to Roger that caused him to nod and illustrate something on his chest. He was good with his hands, his gestures efficient and effortless. Erika nodded in turn.

Jerry considered rejoining the two of them, but decided against it. Instead he retreated to his room and meditated, after a distracted fashion, for half an hour. Then he heard Roger go into his room and close the door firmly. So much for having another talk with him. But Jerry knew there was plenty of time over the weekend, so he went back downstairs, where he found Erika curled up on the couch with a mystery novel. She smiled up at him as he paused in the doorway.

"I'm going for a walk to the old church up the hill. Are you into your book, or would you care to come along?" he asked.

Erika set down the book immediately and rose energetically to her feet. "I need every bit of outdoor exercise I can get this weekend," she explained. "Can you wait a minute while I put on slacks and a sweater?"

"Sure."

The November day still looked sunny but the thermometer had dropped several degrees already. Jerry pulled a light jacket from the rack hanging on the back of the main door. He'd forgotten that he'd left the denim jacket at the cabin and had several times dug through most of his belongings at his condominium in search of it. *I must be getting old and forgetful,* he thought with a trace of self-pity. *No wonder Rachel isn't interested in me. Who wants a dried-up old codger who can't even manage a full professorship after twenty years in the same institution?*

Down the steps clattered Erika in a tight red sweater and black slacks that hugged her thighs in a positively enchanting way. "See? That didn't take long," she called to him, and a huge grin made her eyes seem to sparkle. "Men always think women will take forever when they go to change and it's not always true."

"You're a quick-change artist," he agreed, basking in the glow of her youthful spirits. Maybe he wasn't such a dried-up old codger after all if this playful young thing found him so enjoyable. "I've been thinking about your problem, Erika, and I've been thinking about one of my own, and I think together we may be able to solve both of them."

"Great. There's nothing I like better than solving problems." She laughed. "Well, a few things, but solving problems ranks right up there."

It took Jerry most of the mile walk up to the church to explain his idea to Erika. A pediatric intern wasn't perhaps the ideal person to use, but maybe that was better. Erika would be his test case for instructing residents in some of the areas that were being neglected in her training, and she would gain knowledge that few of her contemporaries had.

Her eyes shone with excitement. "You could do that? You could actually help me deal with all these people better? And take care of myself in the bargain?"

"You bet I can. Every resident should get that kind of training, but there's never enough time or resources." Jerry waved her to a seat on the stone stair in front of the white octagonal church. "Take a patient who's unnecessarily demanding. They're very hard to handle unless you understand the elements that warp how a patient approaches his physician: fear and anxiety and confusion. Being sick makes people behave differently. And when you're confronted by a patient like that, how do you feel?"

"Frustrated, mostly. Sometimes even angry," Erika admitted.

"Right. But you can be taught how to get your patient to tell you what's really bothering him or her. There are clues to help you. And there are words that trigger helpful reactions in patients. These aren't difficult things to learn, and they can make a world of difference in how you perceive your patients, even the little kids, but in your case especially the parents and families."

"How would we do it?"

Jerry thought for a moment, his gaze drifting over the old cemetery. "This weekend I'll give you an overview of what psychiatric residents learn in the first few months of their training about interviewing patients and families. Then during the week let's see if you can spend twenty minutes a day with me when I'm with a new patient—during your lunchtime or when you're finished work. Just whenever you can get away for twenty minutes. I know that's not easy, but if you can manage it, we'll be able to boost your skills in no time."

"I can find the time, if you can," Erika said. She drew a deep breath and gazed up through the pine trees swaying above them to the intense blue of the sky. "I can find the time for anything that will make my work less stressful, anything that will make me a better doctor."

"This will, I promise. And if I have my way, every resident coming through Fielding will learn the same things. But there's no program yet, and you'll be helping me develop it as we go along. Okay?"

"Definitely."

Jerry rose and held a hand down to help her up. As if she needed help, he thought. But she placed her hand in his, trustingly, and allowed him to draw her to her feet. "We've discovered how to get into the church. Come on, I'll show you. And it's nice knowing the devil can't corner us there."

Erika went for the adventure of it. Jerry knew Rachel would have appreciated the irony. Why hadn't he ever invited her to come up to the mountains with him?

Since the change from daylight time it was getting dark so much earlier that Jerry had almost been caught off guard by the gloom in the trees as they made their way back down the hill. The path was barely visible, because it was only marginally a path at all. He didn't want to get them lost when he had Erika in tow. Not that she would mind the inconvenience so much as that she would think him stupid for the mistake, or even suspect that he'd done it on purpose to remain alone with her. Did young women still think things like that? From everything Jerry had seen, Erika was far too sophisticated and sexually open to make such ploys necessary in approaching her—if one were interested in approaching her.

Not that he was. She was now a full-fledged student of his, spiritually if not precisely by the medical center rules, and Jerry had never approved of mentor-mentee intimate relationships. She was a very attractive woman, certainly, and there was no way he was going to obviate that fact. But he'd worked with attractive women before and managed to enjoy their beauty without feeling a need to involve himself with them. He had only to remind himself that he could be useful to her, and she could be helpful to him, and they would get along just fine as colleagues.

The lights beckoned and the smoke coming from the chimney promised a warm log fire as Jerry led Erika into the clearing in front of the cabin. There were even the smells of food being prepared and they banged through the screen door to find that Roger had started making dinner. Jerry's brows shot up. "What's this? I thought you didn't know how to cook."

"I had to learn a little when I had Kerri home. She hated my not eating a decent meal, so she'd tell me how to fix something nutritious and expect me to bring it upstairs and eat with her." Moisture gleamed in his eyes. "Even though she couldn't eat and the smell of most foods made her nauseated."

Erika, hesitant in the face of Roger's obvious sadness, turned to Jerry for guidance. Jerry laid a hand on Roger's shoulder and said, "She must have taught you well. That smells great. Was Kerri a good cook?"

"Yeah. Before she got really sick she used to make me the most amazing things—soufflés and homemade pot pies and apricot scones. I've been thinking of learning to cook some of those dishes, just, you know, to kind of have a connection to her."

"That's a nice idea," Erika said. "Especially the scones, don't you think, Jerry? I love scones."

Roger was sautéing onions and garlic for the spaghetti sauce he'd started. A huge pan of water sat on a back burner, not yet boiling but with a flame curling around its base. "I'd eaten alone for so many years before I met Kerri, you'd think it wouldn't bother me now. But I hate it. I'd rather eat in the cafeteria at Fielding than sit by myself at home and try to get down a meal."

"Do you think that has to do with Kerri being so sick she couldn't eat?" Jerry asked, as if it were an ordinary question. He'd taken up a knife and begun, awkwardly, to chop up the bell pepper waiting on the cutting board. "You were eating alone then, too, only you weren't alone."

"Jesus, Jerry," Roger muttered, not looking at him. "Let's not get all symbolic."

"But things are symbolic. Eating is nourishment. You nourished yourself while you watched Kerri starve. That has to have set up a conflict in you. For her sake you ate, but it was a painful process. You're also a doctor, a healer, and there was nothing you could do to heal her, not even in the simplest matter—that of nourishment."

Roger's hands had stilled. "She wouldn't accept IV nourishment after a while. I begged her, but she'd insisted that Angel tell her exactly what was going on. Angel shouldn't have done that."

"Of course she should have. I would have, you would have, in other circumstances."

"But I wanted to protect Kerri! I wanted to keep the worst from her." Tears coursed down Roger's cheeks and he didn't bother to brush them away. "It was the only thing I could do for her."

"No, you could love her. And you did love her. Our patients almost always understand more than we tell them in situations like that, Roger. They know they're dying. Kerri wanted to face the truth and accept it. But she knew you wouldn't be able to tell her everything so she got the information from Angel. Who probably handled it as well as any of us could have. You know that."

"Yeah, I know that," Roger mumbled, his hand automatically returning to stir the translucent onions and garlic.

A pungent aroma filled the small room where steam misted the windows. From outside the three of them must have seemed wrapped in the warmth and security of the snug cabin. Instead of the expected laughter, however, there was emotional pain. But Jerry thought there was some healing happening, too. And he hoped that Erika understood that.

After the pain comes the healing. And a doctor could help with both, if she weren't too afraid, if she hadn't closed herself off to protect herself. He was going to teach Erika that, to make her life more manageable and more rewarding. He owed her that. He owed every young doctor that. And he was going to fight for the right to give them that knowledge.

Chapter Ten

Rachel was thinking about going to bed early when there was a light tap on her front door. Tricia had left several hours before, so it was unlikely to be her. Rachel stood uncertainly in the archway into the living room, tempted to ignore the intruder. When she heard Jerry's voice she was still tempted to pretend she wasn't there, or wasn't up. She was a little tired from Tricia's visit. But the lights were still on and it would seem rude to ignore him standing out there. Rachel sighed and crossed to the door.

Jerry looked rested and invigorated. Probably from falling in love with a woman young enough to be his daughter, she thought. That seemed to give older men a new lease on life. The thought of a younger man exhausted her. "It's a bit late, Jerry."

"I know. I'm sorry." Not that he waited to be invited in. He gave her a peck on the cheek and shooed her backward with his hands, following behind her. "I'd have called, only I figured you'd say it was too late tonight."

"It *is* too late tonight. Surely whatever it is could have waited until tomorrow."

"Nope. We need to talk right now, before things get set in stone between us."

"Like what things?" Rachel reluctantly followed him into the living room, where he sat down on the sofa and indicated the spot beside him. "Nothing has changed between us that I know of." Except maybe you've just slept with a beautiful young woman and intend to be so taken up with that relationship that you won't have time for me. "You don't have to spend Thanksgiving with us."

He frowned, confused. "I thought we'd settled that."

"I'm saying it's all right if you change your mind, Jerry."

"I have no intention of changing my mind. Aren't you going to sit down?"

Rachel had been debating whether to offer him a glass of brandy. Instead she sat down. "Did you have a good weekend?"

"Hmm. Yes, very relaxing and very productive. I wish you'd come. No, no, I realize Trish was here. How's she doing? Still upset over breaking up with that fellow?"

"To a certain degree, but she seemed better, more interested in other things going on in her life. She's directing the ninth grade play."

"Good, good." But it was obvious to Rachel that Jerry wasn't really thinking about Tricia. "We need to talk."

"So you keep saying. We can talk anytime, Jerry, but I'm a little tired tonight."

"Are you? You don't look tired. You were probably just bored."

Rachel stiffened. "I don't like people telling me how I feel."

His hand went up apologetically. "Of course not. I'm sorry. I of all people should know better than to do that. I just want you to be willing to talk with me now. I've spent the whole weekend working with two people and I want someone to work with me now."

"Come in the kitchen with me, then, and I'll fix us some tea, okay? That'll wake me up."

Before she had even put the kettle on to boil, he said, "It's the sex thing, you know? I'm sorry if I keep harping on it, but I have to understand. Why aren't you interested in sex?"

He had remained standing in the doorway and Rachel considered him for a long moment. Did she want to talk about it with him? Was he her friend, or a psychiatrist, or a man sexually interested in her? Sex was probably uppermost in his mind because he'd spent the weekend around Erika. Possibly they hadn't had sex together because of the situation, but the atmosphere might have vibrated with sex the whole time. And Rachel had been gardening and visiting with her daughter. She sighed.

"I don't know where to start, or how to explain, Jerry. Do you read Ann Landers?"

"The advice columnist?"

"Yeah. Off and on over the years she's had columns about women and how they feel about sex. But no one seems to pay any attention. Certainly not psychiatrists and therapists. If you're not interested in sex, you're half dead or crazy."

"Whoa! That's not true. So what does she say about women and sex?"

"Oh, it's not her, exactly. People write to her and then she'll ask a question that a lot of her readers respond to. Not exactly your balanced study. But the results are interesting. Like that more than seventy percent of the women who responded would be content to forego sex for a little cuddling."

"There's nothing new about that."

Rachel slapped the box of tea bags down on the counter and snapped at him, "Well, you'd think it was, the way women are treated if they aren't interested in sex. Look at you. You come here after a long drive down from the mountains just to confront this little oddity of mine at the first opportunity."

"You aren't an oddity, Rachel. I'm asking you because it's important to *me*, not to you. It makes a difference to me. And it makes me sad to think you're not interested in sex."

"Exactly. It makes you sad. That's a criticism of me, Jerry. Can't you see that? But not being interested in sex doesn't make me sad. It makes me feel released. It frees me from all sorts of traps. And it means I don't have to put up with men I hardly know pawing me because 'everbody does it.' As if I care! This is my body and it belongs to me and that's the way it's going to stay."

Jerry said nothing as he watched her pour the boiling water into a teapot with the tea bags. Rachel wanted him just to go home then. She'd said enough, more than enough, and he was standing there waiting for her to say more. "Do you want milk or sugar?"

"No, thanks."

Rachel pulled a dusty tray off the top shelf and frowned at it, but didn't bother to wash it. When she'd stacked it with the teapot and two mugs,

Jerry came over and took it from her, carrying it back into the living room, where he poured them each a cup of tea. Rachel sat down on the sofa and he handed her a cup. The tea was far too hot to sip but she nestled it in her lap while he sat down beside her. He left his cup on the tray and folded his hands in his lap almost self-consciously.

"From the way you talk about your body it sounds as if it hasn't always been yours to do with as you choose. Have you had a bad experience with someone?"

"That's not how I'd put it."

"How would you put it?"

"That I haven't been able to do what I want, because of my feeling pressured to do what someone else wants." Rachel shrugged. "Men pressure you. And society pressures you. Expectations pressure you. It's simpler to take myself out of the arena altogether."

"Are you talking about the men you've dated since Dan died?"

She sat staring at the mug in her lap, her eyes blinking rapidly. "I suppose so."

"But not entirely."

"Jerry, I don't want to go into this with you. It's really none of your business."

"I wish I could agree with you. It feels like my business. It feels important to me. We can take it slowly."

"What makes it your business? We're friends, Jerry. The definition of friends is practically that they don't have sex together."

"But I'm a psychiatrist, too, and a man who thinks of you as a sexual being. I can't make you explain to me, Rachel, but I need you to try if you can."

What was it that made her want to explain it to him? Rachel felt more than a little confused about that. Was it that he'd developed a good chair-side manner as a psychiatrist? Or because down deep she really agreed that she owed him an explanation, that there was some growing connection between them that demanded it? Certainly there was no other man she'd even consider talking about it with. And strangely, it was the one subject she couldn't bring up even with her best women friends.

"It's difficult to know where to start," Rachel said. "When I was young I was pretty ignorant about sex. I mean, maybe more so than other women. Maybe not. I don't know. It was this mysterious thing that was supposed to be so exciting and so romantic at the same time. I was kind of sheltered as a kid. The boy I went with in high school was probably actually homosexual and didn't know it yet. You know?"

"I can picture it."

"So I didn't get the kind of experience the other girls were getting. Even if they weren't having intercourse they were petting and getting close. But intercourse wasn't something you did in high school, in my time. You were a bad girl if you had sex. At least that was the word and I thought it was what was happening. In college I learned that wasn't what was actually happening. I went to a women's college, where most of our professors were men. I had a crush on this one professor the whole time, though nothing came of that. Still, I wasn't interested in the boys who wandered through my life, because of my crush on him. I really enjoyed the course work, and dreaming about my professor."

"So what did you dream about doing with him?" Jerry asked.

"Not much." Rachel wrinkled her nose in annoyance with herself. "I don't know how it escaped me. Maybe because the books at that time didn't dwell on sex but on a romanticism that seemed exciting but safe. I daydreamed of us at picnics on sunny lawns by sparkling streams, reading poetry and laughing at each other's stories. It seemed so wonderfully safe and endearing. I suppose I knew about sex, technically, but it didn't really mean anything to me."

"You didn't masturbate?"

Rachel felt a flush rise to her cheeks. "See? The whole subject still embarrasses me. I don't know if I can do this, Jerry."

"Well, let's see. You don't have to tell me everything tonight. But it might help."

"I could live without trying to tell you at all."

He nodded and took a sip of his tea. "You're doing it for me. I understand that, and I appreciate it. Everyone has a natural tendency to avoid difficult topics, and some of these are hard issues to discuss. But facing them, bringing them out into the light, helps you come to grips with them. It helps put things into perspective. I wouldn't ask you to do something I thought would cause you even the smallest harm. Do you believe that?"

Rachel slowly nodded.

"Thank you. Let's try to go a little bit further, then. Did you masturbate?"

Her fingers felt frozen and she wrapped them

around her mug. "Not very often. Occasionally. It seemed wrong but not wretchedly wrong. I had a room to myself the last couple of years at college, which gave me a special feeling of privacy. I would daydream about the professor spending time with me in my room, which was a rather romantic garret. I didn't make much of a connection between those thoughts and the . . . masturbating."

"And you feel stupid about that now?"

"Of course."

"So when did you first actually encounter the realities of sex?" Jerry asked gently.

"With Dan. I met him right out of college when I came out to San Diego for law school. I was feeling very brave and adventurous, going to school so far away from my family on the East Coast."

Rachel thought back to those days, trying to remember what the experience had felt like. She tucked her legs up under her and took a sip of tea. "I came out in the middle of the summer, planning to find an apartment and look around before school started. The hotel I was staying in was kind of run down, so I spent as much time wandering around the city as I could. I met Dan on the beach one day and we got to talking. I was so naive."

"In what way?"

"Well, he said his roommate was just moving out and he needed someone else and why didn't I live with him. And I thought that would be adventurous and very avant-garde of me, and so I did."

"What was naive about that?"

"Oh, I might have known what would happen. He might have asked anyone and the same thing would have happened."

"What happened?"

"Just what you'd imagine, Jerry," she said tartly. "We got to know each other real fast and started to fool around and eventually became sexually involved. If I'd been more sophisticated, that might not have happened."

"But that's what was happening in those days, don't you remember? Things were just starting to change from the impossibly Victorian to the loose hippie times. We didn't have AIDS to worry about, and most of us didn't think much about other diseases, so pregnancy was the biggest worry around."

"Yes, and it terrified me. Even though I went on the birth control pill, every month I worried that my period wouldn't come, and that it would be just retribution for my behavior."

Jerry frowned slightly. "Let me understand this, Rachel. You still thought it was wrong to have sex, even though you were having it?"

"Oh, I don't know. You don't change overnight. It had been drummed into us that you didn't have sex until you were married, and I knew everyone else was, but it didn't seem quite right to me."

"Were you enjoying it?"

Tears gleamed in her eyes. "No, not really." She laughed impatiently. "And I thought that was my fault, too. Compounding the problem. I thought I didn't have orgasms because I wasn't married and I felt guilty. And that my problem was spoiling things for Dan. God, the guilt just wouldn't quit."

"So you married Dan to get rid of the guilt?"

"No, no. Oh, I imagine I thought it would help. But I married him because I was madly in love with him. And he was crazy about me. For all the chanceness of our meeting, we really did seem to be a good match. Maybe not externally," she admitted with a rueful smile. "I was starting law school and he was so bummed out on the educational system that he intended to keep his summer job in construction."

"Back to the sex," Jerry suggested.

"It didn't get much better after we were married. I had the odd orgasm, nothing consistent. I felt very responsible for disappointing Dan."

"*You* felt responsible for disappointing *Dan?*"

"Yes. It seemed as though he should have been graced with someone who responded to him appropriately. I mean, what were we hearing in those days: women wild with desire for sex having multiple orgasms and not being able to get enough of it. I could easily have done without."

"Tell me what that was like."

"You sound like a psychiatrist, Jerry."

He shrugged. "An occupational failing, I'm afraid. Rachel, what did it feel like to be having sex with your husband when you didn't want to?"

Leaning back against the sofa, Rachel closed her eyes, afraid they would tear up again. In a voice that sounded strained even to herself, she said, "The poor man would have been happy to make love two or three times as often as we did. So when he wanted to make love, we made love. Well, that's not true. *Sometimes* when he wanted to make love we made love. I could never even the score. I could never be as giving as I thought I should be. It was such a little thing, but I couldn't do it."

"You think it's a little thing to be asked to have sex when you don't want to?"

"Of course. Jerry, what's the big deal?" She opened her eyes and met his troubled gaze. "People have sex all the time. It's not a traumatic event. What was there to object to?"

"What *did* you object to?" He gestured helplessly with one hand. "What I mean is, what about the process made you uncomfortable?"

"Humph. Everything, if it was going wrong. There were plenty of times when I was aroused, but nothing came of it. And the times when I wasn't aroused, everything could bother me. His hand on my breast, even his kissing me." Rachel bit her lip. "Sometimes I had to grit my teeth to get through it. Sometimes, most of the time, I just wanted it to be over with. I wanted to tell him to hurry up and get it over with."

And suddenly the dam broke. Tears welled up and streamed down her face. Unable to speak, she waved aside his hand on her shoulder. Again and again, a wave of sobs engulfed her. She kept rubbing at the tears on her face with a napkin, but more tears would fall to dampen it again.

"Let me hold you, Rachel," Jerry said at last. "Just hold you. Trust me."

"Go home, Jerry."

"I will. I'm going to go home very soon now. Just let me hold you for a minute. I need to hold you."

Through hiccups she said shakily, "It's just one more demand, Jerry. Just one more thing I have to do for someone else."

"No, you're going to do it for yourself, even if it's for me. You're going to do it because it's just me holding you and making you feel loved and comforted. Like a parent with a child, Rachel, not a lover. I'm just going to hold you against me and wish my strength on you, like a blessing."

Exhausted, Rachel turned her tear-streaked face to him and allowed him to put his arms around her. There was comfort in his arms. Her face lay pressed against the denim jacket he hadn't removed when he came in, its cloth absorbing the last of her tears. She could feel his sturdy heart hammering beneath her cheek, and hear his voice saying soothing things into her hair.

She shouldn't have told him. She had to tell him. Torn between these two truths, she lay still against him, absorbing the solace he offered. And despairing that she would never be able to face him again. Sure, he had probably heard this kind of story over the years from patients. But she was a friend, someone he had known for a very long time. Someone who had spent an evening in his hot tub with him. Someone who had developed a fondness for him that she wouldn't even admit to herself, because it was stupid and useless, wasn't it?

"Dear Rachel," he murmured, stroking the back of her head. "You're going to be all right. You're going to feel better. I'm here to help you."

As good as it felt to be held, Rachel gathered herself together and moved back from him with a sigh. Forcing herself to look at him, she smiled and said, "Thanks, Jerry. I appreciate that."

"You're going to be embarrassed about talking to me, aren't you? Don't be. I'm honored that you'd be so open with me. We'll talk again."

Rachel shuddered. "I don't think so, Jerry."

"Don't make up your mind about it, okay? Please. It sometimes helps straighten things out when you talk." He rose and drew her up with one hand. "Remember, it was me who needed to understand. I was the one who insisted that you talk to me. But there's every reason we should do it again."

Rachel made a noncommittal gesture. "I'm exhausted, Jerry. I just need to get to bed."

"I know you do." He bent to kiss her cheek. "See you tomorrow."

Yes, probably she would see him tomorrow, she thought as she carried the tea tray back to the kitchen. And she'd wonder how she could possibly have told him what she had tonight. Revealing secrets she'd never expressed to anyone before, to him, a man, someone important in her life.

But she had had to tell him. Because he had to understand why a relationship between them wasn't possible, even if they grew to care about each other. Rachel would not, could not, put herself in the same vulnerable position again. It wasn't fair to a man, and it wasn't fair to her.

And it was permission, in a way, for him to concentrate his attention on Erika—Erika who radiated a healthy sexual attitude. Not that Jerry had expressed some real interest in Rachel that she had to release him from, but he'd mentioned that he'd been aroused by her in the hot tub and might have considered that a commitment of a sort. Who knew with men? Some of them didn't seem to see a commitment anywhere in their lives; others might see a commitment where it didn't exist.

The whole situation was beginning to make Rachel's head ache. She left the mugs on the kitchen counter and wandered through the downstairs rooms turning lights off. Upstairs, in the single hall light, she stood for a moment gazing at the family portrait on the wall. It must have been taken almost twenty years ago, when she and Dan were in their late twenties and the girls were adorably young. So very long ago. In another life.

Rachel touched the portrait like a talisman, sighed, and headed for the bedroom.

"Jerry? Is this a bad time?"

Jerry looked up to see Erika standing in the doorway of his office, looking fresh and relaxed. "No, no. Come on in. Is this for one of our twenty-minute training sessions?"

"If you have the time." Erika slipped onto the chair opposite him that so many patients had occupied over the years. "I'm waiting for some lab results and no one will miss me."

"Don't sit down," he teased, bounding to his feet. "We'll go on a mini rounds with my new intern. It's actually perfect timing."

The young man who had just joined him on the ward was still uncertain of himself around psychotic patients and Jerry was trying to teach him to accept psychiatric illness on the same visceral level as he accepted physical illness, and to deal with it in a professional and competent manner. But the intern, Ed Morrison, was exceptionally good at interviewing patients, and this was what Jerry wanted to show Erika. He met Ed in the corridor and asked if he and Erika could observe the intern's interaction with his first patient of the day. "Erika needs to learn some of the techniques you've acquired already in your training, Ed. Will your patient mind?"

Ed, appearing both flattered and flustered, said,

"Who, Mr. Farber? He won't even know you're there."

"Literally?" Erika asked as they took their places in a small conference room near the nurses' station.

"Yeah. He's kind of out of it."

Jerry whispered as Mr. Farber shuffled in, "But watch how Ed handles that, Erika. He's learned to keep the interview on track no matter how far afield Mr. Farber wanders."

And Mr. Farber wandered far afield. Sometimes he thought he was in a munitions factory during World War II, sometimes he thought he was talking to his son. Through the whole exchange Ed Morrison kept a thread of reality running that seemed to draw the old man back time and time again. When Erika's twenty minutes were up and Jerry excused themselves to an oblivious Mr. Farber, they stood outside the interview room for a minute.

"Did you see what he was doing?" Jerry asked. "That doesn't work just with delusional patients. The same focus can help with any interview."

"That was great." Erika's eyes gleamed with excitement. "You think I can learn to do that?"

"Of course you can." Jerry walked with her to the elevator. "I have a psych consult with a teenage cancer patient later today. Would you like me to page you so you can be there?"

"You bet. Thanks, Jerry." She seemed to catch herself. "I'll remember to call you Dr. Stoner around the patients."

"Fielding Medical Center will no doubt be pleased; it doesn't make the least difference to me."

Jerry watched her walk into the elevator but his thoughts were already elsewhere. His day was shaping up to be unremittingly busy but he had to talk with Rachel today, even if she didn't want to hear from him. He had to be "in her face," as the younger people said, so that she didn't have a chance to build up a resistance to him, to shut him out of her innermost life.

What an extraordinary woman! It would have taken a great deal of courage to tell him what she had. And a great deal of trust and faith in him. But what it meant for a relationship between the two of them he couldn't imagine. Obviously her intent in explaining her situation to him was to discourage him from even thinking about something more between them than the friendship they enjoyed. But that wasn't *his* intent, and Jerry could be very persuasive when he chose to be.

The dilemma was going to be achieving what he wanted while not unduly influencing Rachel in her vulnerable state. A bit much to ask, even of a psychiatrist. Jerry shook his head and trained his attention on the approaching nurse.

Chapter Eleven

Rachel was afraid, every time the phone rang, that it would be Jerry. She wasn't ready to talk to him yet but she knew that wouldn't deter him if he thought she was avoiding him. He was, in his own way, a very determined man. Not that the easygoing, laid-back style was a façade. It was more that he had definite opinions about what was best for people and he tended to make sure that they knew about them.

When the phone rang and it was Nan LeBaron, Angel Crawford's roommate until a few weeks ago, Rachel was relieved and more than happy to have the neurology fellow come down to discuss a problem with her. Though Rachel knew that Angel and Cliff were back from their Hawaiian honeymoon, she hadn't actually seen either of them and hoped Nan would pass on the latest information. Such an attractive couple, headed for some interesting career conflicts if they didn't both stay on their toes.

Nan entered looking slightly harassed, which was not her normal frame of mind. She was tall, at least five-ten to Rachel's five-five, with straight blond hair and a generally soothing if somewhat acerbic manner. Rachel rose to shake hands with her and raised her eyebrows in mute question.

"Oh, you're not going to believe this one," Nan told her as she dropped wearily into the chair opposite Rachel's desk. "I've always thought, especially as a neurologist, that a durable power of attorney for health care was a terrific idea. And now I've got a patient in a coma who has one and I'd give just about anything if the sheet of paper on which it's written would spontaneously combust."

"Why?" Rachel leaned back in her chair and folded her hands across her abdomen. She felt like a psychiatrist.

"Because this poor young woman, Pamela, gave the power of attorney to her husband."

"That's usually the case. Is he a jerk?"

"Worse than a jerk. He's an asshole and means to use any power he has to do her in."

"Wow! Can he?"

Nan sighed. "Oh, it won't come to that, I don't think. We can stall until we see what's really happening with her. She's one of those marginal cases. She might be brain dead, she might not."

"Surely he had nothing to do with whatever caused her condition."

"No, no. That was from a car accident. He wasn't anywhere around. And he didn't tamper with the car. This isn't Perry Mason time. But what he is is separated from her. Her sister explained that to me early on after Pam was brought in."

"Not good," Rachel murmured. "A divorce automatically ends an ex-spouse's rights under the durable power of attorney, but there's no provision for a separation. Is the sister named in it at all?"

"No, it was made up several years ago when the sister didn't live close by and there was no trouble in the marriage, apparently. This guy really seems to think he can force us to pull the plug even if she's not been determined to be brain dead."

"Well, he's wrong of course, but he sounds like the type who'd search around for another opinion until he found someone who would say she was brain dead—if he could find someone."

Nan shuddered and stretched elegant hands out in a gesture of supplication. "Would you talk to him? He might listen to you. He talks to doctors like we're auto mechanics. God, I'd hate to be his car mechanic. He's incredibly rude, always assuming you don't know anything, or that you're making a mistake, or that someone else could do a better job. It's almost as if he doesn't acknowledge you at all as a person, you know? You're a mechanic and you're trying to get away with something that he's not going to let you get away with. The guy gives me the creeps. How this poor woman stayed with him for five years *I'll* never know."

Rachel had severe doubts about what good she would be able to do in the situation, but she agreed, because she felt it was her job, to see the man. "Want him to come here, or me to go there?"

"Make him come here," Nan suggested as she rose. "Anything you can do to put him at a disadvantage is going to be helpful to you. And, Rachel, I'll owe you one."

"It doesn't sound like I'm going to be able to do

much, but I'll try." Rachel stood up and shook hands with the young woman again. "Have you talked with Angel? How was the honeymoon?"

Nan grinned. "Fantastic. And I remember the time less than a year ago that she left that man standing at the door ringing the bell and refused to see him." Nan shook her head in amazement. "Who would have guessed?"

"Are you keeping the apartment the two of you shared?"

"At least until the end of the year. I really don't want to bother getting another roommate right now, but I don't want to pay the whole rent forever, either. Maybe I'll look for a smaller place, but I kind of like the company of another person, you know?"

"Yes, I know. Well, send him down to me, Nan. What's his name?"

"Bill Enderling. Hers is Pamela and the sister is Beth Sawyer. The medical situation is pretty much like the Lee case last week, so you know all the options. Thanks, Rachel."

Because she was caught up in her thoughts about Nan's patient, Rachel answered the phone without anticipating the caller. "This is turning into a killer day," Jerry said without preamble. "I had hoped to get over there to see you, but there's no way. How are you doing, Rachel?"

"I'm just fine, Jerry. About to talk with a young man who wants to pull the plug on his soon-to-be ex-wife."

"And people think medical ethics is boring." He hesitated. "I wanted to ask you to dinner tonight but I can't even guess at when I'll be done here. Is it okay if I call you later?"

"I was thinking of going out to a movie."

"Alone?"

"Jerry. Yes, of course alone. I don't have any young acolytes swarming around me."

"Is that supposed to mean something?"

"Probably. I'm sure I'll talk with you soon, even if I'm not home tonight."

"You wouldn't go out just to avoid my call would you?"

"Why not? That's the door, Jerry. I'll talk with you later."

He was a three-piece-suit man, Bill Enderling. In his right hand he carried a briefcase and Rachel knew without asking that he was an attorney. Well, she had the advantage of age and experience on him.

Behind him was a young woman who looked so incredibly sad that Rachel felt an instant sympathy with her. She would be the sick woman's sister, Beth Sawyer. Though Rachel hadn't expected her, and felt she might be a complication, she welcomed the two of them and asked Enderling to move the second chair from between two file cabinets.

"They don't give you much space here," he said, with something of a smirk in his voice.

"No, most of my meetings take place on the nursing floors or near the ICUs. You can leave the door open if you're claustrophobic."

It was the kind of game lawyers played and he glanced over at her sharply but said nothing. Rachel shook Ms. Sawyer's hand and indicated the chair opposite her. "I'm glad you both came because it's really the two of you who are going to have to work this through. I'm very sorry about

Mrs. Enderling's condition, but my understanding is that the doctors aren't satisfied that there is no brain activity."

Enderling had taken charge of his chair like it was an animal to be subdued. "There's virtually no brain activity on the scans," he insisted. "Pam has always been very clear about the circumstances under which she would want mechanical measures to be stopped. The idea of having her body maintained by ventilators and drugs when her mind was gone was abhorrent to her. She even spelled that out in her durable power of attorney for health care when she appointed me her voice in such a situation."

Beth Sawyer had sat through this recitation with moist eyes and a frightened expression. "But the doctors say they can't be sure yet if her mind is gone."

Enderling sneered but Rachel said calmly, "That's right. Generally they check for activity over a period of time. There have been a number of instances of people recovering from severe head trauma when there was very little activity during the early period. You do agree, Ms. Sawyer, that your sister would not want extraordinary means taken if she is indeed brain dead?"

The young woman nodded her head, her lips pressed tightly together to prevent her from crying. Rachel wanted to say something consoling, but before she could Enderling said flatly, "Which is her condition right now. This hospital is prolonging her life unnecessarily and I could sue them for not regarding Pam's wishes."

"Nonsense," Rachel said sharply. "You don't seem to realize, Mr. Enderling, that it is the doctors who determine brain death, not someone's husband or their dog. When and if they determine brain death, they will be more than willing to abide by Pamela Enderling's wishes. I think what you fail to grasp is that you're putting yourself into a very slippery position here. Should you by some remote chance manage to have life support removed before the Fielding Medical Center doctors have determined brain death, you could yourself be sued for acting precipitately. You already appear ghoulish to the staff, Mr. Enderling, and you must appear quite Machiavellian to your wife's sister. A little proper respect for your wife in her tragic situation would seem a far more reasonable and ethical position for you to take."

Beth Sawyer blinked at her and Bill Enderling snorted. "I know very well," he said, "that medical ethicists have no real power. They can make suggestions but they haven't any authority whatsoever. I only came here to shut up that arrogant Dr. LeBaron and get on with the process."

"Well, you'd do better to listen to my suggestions than to mock them," Rachel said. She surprised herself by feeling perfectly relaxed and in charge of the situation. If she had very little power here, Enderling had none at all. Of course, chances were that he would "win" ultimately. That his poor wife would be declared brain dead and the life support removed. "Your insistence on removing life support at this point would appear very shaky to the American Bar Association," she reminded him. "And I for one would be perfectly willing to bring the matter up before them if you don't respect the intent of your wife's directives. If and when she is declared brain dead, no one will object to her removal from life support. Until then, my advice to you is to leave the hospital and allow Mrs. Enderling's doctors to do their job and her sister to sit with her when possible to provide what comfort she can."

Enderling didn't bother to answer her. He shoved back his chair, which barely remained upright, and grabbed his briefcase. Shaking his head in mute disgust, he left the room, but Rachel knew he would also leave the hospital. Because her threat of reporting him to the ABA was not an idle one. He was certainly trying to manipulate to his advantage a situation where he had a decided conflict of interest. And he knew that when and if the doctors called to say they had determined that Pamela Enderling was brain dead, he would get exactly what he wanted. All Rachel had done was give him a good reason to be patient. She turned then to Beth Sawyer.

"I'm sorry. Your sister's case is tragic enough without running into this kind of nastiness. Is there anything I can do for you?"

Beth rose and extended her hand. Then with a shaking breath she said, "You've done the only thing I could have reasonably asked for at this time, Ms. Weis. Thank you."

"You're very welcome. I hope things will work out well for Pamela."

The young woman bit her lip again. "Dr. LeBaron told me there was only a smidgen of hope, you know. I understand that. It was just so awful having Bill there making things worse. I want to at least be able to say goodbye to Pam in peace."

"Of course." Rachel came around her desk and

gave the young woman an impulsive hug. Somehow she was reminded of both of her daughters, close to Beth Sawyer's age and unfaced with this kind of catastrophe. "Let me know if I can do anything to help."

When Ms. Sawyer had left, Rachel felt too restless to sit down. She grabbed her swimming bag and took off across the Fielding campus to the pool. Fifty laps later she felt more relaxed, ready to go back to her office and face what might be on her voice mail.

Crossing the medical campus Rachel was overtaken by Erika, who slowed her energetic pace to fall in line with the older woman. "Hi, Rachel," she said, her voice filled with excitement. "This has been the most incredible day!"

"How so?" Rachel wasn't sure she wanted to hear, but didn't really feel she had a choice but to ask.

"This morning Jerry let me sit in on an interview one of his interns did with a psychiatric patient. It had all the classic points Jerry had told me about over the weekend, and it was fascinating to watch. And then this afternoon! God, I've never seen anything like it."

Rachel loved young enthusiasm, but there was a note of idolatry here that alerted her. "You watched Jerry work," she guessed.

"How did you know?" Erika's eyebrows rose in astonishment. "Oh, you've probably seen him with lots of people, haven't you? Well, he was fantastic! This girl, a teenage patient with cancer, has been absolutely unreachable. No one could get her to talk or make sure she was understanding what we were telling her. And then Jerry talked to her. You wouldn't believe how changed she was within a few minutes! And every one of us had been sympathetic before, honest. It was just the way he has. And he says he can teach it to me."

"I'm delighted for you, Erika."

Erika almost hugged herself with delight. "This is going to make such a difference, Rachel. I know it won't solve everything, but it will sure come in handy. Like with that family last week. Jerry says he'll spend some time with me every day until I grasp the essentials."

"He's a terrific teacher." Rachel wanted to add that Jerry already had a lot of duties without taking on the burden of one more, but she suspected that this particular one wasn't a burden, and that any comment along that line would not only dampen Erika's enthusiasm but prove what a wretched human being Rachel was, so she refrained. No wonder Jerry was so busy today, finding time for Erika *twice*, when he could barely make a minute to call Rachel at all. Yes, indeed, Rachel assured herself, she was becoming a first-class bitch where Jerry was concerned.

Erika gave Rachel's arm a quick squeeze. "I've got to get back to the floor, Rachel. Talk with you later." And she was gone, the edges of her lab coat flapping as she raced off across the lawn. Rachel watched after her until she disappeared inside the hospital door. Erika was without doubt a beautiful and charming young woman. A kind, lovable human being, as well as a sexy, approachable person. Just the sort of woman a middle-aged man could not resist. Why should Jerry be any different from his contemporaries? Her own daughter was seeing a man almost twenty years older than herself, and apparently found him irresistible. And, really, what difference did it make to Rachel?

A lot, she sadly admitted to herself as she picked up her own pace. Jerry had somehow recently invaded her heart in a way he hadn't managed to touch it for the previous three years. It wasn't just his friendship she'd miss if he became involved with Erika. Rachel reminded herself that she didn't have enough to offer Jerry, that he would be better off with Erika. And maybe, somehow, they would at least manage to remain friends.

What was on her voice mail was a message from Jerry saying, "Don't go to the movies tonight, Rachel. Let me bring over a video and some microwave popcorn. I'll come as soon as I can get there—probably by eight. Pretty please? Page me if you can't. Otherwise I'll be there."

Oh, sure, leave it up to her to call it off. And how was he going to know what movies she had or hadn't seen? He'd probably bring some psycho adventure thing that she couldn't stand. Actually, she'd been to the movies with him as often as with anyone in the last few years and they seemed to have similar taste. She decided to let him come, against her better judgment. Why torture herself, or embarrass herself? But his suggestion of a movie seemed to say that he wouldn't pressure her into discussing sex again, didn't it?

When Jerry arrived, at eight-thirty, he had brought not only the video and popcorn, but a bottle of English cider, her favorite. "Lovely," she said, taking it from him. "This always reminds me of pubs in country villages. It's about time I got back to England again. A friend keeps writing to offer me her cottage in Somerset for a week."

"Wait until spring and I'll go with you," Jerry suggested.

"No one said you were invited."

He cocked his head at her. "Oh, come on, Rachel. I'm the perfect companion: I speak the language and I can take care of you if you have a nervous breakdown."

"What a fantastic recommendation. I'm not planning to have a nervous breakdown." He had followed her to the kitchen where she handed down two glasses for him and set the microwave oven to three minutes and twenty seconds.

"Well, maybe your friend will have a nervous breakdown," Jerry said.

"Unlikely." Rachel got out napkins and a large red bowl. The tray she'd washed that morning still stood upright in the dish rack. When the popcorn had finished popping she poured it into the bowl and carried the tray into the living room, where she'd pushed two chairs forward with an end table between them for their refreshments.

Jerry surveyed the arrangement critically. "I thought we could sit on the couch."

"This way there's a place for the popcorn and cider," she said reasonably.

"I brought *The Big Easy.*"

Since by the tone of his voice this seemed to carry some significance, she replied, "I don't think I know it."

"It's not new. Dennis Quaid and Ellen Barkin. You haven't heard of it?"

Rachel shrugged and shook her head. "Should I have?"

Jerry grinned. "Probably. But never mind. I think you'll enjoy it."

An understatement. Ethical issues aside, the movie was sexy and exciting and pulsed with life, but mostly it was sexy. Rachel soon understood why Jerry had wanted to sit on the couch. They remained in their chairs, eating popcorn and drinking cider, during a scene so steamy that Rachel involuntarily said, "Wow!" Jerry winked at her and blew her a kiss but made no move to touch her. Still, she could feel the tension rising in her body during the rest of the movie. "This isn't fair," she muttered at one point.

"All's fair in love and war," Jerry reminded her.

"Is this love or war?"

"We'll see."

The lights in the room were dim and Rachel sat curled into herself as though she couldn't be seen. When the movie ended, Jerry automatically pushed the rewind button. "I've been told, by several women, that that's one of the sexiest scenes they've ever seen," he said.

Rachel cleared her throat. "And that's why you showed it to me."

"We'll get to that. First I want you to tell me if you agree."

"Yes, I agree." Rachel glanced over at him. "Who were these women telling you how sexy it was?"

"Oh, just some friends talking at a cocktail party, and people I've subsequently asked."

"You just go up to people and ask them about a thing like that?"

"If I know them well enough." He shrugged. "They consider it scientific research. Psychiatrists have a reputation for being obsessed with sex."

"And are they?"

"No," he said judiciously. "At least, I don't think I am."

They had long since finished their popcorn and cider. Jerry stood up and held a hand down to her. "Come on. Let's discuss it further on the couch."

Rachel reluctantly allowed him to draw her to her feet. Her body seemed to hum with physical desire—so much so that his hand clasping hers felt like a magnet drawing her to him. She automatically raised her face for his kiss. How many years had she known him? And he had never more than brushed her cheek or her lips with his. Now he held her against the length of him and warmed her mouth with his. His lips felt firm and gentle, giving and challenging at the same time. Rachel felt a response deep inside her body and shuddered with the strength of it.

He guided her to the couch and pulled her down onto his lap. His lips scarcely seemed to leave her mouth, where they promised her excitement and satisfaction. His hands . . . for an electric moment one hand rested on her blouse, cupping her breast. Then it moved to begin unbuttoning the untucked blouse. Rachel felt his fingers move from one spot to the next, sure, unhurried, determined. When the last button was released he drew back the blue silk to reveal the blue bra beneath. His hand came to caress her breast, to cup, and swirl and stroke her through the satiny fabric. And then his mouth came down to nudge the material down and draw the nipple in. Rachel moaned with the excruciating pleasure of it. Her breathing was coming more rapidly now, her whole body pulsing with physical desire.

"Do you want me to stop, Rachel?" Jerry asked in a soft whisper at her ear. "I want to make love to you but I don't want you to do something you don't really want. Can you tell me the truth?"

His voice seemed to blend in her mind with the heady excitement but Rachel tried to sort out her emotional needs from her physical ones. This was Jerry. Jerry who had swum beside her in the pool and whose buttocks even then had given her a twinge of desire. Jerry who had sat in the hot tub with her, naked. It had not been easy to ignore his need or hers then, either. His hands remained untouching of her while she decided. But she wanted his mouth on her breast, she wanted to see him naked again. She wanted him to fill the empty space in her momentarily and with exquisite joy. Because he was Jerry, and not just because she was turned on by the movie.

"Let's go up to my bedroom," she said. "But, Jerry, this is just for tonight."

"If that's what you want."

She moved through the dimly lit house with a feeling of wanton abandonment. For once her body was leading her instead of her mind. Her body *wanted* Jerry's. She needed him. She trusted him to satisfy that aching longing deep inside her. For now, for tonight, just this once.

By the time they reached her bedroom, he had pulled his shirt over his head and unzipped his jeans. Rachel stood uncertainly inside the door of the room, not knowing what to do first. Jerry hugged her to him and allowed his jeans to drop to the floor. She could feel the fine urgency of his penis against her crotch and how her own body seemed ready to open up to him, to spread like a flower before him. His lips pressed hers, and strayed to her nose and eyes, then down to her neck and finally, once again, to her now naked breasts.

She wanted that desire to continue forever. That moment of rising hope and need and expectation. Rachel felt his hands unfasten her trousers and push them down. She felt him slide her underpants after them and knew the moment when he released his penis from his own boxers. His flesh pressed against hers, rigid with uncomplicated need. She grasped his buttocks firmly and pulled herself against him, knowing an almost unbelievable urgency. They swayed together for several minutes, close but not joined, each savoring the moment.

Then Jerry danced her to the bed, humming in her ear, smiling down at her, dipping her back until she realized that she'd touched the pillow. He drew back the covers and settled her onto the playful flowered sheets, bending to take a nipple into his mouth, to draw on it until the cacophony inside threatened to overwhelm her, and then withdrew, saying, "I have to admit I came prepared, Rachel. Hold that thought."

When he rejoined her he slid beside her on the bed, the whole length of him along her body. Flesh touching flesh from face to toes. And then he began to stimulate her all over again, his lips and tongue wandering like a symphony over her skin, calling forth music she hadn't known was in her. Laughter from his tickling her neck, a moan from the deep suction at her breast, a purr as his tongue slid over her stomach and thighs. But nothing to compare to the thunder that pounded through her at the touch of his fingers, the caress of his tongue between her legs.

"Oh, God," she cried. "I don't think I can stand that."

"Oh, I think you can. Just let me touch you and taste you, Rachel. I've wanted to for so long. Do you like that?"

"Yes, you could do that forever. Oh, God, Jerry, I'm going to explode."

"I want you to explode. I want you to come for me, with me. Will you do that, Rachel?"

It was unnecessary to ask. Already she realized the crescendo in her body, the peak scaled and rewarded. Rachel felt Jerry come inside her and ride with her wave of fulfillment. The release from the strain of such a long period of physical tension made her grin, and then chuckle, and finally laugh out loud. Once she had started, she couldn't seem to stop, the waves of laughter coming like a second orgasm, flooding and filling her, only gradually tapering down.

Jerry hugged her with delight. "Now that's the kind of response I like to my lovemaking. So many people take this whole process so terribly seriously."

"Don't tell me about other people you've made love to, Jerry. Right now I want to believe you and I are the only two people who have ever made love in the whole world. There's nothing naive about *my* fantasies."

"It's a lovely fantasy." He smoothed the damp hair back from her forehead and kissed her gently. "You have a beautiful, responsive body, Rachel. Do you think I could interest you in sex now and again?"

"You tricked me," she said, but without rancor. "I didn't say I couldn't be seduced. I just have a better guard up most of the time."

"Tell me about it."

She looked surprised. "You mean you've tried before? Oh, you mean the night we were in the hot tub. I was flying that night, Jerry. I didn't need sex, even good sex."

"Is there some other kind?"

Rachel frowned. "You know there is. That's what I was trying to tell you about last night."

"Tell me what constitutes the bad part."

"The bad part is not wanting to be there, not wanting to expose yourself again to failure. The awful part is having your body touched when you don't want it touched, and not being able to say so because you'll hurt someone else's feelings. You let yourself be used because someone else can't handle what they think is rejection."

"Isn't it?"

"Rejection? That's not what it feels like to me. If I'm supposed to keep my body in constant readiness for a man, then not being interested must constitute some kind of bad behavior on my part, not a rejection of him. I must be a bad person if I don't want to be touched, to open my most private self at any given time."

"You don't think men are opening their most private selves to women?"

"No, I don't." Rachel rolled away from him and

stared up at the ceiling. "Sex is different for men. They're proud of their naked bodies and their virility. They think it's their penises that grind out orgasms from women, that they're responsible for—no, not responsible, they're the *givers* of orgasms to women. They don't think of women as giving *them* orgasms. They're also the givers to themselves of their own orgasms. Kind of a nice situation to be in, isn't it?"

"It can be a burden to men to think they're responsible for women's orgasms."

"No, Jerry, not the way I see it. Men think that if women don't have orgasms, they're frigid, or withholding, or mean. Or defective. Let's not forget defective. Men give what orgasms there are to be given, but if women don't have them, the women are responsible for that."

"Wow. That's quite a proposition, Rachel."

"That's the way I see it." She was holding her body rigid and when he reached out to her, she pushed his hand away.

"For tonight, I'm going to accept your premise," he said, sliding over to lie close to her but keeping his hands to himself. "And I'm going to accept that you've never really been able to have sex on your own terms. There's too much baggage around it for you. And I'm going to promise you that I'm not going to touch you sexually any more tonight, that all I want to do is snuggle next to you and hug you. Would that be all right?"

Rachel felt a sob catch in her throat and she turned her head away from him, but she nodded. Jerry curved his body to fit against hers. His hand came around her waist, holding her snugly. He kissed the back of her neck and whispered, "Good night, Rachel. Thank you for trusting me."

And she fell asleep almost instantly, feeling safe and secure.

Chapter Twelve

She had mumbled that she would make him breakfast, but Jerry had refused, saying, "I need to get home to shower and shave. I have an early appointment." He had kissed her lightly, on the lips, and felt an answering pressure, though she was just barely awake. Jerry had loved the sensation of dressing in her bedroom, of going downstairs through the silent house and gathering up the video (though he'd been tempted to leave it) and returning the tray of dirty dishes to the kitchen. For a moment he'd stared out into the garden where the late fall flowers bloomed, and wondered if he would stand there again, at this early hour of the morning. Then he left her house with her asleep in the room above, and drove to his condominium.

In the hallway outside his unit he found Roger sound asleep, in a rumpled jacket, his hair sticking out untidily. Jerry, frowning with worry, stooped down to make sure the younger man was all right. His breath seemed to come naturally, and his face, partially hidden by an arm, looked a reasonably healthy color. Jerry gently rocked his shoulder. "Wake up, Roger."

"Christ!" Roger, from years of practice no doubt, was instantly awake. "What time is it?"

"Six-thirty. What are you doing here, Roger?"

"What do you mean it's six-thirty?" the anesthesiologist demanded. "Didn't you come home last night? One of your neighbors let me in downstairs and I was just going to wait until you came home."

"Well, I'm home now." Jerry opened the door to his condo and waved Roger into the living room. "Have a seat. Or do you have to get to the hospital?"

Roger considered this uneasily. "I should be there at seven. Seven-fifteen will do. I need to talk to you, Jerry." And then he gave his companion a sharp glance. "You weren't with that beautiful young thing, were you? With Erika?"

"No, I wasn't with Erika." Jerry raised a hand. "It's none of your business, Roger. What did you want to see me about?"

"I can't sleep."

"You were sound asleep when I found you."

Roger shrugged this off. "You know what I mean, Jerry. Though I must say if I'd known how easy it would be to fall asleep waiting in your hallway I'd have tried it before."

Jerry took a seat and motioned for him to do likewise. "Maybe you've learned something useful, then," he suggested. "Maybe it's your house with its memories of Kerri that makes it especially difficult for you to sleep there. Maybe you should try moving."

"I couldn't do that. I need the memories of her there." Roger raked a hand through his ragged hair and Jerry could understand why it looked so unkempt. "Besides, I like the house. I couldn't just sell it and move somewhere else."

"Temporarily then. Just live in a hotel or something for a few weeks." Jerry had a flash of inspiration. "Better yet, how about taking over Angel's room in the flat near the hospital? You've met her roommate, haven't you? A neurology fellow named Nan LeBaron? Nice woman. Wouldn't interfere with you. She's seeing an architect, I think."

"What's the point?" Roger asked. "I'd just have to go back to the house eventually."

"Sure, but later, when you're ready. The point is to make things easier for yourself. If you're going to keep on working and try to carry on your life, then you need to take better care of yourself, Roger. Otherwise you'll end up drinking too much or taking more pills than are good for you. And I'm going to give you the name of a grief support group. I expect you to go."

"Christ! Give me a break, Jerry. You're trying to get me to change my whole life around."

"Just because it would be good for you," Jerry reminded him with a self-righteous wink. "Seriously, you need some help and this is my suggestion. I'm always here for you to talk to, and I'll give you the name of a good therapist you might try, but for the time being I think a change of venue and a support group would be ideal."

Roger grumbled, and yawned, but did not disagree. "All right. I'll give it a try. But is this woman going to want me to live with her?"

"I don't think she'll mind. If that doesn't work out, we'll find something else."

Roger, with a mischievous grin, asked as he

rose, "How about here? Don't you want me to stay with you? Would I be in the way?"

"No, I don't want you to stay with me. Run along to the hospital, Roger, and keep awake for your patients."

"Hey, I'm a professional." He was already at the door with a hand smoothing down his hair. "Thanks, Jerry. They aren't bad suggestions."

"I'm glad you think so. Out!"

In his role as a psychiatric liaison for Fielding Medical Center, Jerry saw patients on the regular medical floors who had psychiatric problems. It was to one of these missions that he'd been appointed this morning, and he stopped by his office on the way to meet with a patient suffering from chronic ulcerative colitis. Though it was early, he found Erika there, studying something in the folder he'd given her about interviewing patients.

"You can come with me, but this is going to take more than twenty minutes, I'm afraid. Act as if your pager has gone off if you need to."

"Okay." She jumped up, looking so fresh and eager that it made Jerry feel quite elderly in comparison. "You're not going to make me say anything, are you?"

"Not this morning. But for tomorrow I want you to choose a patient of your own, or one of the families, and I'll sit in with you while you talk with them. Agreed?"

Erika looked uncertain for only a moment. Then she nodded. "Sure. That's the best way for me to learn, isn't it?"

"Ultimately." As they walked briskly down the corridor, Jerry began ticking off points on his fin-

gers. "Remember the five points for chronic illness are identity, intimacy, meaning, hope, and
control. Give me an example."

"Well, first the patient wonders who he or she is
with their illness and if they're just their limita-
tions and needs. They're not sure they're a worth-
while person."

"Good. How about intimacy?"

"Patients worry about being rejected for being
ill, so they're afraid to let people close to them."

"Right. That's important. It applies to physicians as well as nonmedical people. What about
meaning in their lives?"

Erika frowned and shook her head. "It's not that
I don't remember what I've read, Jerry. It's just
that this one confuses me, too. Patients almost all
ask, 'Why me?' at some point. And I understand
that. I'd do it, too. What's harder is trying to work
out what it means that they've gotten sick. I mean,
do they blame it on themselves?"

"Sure, sometimes. Even the kids you deal with
occasionally believe they've brought on their own
illness by being bad or doing something wrong. It's
important to help them dig that out; it's much too
big a burden for them to carry. What else?"

"With adults, apparently they wonder if their
life can have meaning if so much of their attention is focused on their medical problems. I guess
they kind of get obsessed, huh?"

"With reason, usually. Today's medical problem,
ulcerative colitis, can really be a consuming problem. You'll hear. Just leave yourself open to taking
in what he says."

Erika smiled almost coquettishly at him. "And
hope. That's the fourth point. It seems to me no

one helps them regain their hope the way you do. You know, I saw you with that patient yesterday, and with Roger in the mountains. You're really great at that."

"People can usually find a reason to keep going, if you help them past their feeling of despair. And the best way to do that is to put their problem in perspective." Jerry regarded her curiously. "You sometimes sound like you've never known anyone who was sick."

"It's funny," she admitted. "I really haven't. Like, until I went to medical school and all."

"Then what interested you in medicine?"

Erika looked self-conscious and produced something very like a blush. "I had a boyfriend in college who was premed. I wanted to be in all the same classes he was, so . . ." She shrugged. "I found I was good at those classes, and went ahead and applied to medical school. The rest is history."

Jerry laughed. "I presume you didn't tell this to the med school admissions committee."

"No, I didn't think it was any of their business. It's sometimes made me feel like a fake, though, you know. Except that I do love it. I just have a few problems, such as this one you're helping me with."

"Everyone feels like a fake about something," Jerry assured her. "And most of our weaknesses can be strengthened or worked around. What's the fifth challenge?"

"Control. Patients with unpredictable illnesses lose their sense of control. They need to find ways to regain it."

"And you can help them." Jerry pushed open the stairway door onto the third floor. "Mr. Torres has been suffering from ulcerative colitis for five years. He's getting close to the point where he may need a colostomy, which is a truly heavy burden to lay on anyone. So he's been employing denial but that has started to fail him, and he feels despairing. And unable to give permission for the surgery. Which, of course, drives the surgeons nuts, so they call a consult. But we don't have to provide them with what they want when we do a consult. Our object is to help Mr. Torres, not necessarily to satisfy the surgeons."

"I'll bet they don't see it that way," Erika said as she followed him past the nursing station.

"They want what's best for him, but they're not a particularly patient group. And they *always* know what's best for their patients." Jerry tapped at the patient's door and then went in with his protégée following close on his heels. Mr. Torres, who sat slumped dejectedly on his bed, was going to be a challenging case, all right. Having Erika with him might inspire him to perform at his best, and probably she'd learn something useful. Still, he would have preferred it to be Rachel who observed him, and admired him, and learned what a truly talented psychiatrist he was. Or something like that.

Oh, hell, what have I done? Rachel wondered when she lay finally awake in her bed. Not that she regretted last night. Not really. It was the future that worried her. Jerry was going to expect something from her, and that's just what she'd been trying to avoid.

On the other hand, Rachel couldn't help grinning at the memory of the previous night's encounter. He had been so dear, and so concerned about her. And he had guided her to such pleasure! Her body this morning felt voluptuous in a way it hadn't for a very long time. At her age! Really, it was almost undignified, she thought with a smile that seemed to reach right across her face. She stretched luxuriously and reluctantly climbed out of bed.

Maybe he didn't expect anything of her, though. Maybe last night had been in the manner of a gift, because they were friends and he wanted to help her. Maybe he'd just been a sort of sex surrogate for her, to show her that there wasn't anything wrong with her and that she could respond as well as any other woman, given the right circumstances. The right circumstances in this case being a sexy movie, a thoughtful lover, and her own attraction to Jerry. Rachel didn't actually want Jerry to know how attracted she was to him; it could only make things more complicated. As if just sleeping with him didn't make things complicated enough. Hadn't they had a perfectly good relationship for the past three years when they'd just been friends?

Rachel went down to the living room and found that Jerry had removed all traces of their previous evening's entertainment. She was glad, when she entered the kitchen, to find the tray with the popcorn bowl and their glasses. It hadn't been an erotic dream after all, though it wouldn't have been the first one she'd had starring her favorite shrink. That was another thing she didn't plan to tell him.

Before her bagel popped up in the toaster the phone rang. She felt a moment's hesitation, not knowing what she'd say to him. But she picked up the portable phone and offered a cheerful greeting before she found out that it was her daughter Jennifer.

"Oh, Mom, I'm so glad I caught you. Can you talk?"

"Sure." Rachel popped up the toaster prematurely and left the bagel there to cool. "What's up? How was the weekend?"

"Yummy." Jennifer made a noise that sounded suspiciously like a giggle. "Oh, Mom, I think I'm in love!"

"Oh, sweetheart, how wonderful!" Rachel had been bracing herself for this. You didn't rain on your daughter's parade, no matter what your own doubts and reservations. "Tell me all about him."

"Well, of course it's Fred, Caitlin's uncle. He's just so amazing. He knows so much and he's done so much and he doesn't have any doubts. You know? I don't mean he's opinionated or anything like that. He's very open-minded, actually. But he's so sure of himself and he's so good to me. And he's so handsome and so athletic and so smart! Oh, I wish you could meet him right now."

"I wish I could, too. I take it the weekend was everything you could have wished for."

Jennifer's exuberant laugh rang over the phone. "Oh, yes. He's just . . . incredible. We talked and talked and talked for hours. And we, you know, got along really well in other ways, too. I think it makes a difference that he's older."

Undoubtedly his being older had given Fred years to learn a few things about making love to a woman, experience most men Jennifer's own age hadn't had a chance to acquire yet. "As long as he's responsible and considerate, he has my vote of confidence," Rachel said. "Tell me more about him."

"Well, I told you he's in television advertising. But he's done all kinds of things before he wound up there. Exciting things, like leading photo safaris in Africa and bringing computers to inner-city kids. He took this job because it pays so well and one of his kids is in college."

Of course. At forty-five you'd very likely have a kid in college. "Does he have more than one child?"

"Two others, girls. They live with their mother in Connecticut. She's remarried and Fred gets along with her okay. The kid in college, Jeff, lived with him the last few years of high school because he needed a male role model."

Was this Rachel's daughter talking to her? Or was Jennifer repeating what she'd heard Fred say? In either case, Rachel thought with a sigh, it was probably true. At least everyone seemed to think boys needed a man in their lives to teach them manly things. It was Rachel's opinion that boys could well do without any number of the manly things men taught them to do—like making war and being macho.

"Is it Jeff's first year of college?" she asked.

"Yeah. He's nineteen and he goes to school in New York. I haven't met any of them yet."

Yet. Well, of course it was inevitable Jennifer would meet them. And thank heaven the boy was six years younger than Jennifer. It couldn't be comfortable contemplating stepchildren almost your own age. Rachel realized that was a jump—to thoughts of marriage for her daughter—but it seemed entirely possible, the way Jennifer was talking. Of course she would say nothing of that eventuality. It must be Jennifer who brought it up.

"He's not Jewish, Mom," Jennifer was saying. "Does that bother you?"

"No, not really. On the other hand I hope he's not particularly religious, since you aren't."

"He was raised something Protestant. I can't remember which. But he hasn't been in church since his wedding. And he's been divorced for five years."

So he'd had more than enough time to adjust. He would not be going out with someone for the first time. Or maybe the hundredth. Rachel had heard what it was like out there: men dating women and seeming completely in love with them, and then just one day never calling again. Fred wouldn't be one of those. Jennifer was a good judge of character. Better than her sister, and better than Rachel.

"He sounds like a good match for you," Rachel said, pumping enthusiasm into her voice. Her doubts were unnecessary and unbecoming. Let Jennifer know how pleased she was that her daughter had found a warm, loving man to add pleasure to her life. That was the important thing, not all the little details about his age and his previous marriage. Jennifer could cope with that. She was a strong, resourceful woman. "I'm so happy you're excited and pleased with him. Have you sent me a picture yet?"

"I'll have one in the mail tomorrow. I promise. I didn't get it mailed off before we went to the Cape and I've been busy since. How are things with you?"

"About the same," Rachel replied cautiously.

Not the time to interject Jerry into the conversation. "The new work is going well. I really enjoy it. It was the right move."

"Great." Then, with scarcely a pause, Jennifer went on to describe an episode that would illustrate Fred's cleverness, and then one showing his thoughtfulness.

"He sounds wonderful," Rachel said, at least half believing it. "I can't wait to meet him."

"Well, I'm not sure when that will be." Jennifer had become a little evasive. "I may stay here over Christmas and . . . make plans with Fred. I'm not sure. It's a little soon to know. That would be okay, wouldn't it, Mom?"

It would be the first Christmas she hadn't been home. "Of course, sweetheart. We'd miss you, but you've got your own life to live now. I understand that, so don't worry about me. Trish will probably be here, and maybe Jerry. Jerry's going to have Thanksgiving with us."

"That's great. I'm not sure about Thanksgiving. Fred had already made plans but I'd like to take him with me to Betty's if he can change them. We'll see."

"I hope he can. Jen, I've got to get to work now. I'm very happy for you. We'll talk soon, okay?"

"Sure. Love you, Mom."

"I love you, too."

Jerry was surprised to have an urgent message from Carl Norridge when he returned from a psych consult that morning. The chairman of the psychiatry department made him wait five minutes, though no one emerged from his office and there was no light lit on his secretary's phone console to indicate that he was on the phone. When Jerry entered Carl's office the chairman wore a portentous frown and waved Jerry to a chair rather than rising to shake hands with him.

Carl's tie was a particularly dull one today, one that would have won Jerry's amused attention if the atmosphere in the room hadn't been so downbeat. Both Jerry and Carl knew the virtue of the pregnant pause, but Jerry was on Carl's turf and he needed the advantage, so he merely cocked his head attentively and waited.

Carl's affect could probably be described as sad and concerned, Jerry decided. And yet it was that judgmental kind of concern that he'd witnessed as a child in school—the authoritarian figure about to plunge the thoughtless child into a bath of cloying guilt and recrimination.

"I don't suppose you understand the gravity of the situation," Carl began.

Jerry nodded. "It would be difficult to understand when I haven't the slightest idea what you're talking about, Carl. Fill me in on the situation first."

"I'm speaking, of course, of your indiscreet affair with Erika Amundsen, a girl, I might remind you, of almost half your age."

"To be entirely politically correct, Carl, which I'm sure you'd wish to be, you would not call Erika a girl. She's a woman, or a young woman if you must; never a girl. She's a pediatric intern here at Fielding and we don't employ girls as pediatric interns." Jerry regarded him thoughtfully. "Then we need to consider your words 'indiscreet' and 'affair.' What could possibly have given you the idea that I'm having an affair with Erika?"

Carl leered at him. Yes, Jerry thought, it was decidedly a leer. Carl could hardly have made his belief more clear. But he did. "You took her to the mountains with you for the weekend."

"I also took Roger Janek. Did you think I had an affair with him, too, or did you assume that he also had one with Erika?"

"Don't be absurd," Carl snapped. "Roger Janek has just lost his wife."

Jerry considered this as a reply. "So you don't think I slept with Roger, or that Roger slept with Erika. So why did I take him with us?"

"God only knows."

Jerry laughed. "Maybe it was the indiscreet part. I took him along so he could witness our affair, so we could embarrass him by flaunting our sex in front of him. That sounds like the sort of thing I'd do, doesn't it, Carl?"

"Are you denying that you're having an affair with this young woman?"

"Of course I'm denying it. The idea is ludicrous. Since when did you start manufacturing rumors about people's sexual involvements, Carl? I'd think that was beneath you."

Carl was smug in his knowledge. "I have it on very good authority, Jerry, that the young woman comes to your office every day and spends time with you. I'm also very aware that men in positions of authority all too readily take advantage of the admiration with which younger women view them."

"Are you, Carl? Yes, I've seen it happen any number of times in our own department, but I've never heard of your censuring anyone about it. Why me? No, don't bother to tell me. I can guess.

You're trying to find a reason to deny me a professorship. To think of a sordid reason why I shouldn't have the promised vice-chairmanship. Well, it won't wash, Carl. I'm not having an affair with Erika. I've never slept with her and I never will sleep with her. Is that clear enough?"

Jerry had risen but Carl was apparently not through with him. "Your denials don't carry much weight in view of the very obvious nature of your involvement. Hospitals are small communities, Jerry, and word of this sort of thing circulates quickly. Everyone is aware of the situation between the two of you. We don't have any absolute rules at Fielding against such involvements but the guidelines are clear."

"I'm not in a position of authority over Erika," Jerry reminded him. "She's in an entirely different department than mine and we wouldn't for the most part have much contact with each other. However, Erika was having some difficulties with her own department and I offered, generous man that I am, to try to help her out."

Jerry had remained standing, looking down at the department chairman lounging behind his massive desk. "You'll remember I told you my plan for teaching all the new interns some of our psychiatric methods of interviewing and dealing with patients? Well, Erika is my test case. I've become a mentor to her and she's coming along very well in our little program. Don't try to make something more out of this."

"It's perfectly clear that the girl . . . young woman is completely taken with you," Carl replied. "She's told several people in her department that you're"—he smirked—"just incredible. I think we can all read between the lines."

"So you're accusing me of not only having an affair with her, but of lying to you now?" Jerry asked, his voice sharp. "You are completely discounting what I've said because you wish to read the situation another way? I'd tread a little carefully, Carl. I don't like having my word doubted. I don't like playing games and I don't like having my reputation trashed. But I especially object to your slandering Erika with your insinuations."

"She's hardly blameless."

"You're beginning to irritate me. The only mistake Erika could possibly be blamed for is agreeing to let me teach her a few principles about interviewing patients and their families." Jerry shook his head. "I'm not going to let you screw around with me, Carl. You've made me promises that you're trying to break, and in a really despicable way. I'll insist that you call a meeting of the psychiatry faculty. That's my only option, since otherwise you have all the power here."

"You're putting yourself in a really untenable position."

"Am I?" Jerry scratched a graying eyebrow thoughtfully. "Fielding isn't the only medical center in the Bay Area, Carl. I'm not going to starve if I get booted out of here."

"Your reputation would be ruined."

"For what? Being accused of having an affair with a pediatric intern I'm mentoring? I think not, Carl. Especially since it's not true. Where's your sense of proportion? It's done all the time. I should get a medal because I'm *not* fooling around with her, by your lights. Give it up, Carl. This horse won't run."

"We'll see about that."

Jerry shrugged with frustration. "I have work to do. See you around, Carl."

Chapter Thirteen

Rachel had found a message on her voice mail when she got in. Jerry's baritone had assured her that he had every intention of talking with her sometime during the day, but that it was stacking up to be another killer one. "We have a lot to talk about," he had said, "and I'm not going to let you avoid me any more than I did yesterday. At least not if I can help it. Take care."

Rachel had smiled ruefully and erased the message. Maybe she'd be in luck. Maybe he'd literally be too busy to make any time for her the whole day. There were enough ethics concerns to fill her whole day as well, so she dug right into the stack of folders she'd left on her desk the previous evening. It wasn't until late in the day, when she wandered into the cafeteria to get coffee, that she ran into Angel Crawford, tan from her honeymoon.

"Wow! You look great," Rachel said. "Nan said you were back. How was Hawaii?"

"Better than I expected," Angel confessed. "I don't know. I'd heard about Hawaii for years and I thought it would be a dead bore, but who cares when it's your honeymoon? But it was great. Cliff says he'd even go again, if we weren't going to be in Wisconsin by the next time I can get a few days free. Of course, he exaggerates."

"A common failing among surgeons, I've heard." Rachel filled a large Styrofoam container with coffee and considered whether she wanted any sweetener. "It was a lovely wedding, Angel. I'm glad Jerry brought me."

"Oooo. That reminds me. Have you heard the latest rumor? Actually Cliff called me about half an hour ago to tell me that it's not even a rumor. He ran into Jerry at lunch."

Rachel felt a prickling at the back of her neck. "No, I haven't heard anything. I've hardly been out of my office all day."

"Apparently Jerry's department head reamed him out for having an affair with Erika Amundsen. You remember her; she was at the wedding, too. A beautiful young woman, pediatric intern. Well, apparently Norridge accused Jerry of having an affair with her and insinuated that he wouldn't be an appropriate choice for vice-chairman or to get a professorship because of it. Jerry was livid."

Rachel didn't know what to say. *Was* Jerry having an affair with Erika? Surely not. He wouldn't have . . . But then, maybe he would. How was she to know? Men frequently did things that were incomprehensible to Rachel. "What's he going to do?"

"Well, it isn't true, of course," Angel said.

Though she continued to discuss the situation, she'd lost Rachel, whose thoughts went something like: Angel had said it wasn't true. That meant Jerry had told Cliff that it wasn't true. Which meant it wasn't true. Presumably Jerry would have no reason to lie to Cliff. But what a mess for Jerry.

All the appearance must be there, with the weekend in the mountains and his continuous association with Erika. And the intern's obvious idolatry would suggest an infatuation to at least the older men on the staff. Especially Carl, who Jerry had once told her saw a sexual connotation in everything. Jerry was in a rather sticky position if Carl couldn't be brought to believe him.

Rachel found herself at the cashier, where she pulled out her wallet and searched for change to pay for her coffee. Angel was behind her, pushing a tray laden with a late lunch, and Rachel still couldn't think of anything to say. Angel regarded her curiously. Jerry was, after all, such an old and good friend of hers.

But what could Rachel say? She wasn't going to tell Angel what had happened last night. She wasn't going to claim some inside knowledge of Jerry's problem, and she didn't want to make some inane, nonsensical comment that indicated she *didn't* have any emotional investment.

"I'll talk with Jerry," she said finally. "Maybe I can help."

"Could you?" Angel's look of curiosity had deepened, but she was far too polite to say anything. "Cliff will stand behind him, of course, and that has to carry some weight. But Norridge has the psychiatry faculty pretty much under his thumb. At least that's what Cliff thinks. I don't really know the department very well. You may know it better from going to functions with Jerry."

Rachel considered the faculty she'd met on various occasions. A singularly uninspired group, except for Jerry. Too willing to sway in any wind that swept through the department, too puffed up with their own expertise. And far, far too few women to be representative of the field. Jerry had made very little effort to ingratiate himself with his peers, though the interns and residents always admired and respected him. He might very well have let himself in for a very difficult time.

"Like most academics, they're uncomfortable with someone who doesn't play the game," Rachel finally said. "I think they secretly admire his courage, but that only makes them resent him because they aren't capable of doing the same thing. They tell themselves you have to act as a *team*. You can't have any iconoclasts disrupting the service."

"God, I'll be glad to get out of academia!" Angel raked long fingers through her auburn hair, a gesture she seemed to have picked up from her husband. "I don't know how Cliff stands it, but he seems to thrive here. I hope he won't be disappointed in Wisconsin."

"He won't," Rachel assured her. "Look, I'd better go. It's good to see you, Angel."

Angel's parting words were, "See what you can do for Jerry."

Easier said than done, Rachel grumbled to herself as she trotted back to her office. Especially when she hadn't even been sure Jerry *hadn't* slept with Erika until Angel had said so. After all, Erika was a beautiful woman, sexy and bright and obviously infatuated with Jerry. Who could resist that combination? But obviously Jerry had. Why? Because of his inherent honorableness, or because of his attachment to Rachel? Maybe both.

There was no further message from him on her voice mail when she returned from the cafeteria.

Rachel sat and sipped her coffee for several minutes, debating what to do. She would have to call him, of course. But what could she logically offer to do for him? The possibilities made her shudder. If Norridge wasn't going to believe Jerry, why should he believe her? Rachel forced herself to pick up the phone and dial Jerry's number. She assumed she would get his voice mail and was unprepared for his crisp "Stoner here."

"It's Rachel, Jerry. I hear you're having some trouble with Carl Norridge."

"Jesus, news travels fast," he muttered. "Let's not talk about that."

She heard his office door bang shut and pictured him giving it a shove with his foot so he could have some privacy in talking to her. "I think we probably have to talk about it," she said.

"Well, at least not until we've talked about last night. Are you okay about last night?"

"I think so."

"Good. I'm more than okay about last night, Rachel. I've wanted to be that close to you for ages."

"Since the hot tub."

"Since before the hot tub. But I admit it's been coming on gradually, so that I didn't really suspect until we went swimming together. And it isn't just lust, Rachel. You understand that, don't you?"

"I'm not sure. Jerry, I'm very fond of you, but one sexual encounter doesn't wipe out my concerns. You must understand that. I can't just get involved with you when I know I'm not able to offer what you or any man would want in the way of a relationship."

There was silence for a minute before he said, "Okay. Let me think about this, will you? Obviously we have to talk but this isn't the greatest time for me. I have two consults to do before I can get out of here and several meetings with residents. I don't know when I'm going to finish."

"What can I do to help with Norridge?"

"Nothing. I'll work it out. God, this stuff pisses me off. All of a sudden after twenty-odd years here I'm fighting for my life."

"I'm sorry. Let me help if I can."

"There's nothing you can do. But thanks for offering. I'll call you later."

Just as she was about to put down the receiver, she heard him yell, "Wait! Are you still there, Rachel?"

"I'm here."

"Rachel, you do understand that I haven't slept with Erika, don't you? There's no doubt in your mind about that, is there?"

Rachel swallowed against the lump in her throat. "No. There's no doubt in my mind about that." Not now. Not if he said he hadn't. She allowed the phone to drop back into the cradle with a slight click. Her head had begun to ache.

Before Jerry had a chance to leave his office there was a hesitant knock at the door. He called to come in and Erika opened the door but remained standing there. Jerry smiled ruefully at her. "Come and sit down. We need to talk."

Erika frowned as she took the chair opposite his desk. "I don't understand what's happening, Jerry. People are looking at me funny and one of my attendings made some kind of crude comment abut the two of us?"

Her voice rose in a question and he could see

that she was holding herself stiffly away from the back of the chair. Poor kid. She probably thought Jerry had been bragging about his probable conquest of her. He would have closed the door, to give them privacy, but such an action might serve merely to inflame the gossip already circulating on the floor.

"Hell, I seem to have gotten the two of us in a bit of a bind. I don't mind so much for myself, but I don't like your being caught up, too. What it is, Erika, is my department chairman thinks we're having an affair."

"But that happens all the time," she protested, leaning forward as if that would help her better understand. "No one ever gets particularly excited about it. Besides, you could tell him it isn't true."

Jerry snorted. "I've tried that. It's a political thing, Erika. Norridge doesn't want to believe me because he thinks he can use an affair against me to renege on a promise." He tilted his chair back and contemplated the peeling paint on the ceiling of his office. "Damn it, this is really beginning to tick me off. And I don't quite see how I'm going to keep you out of it. Forgive me. I only meant to help you."

"You *are* helping me. You should have seen me this afternoon when one of my patient's parents started having a fit about something. Straight out of the Williams and Lowe article you gave me. 'Characterologically angry patients'—maximize the patient's, or in this case, parents', areas of mastery and competence. I did it, Jerry! You would have been proud of me. And then that jerk makes some kind of comment about you and me when I was telling him how much you'd helped. I wanted to kick him in the shin."

"You probably should have." But Jerry was grinning. "That's great, Erika. You're going to get so good at this it will make your whole residency better, I swear."

"If I get to continue working with you," she said soberly. "It probably wouldn't be good for either of us to meet the way we have been. And, you know, Jerry, I almost wish it were true, that we were having an affair."

Jerry hadn't quite seen that coming, but he knew he probably should have. He sighed and held her gaze firmly. "That's just the part of you that admires my experience, Erika. Actually, I'm an aging hippie who has sons almost your age. Not exactly a proper object for a beautiful young woman's desire. Will you believe me that it's a passing fancy, and one you'll be glad you never acted on?"

"You might be glad. I don't know if I will be."

"Will how you feel make it hard for us to work together?"

Erika rose and shook her head. "Not for me. But maybe we'd better let things die down for a while."

"I hate doing that. It's like an admission of guilt, or as if they can ruin our plans with their innuendoes. Think about it overnight and we'll talk tomorrow. I don't like interrupting our progress when things are going so well for you, but I don't want to see you the brunt of damaging rumors, either."

"I'll let you know."

* * *

Rachel was a very private person. She was also a very pragmatic person. Having worked for years in a legal setting, and then for many more in a medical setting, she knew how entrenched people could become on one side or another of an issue, given only a matter of days. If something was to be done about Jerry's predicament, and by extension Erika's, it would need to be done swiftly.

Alternatively Jerry would marshal his forces, and Carl Norridge would marshal his, and in time the two sides would do battle. Whichever way the battle was decided, and it could hardly be decided without severe damage to Jerry's position, there would be hard feelings and acrimony left behind. Rachel was inherently impatient with the waste of time, energy, and accord this sort of battle entailed. But she was also very reluctant to expose her personal situation in an effort to make the battle unnecessary.

She sat for a long time sipping at her coffee, her lips twitching with frustration. Why should she have to reveal herself in order to end the stupid game some middle-aged cowboys were intent on playing? Really, in many ways it was none of her business. Jerry had done some ill-advised things recently, and there was no reason he shouldn't have to explain them. But Carl Norridge wasn't interested in Jerry's explanations, or even in Jerry's sex life, but in keeping Jerry from achieving a position of any power at Fielding.

And why? Because Jerry refused to fit in with the department, refused to play their silly but required games, refused to compromise his own principles for a bunch of unnecessary rules. Jerry was an important feature at Fielding. His concern for patients was legendary, his respect for the staff and their professionalism was unquestioned. How could Rachel not protect Jerry if he needed her protection?

Rachel crumbled the large Styrofoam container and tossed it irritably into her wastebasket. She was tired of protecting men. Let them take responsibility for their own actions and not expect women to cover for them. Not that Jerry had asked her to protect him. It was just that she knew, she *knew*, this would turn into some macho standoff if she didn't intervene.

Well, she would save Jerry. But that would be the extent of it. She wasn't going to place herself in jeopardy again. She wasn't going to make someone else miserable. Certainly not Jerry. And she wasn't going to trap herself. Life was too short.

Rachel picked up her briefcase and lifted down her coat from the hook on the back of the door. With any luck Carl Norridge would not have left his office yet.

It was after nine when Jerry arrived. Rachel had expected him to call, but not necessarily until the next day. When she opened the door to him, the first thing he said was, "What the hell did he mean, he didn't know about us? For God's sake, Rachel, there was no need for you to talk to Carl. I don't even think I *like* your having talked to him."

"No, I didn't think you would, particularly. You'd rather have a shoot-out at the OK Corral, wouldn't you?" Rachel's temper had not improved since she'd decided to see Carl and she was in no mood to have an edgy talk with Jerry. "Look, I talked to him, he apologized for not understanding the situation, and you're back to square one about this whole thing. He still doesn't want to make you a professor, or, heaven forbid, the vice-chairman of the department. Those are things you have to handle yourself. I decided I wasn't interested in seeing Erika's reputation damaged."

"Oh, sure," he growled, letting himself into the hallway without much encouragement from Rachel's body language. "I'm sure you did it for Erika. And why did he listen to you, anyway? He wouldn't listen to me."

"Well, Jerry," she drawled, "Carl asked me out about a year ago. No big deal to you high-rolling psychiatrists, but the man is married, after all. I didn't accept his invitation, but it's something he would rather forget about if possible. And I'm sure you're far too honorable to repeat what I've just said. Mostly, though, Carl finds it too difficult to believe that you could be screwing two women at the same time. He's rather provincial that way. Or he doesn't think you have it in you."

"You didn't need to tell him we were involved. I hadn't told him. It's none of his business." Jerry stomped into the living room and dropped sullenly onto the sofa. "I was trying to protect your reputation," he added nobly.

"Yes, I know." She had followed him into the room but remained standing near the door. "I didn't particularly like having to tell him, but it was the only way I could think of to put a stop to a lot of unnecessary feuding. And it didn't seem fair to Erika to let things stand as they were."

"I would have taken care of everything."

"Oh, sure. You and Dan." She lowered her voice

to mimic John Wayne's: *"I'm the man and I'm in charge here. I can handle anything. Anything you care to challenge me with. Raging bulls, loaded guns, irate women."* She stuck her thumbs in the belt of her jeans and swaggered about the room, getting into the role. *"I can manage it all with my little finger, because I'm a man. And I know what I'm doing, little woman."*

Jerry laughed and insisted that that was not his meaning.

"Oh, no? Maybe not ostensibly. But that's what men *do*, Jerry. Especially around sex. They're men and they know how it's supposed to be."

He cocked his head questioningly. "Did I do something wrong last night?"

"No, you didn't do anything wrong last night! You were wonderful! You knew exactly what I needed! You see? You did it just right because you're a man and you know what to do. And I'm a woman and I should be grateful for what I get."

"Rachel, I somehow don't think we're talking about last night, precisely. Would you come and sit down by me?"

"No, I won't sit down by you! I don't want to come anywhere within ten feet of you. In fact, I'd be happier if you went home."

"I can see that, but it hardly seems fair. Let me try to understand this. You're upset because you felt you had to go to Carl to save me, though I hadn't asked you to. Is that right?"

"Oh, sure," she muttered sarcastically. "Blame it on me. Who got you into this situation? Not me."

"Right. And you're also upset because we had a good sexual encounter last night. I gather what upsets you about it is that I acted as though I knew just what you needed, that I was smug and chauvinistic."

"I didn't say you were smug and chauvinistic."

"Was I?"

"No."

"But I shouldn't have known what you needed."

"You make it sound unreasonable of me. And it isn't. If you knew this time, it doesn't mean you'd always know. It doesn't mean you're born knowing what *I* want. Or that all the experience you've had with other women would tell you what *I* need."

He caught her hand as she passed by and drew her, only slightly protesting, down onto the sofa beside him. "First, let's get it clear that I don't have a vast experience with women. But I do have a long experience with one woman and I learned from her. How could I help but learn from her? And I realize that doesn't mean I'll know what *you* want. But I can learn what you want, can't I?"

He had not let go of her hand and he pressed it now, firmly, between both of his. "This has something to do with what you were telling me the other night, doesn't it? About why you weren't interested in sex. About why it feels like a trap to you."

"I suppose so. Oh, Jerry, it's so very complicated and I can't explain without seeming to be speaking ill of Dan. And I don't want to do that. He was a good man and a wonderful father. He was vital and honest and he loved me."

"But there was something wrong with your sex life, something that's still crippling you." Jerry ran a finger soothingly along the outline of her hand. "You don't have to convince me Dan was a fine person, Rachel. I know that. And maybe it would help you to know that Dan talked with me, a very little, about sex."

"Talked to you?" Rachel blinked at him. A shudder went down her spine. "He talked about our sex?" she asked in a shaking, small voice.

"No, not about your sex. About sex in general. Asking me questions as a doctor and a psychiatrist. He knew that I knew they were about the two of you, but he was very circumspect. Rachel, I hear questions about sex all the time."

She withdrew her hand from his and wedged herself into the far corner of the sofa. "When did he talk with you?"

"It's hard for me to remember, Rachel. Probably about a year before he died. Maybe six months before he got sick the first time."

Well into her campaign. Perhaps even at the turning point, where things had started to get better. Surely she didn't have Jerry to thank for that. She drew in a wobbly breath, knowing she was close to tears, and close to telling the truth. She would tell Jerry the truth, as she saw it, and then he would understand her reluctance to get involved. Or maybe he wouldn't.

"For a long time Dan refused to believe there was anything wrong with our sex life. I mean, that there was anything that could or should be done differently. He thought that it was my problem for being uptight, that if only I could relax I'd enjoy sex and have orgasms. He was so very sure of himself, about that and everything. And I was insecure sexually. I thought he was right, for the better part of two decades. Years and years when I had a few orgasms a year, and when I was crushed with shame for being so unwomanly."

Tears had welled up in her eyes but she willed them down and kept her head slightly averted from Jerry's sympathetic gaze. She caught her lip between her teeth and exerted enough pressure to steady herself. "Do you know what that does to a person?"

"Yes, actually, I do. I'm sorry, Rachel. You never struck anyone as being insecure about anything. You're a very capable woman."

"Well, that was a good side effect of the problem," she said, almost with humor. "If I couldn't prove myself as a sex object I was certainly going to do it in every other area I could attempt. Superwoman before superwoman existed. A lawyer and a mother and a homemaker." A bitter edge crept into her voice. "Just a bit of a failure as a wife and a woman."

"Ouch. I'm sure Dan didn't want you to think that."

"What other choice did I have? If he was right, I was wrong. For a long time it didn't occur to me that I could be right, or at least that there might not be anything wrong with me. I could only see things as they stood. I felt like one of those conditioned rats in lab experiments. For years, all the early years, my body had gotten aroused time and time again, only to be unsatisfied. Finally it said, Enough. Forget this. I don't need the frustration of always being disappointed. I won't bother to get aroused. Then I can't be thwarted." Rachel sighed and rested her head back against the sofa, her eyes closed. "At least that's how I now see what was happening. I didn't see it at the time."

"But you decided to do something about it."

"I had to. Dan had become more difficult to

deal with. Well, naturally. The less my body responded, the less I was interested in sex. Dan's touch became an irritant. I was interested less often, but I couldn't always say so, because Dan expected it of me. He was hurt and felt rejected if I didn't go along."

"But if you did go along you felt . . . what?"

Rachel sat for a long time, slumped now, her head almost down to her chest. Her voice was a whisper. "Sometimes just irritated, wanting to get it over with. Sometimes—violated. I know that sounds awful. And I shouldn't have felt that way, but I did."

"Why shouldn't you have felt that way?"

"Because he was my husband. Because it was my fault that the whole situation existed. Because it was so little to ask, that we make love, enjoyably, happily. I was ruining everything. And I made it worse."

"How?"

"I started reading, and finding out that there were a lot of other women in my position. God, if I'd only done that sooner. All those years I wasted! And then Dan wouldn't buy it. He couldn't accept that maybe the way he made love to me wasn't what I needed. He tried to discount that but I insisted. I told him he had orgasms all the time and that I didn't and I resented it. I told him there was nothing wrong with my body, that I could have orgasms. That we weren't going to have sex anymore unless he spent the time and attention to help me have an orgasm."

"So what did he do?"

"He tried to ignore me. But I wouldn't be ignored. Our sexual encounters became tinged with hostility and unhappiness. I stood my ground. After all, what could be so hard about his paying some attention to what I needed?"

"He took it as a criticism of his lovemaking. That can be hard on a man's ego."

"Well, twenty years of being treated as a deficient woman was hard on me, too," Rachel said. She managed to look at Jerry then. He was not, as she had feared, showing any signs of losing sympathy with her. "Hell, Jerry, I listened to him every day. I tried to show him how much I appreciated him. If I was constantly accommodating him, why couldn't he accommodate me in this one little area?"

"Unfortunately," Jerry said sadly, "it's not a little area to men. They think they're expected to know everything about sex from the moment they reach puberty, instinctively. No woman can tell them what they're doing wrong, because they can't afford to be wrong. No woman can tell them her body responds in a particular way, because all women's bodies are supposed to respond in a way men already know about."

"You'll have to excuse me if I don't feel real sorry for them," Rachel grumbled. "It's a burden they put on themselves."

"Not necessarily. Women expect them to know a lot, too. Like you did when you first had an affair with Dan. You felt ignorant and thought he was a lot more knowledgeable."

"He was. From everything I can see, most men have more experience. The problem is that it may not be useful experience. And what's worse, things are set up so that if women question the value of that experience, we're ball-busters or bitches or lesbians. It's a double bind, Jerry."

"I know. It's not fair to women. But things have been changing."

"That's what everyone always says. And I know it's true. But what do I do about all those years I didn't catch on? About all those years I let myself be a victim?"

"Forgive yourself. That's all you can do, and it's a very powerful thing to do, Rachel. We all need to forgive ourselves for certain things."

"That's not the only thing I have to forgive myself for, Jerry. How can I not feel guilty for making the last year of Dan's life miserable? Because it was miserable for him, even before the tumor. He was angry with me, and starting to question his own masculinity for not being able to satisfy me like he thought he was supposed to. And wondering if he'd been wrong all that time."

Jerry nodded. "That was unfortunate, his illness coming then. But it was something you had to do."

Rachel moved restlessly, her energy propelling her to her feet. For a while she paced around the room, only coming to a stop when she was standing in front of a framed photograph of herself with Dan that she kept on the mantel. For a long time she stared at the picture before turning slowly to look straight at Jerry. "I used to lie awake at night, when he was sick, when he was dying, thinking about how I could have made his last year so much more enjoyable if I hadn't fought him on that issue. If I'd steeled myself and continued doing things the way he'd wanted them done." A lone tear coursed down her cheek. "Sometimes, deep inside me I'd find the fear that I'd actually caused his illness. Like I'd implanted in his brain a seed of doubt in himself that had grown into a tumor, a malignant tumor, that wormed its way so deep that even the neurosurgeons couldn't get all of it out of him, no matter how hard they tried."

Never before had she voiced that fear, one that still haunted her sometimes deep in the night. Jerry had come to stand beside her, moving to hold her tightly against himself.

"Poor Rachel," he whispered against her hair. "How much pain all of this has caused you, as if just losing your husband wasn't enough. I'm sorry I didn't understand. Maybe I could have helped you. Maybe I still can help you."

Her head rested in exhaustion against his shoulder. "I had to tell you all of it, Jerry. I don't know what I'm going to do about it. Everything seems so confused again, because of how I feel about you."

"You don't have to decide anything tonight, Rachel." He kissed the top of her head. "Let me spend the night and hold you. Nothing more. Just let me be here with you."

She was too spent, and too grateful, to object.

Chapter Fourteen

Jerry's pager went off late in the night. He was disoriented for a moment, unable to place himself, though he felt particularly comfortable snuggled close to a warm female body. Rachel, his mind assured him, and he very nearly fell back to sleep. He was not accustomed to his pager going off at night because in an emergency the hospital simply called him and he answered from his bed.

But he wasn't in his bed, and after a moment the realization came that he would have to do something about the interruption. In the bathroom he peered at the number on the pager and then went downstairs to phone in. Emergencies didn't so much start his adrenaline running as call for a focused attention that made him feel challenged and useful. This emergency—the resident on call had been attacked by a patient—called for his immediate departure.

He kissed Rachel lightly to waken her. Her eyes fluttered open and she smiled slightly. "Are you leaving?"

"Yes. An emergency at Fielding." He was pulling on his pants as he spoke. "I'll probably just spend the rest of the night there."

"I'll see you sometime during the day, then."

"Right." He struggled into the sleeves of his favorite blue sweater. "And, Rachel?"

"Mmmmm?"

"Thanks for sorting things out with Carl."

"You're not annoyed with me for that?"

"Actually, I'm relieved. But you shouldn't have had to be involved. Our relationship is none of Carl's, or anyone else's, business."

"Hey, we both work at a hospital. Whether we like it or not, people are going to talk. It's just better if they don't get it wrong. And it could have been very damaging for Erika."

"I know. I shouldn't have let Carl put my back up that way. I'd probably have tried to talk him around if he weren't intent on messing with my future. Hell, you're half asleep. We'll talk about it later."

Rachel nodded and snuggled her head against the pillow. "Good night, Jerry. Thanks for listening to me."

"Thank you for telling me. We'll get it sorted out." She made no reply. Jerry wasn't sure whether that was because she'd fallen asleep or because she wasn't really convinced that they could work it out. In any case, he had to get to the hospital, and he wasn't going to have time to think about their situation until much later. Though her eyes were closed and her breathing had become deep and regular, he blew her a kiss, and wondered when he was ever actually going to eat breakfast with her.

Jerry was relieved to find that the resident who had been attacked was not physically injured. Chances were, however, that this would leave psychological scars if the situation wasn't dealt with quickly. He called the young man into his office and talked the situation through with him for the next hour. Jerry was honest about the possibilities of such an event happening again, but he was also encouraging in his conviction that most psychiatrists learned to handle the fears that went along with the job. By the time the young man left his office, Jerry felt confident that the worst of the experience was past.

"But if you start worrying about it, please come to me. We'll find a way to work through it." Jerry laid a hand on the man's shoulder and met his searching gaze. "Almost anything can be handled if you're willing to face it and find new options for looking at it."

The resident seemed to accept his assurances. As Jerry watched him walk away down the corridor he wondered if Rachel would be as easy to convince. He was not trying to tell her that her situation was easy, or that there was a simple solution, just that if she was willing to discuss the matter, he was sure they could find ways of coping with her problem. Because it had, in some unique way, become his.

Jerry hadn't realized that the day staff had come on until he noticed Carl Norridge standing by the nurses' station. Carl indicated that he wanted a word with Jerry and Jerry motioned him into his office. When the two men had seated themselves, Carl pursed his lips and said, "I've been talking with Tsu in the pediatrics department. He seems to think this . . . training you've been giving Ms. Amundsen has been moderately useful to her. Useful enough, let us say, that he'd be willing to consider making time for it in all his residents' schedules."

A major victory. Not that Norridge was going to phrase it that way. In fact, Norridge wasn't quite ready to concede. He went on, "My suggestion is this. If you'll take someone from a more demanding residency, what I'm talking here is surgery, and provide the same training, I'd be willing to evaluate the results and consider applying for funds for a program. Is that something you'd be interested in doing?"

"Sure. What we're talking here is a tradeoff, is it? Instead of the vice-chairmanship, you'd make me director of this program?"

"Only if I thought it had real promise."

"Well," Jerry said with a grin, "let's say you thought it had real promise. And I'm sure you will. Do you think you'd be able to see your way clear to make me a full professor at the same time?"

Norridge hated to be pushed. Jerry watched expectantly as he fiddled with a tie clasp almost as abominable as his tie. After a long pause, he said, "I'll have to think about it."

"Fine. Just so we're clear, though, I want you to know those are my terms. The directorship of an interview training program and the professorship go together."

"I'm not even convinced about the training program yet, Jerry."

Jerry shrugged. "We'll talk about it when you've seen a little more information."

Apparently Carl did not feel comfortable leaving it that way. "What would you do if you didn't get either?"

"I'm not sure. I'd have to think about it."

Norridge rose and dusted off his pants with a manicured hand, as though Jerry's office seating was dusty. Maybe compared to the seating in Norridge's elegant office it was. Real live patients came here, though, and talked and laughed and cried. Unlike Carl's office, where mostly administrators conferred and members of the faculty agreed with their chairman. Jerry wouldn't have traded places with Carl for a doubling of his salary. And though there were things he might be able to accomplish if he were vice-chairman, he would far prefer the autonomy of running the kind of training program he had proposed. But Carl didn't need to know that.

Just as he was about to leave the office, Carl turned to ask, "Was it a medication problem, the patient who attacked our resident?"

"I think so. He'd hidden his pills under his mattress, according to the nurse who searched there afterward. Some of them get very clever that way."

"Yeah. Well, thanks for handling the resident. It's one of the things that turns them against psychiatry if it isn't handled correctly."

Which was as close as Carl would come to a compliment to Jerry, and it was close enough. Jerry said, "He's going to be a good psychiatrist. He'd probably benefit by your telling him about your experience back in '82."

Carl laughed reminiscently. "He's probably already heard about it, but I'll make a point of telling him. See you around, Jerry."

And that was the end of the whole episode about Erika. When she arrived for work that morning she found a message from Jerry explaining the situation. Within the hour she had managed to present herself on the psych floor, ready to continue her lessons, and unembarrassed about her admission that she wouldn't mind having an affair with him.

Jerry admired the flexibility of the young. He was not going to be nearly so flexible if Rachel decided that the two of them weren't going to have an affair. And something a great deal more important than that.

At Rachel's request they didn't see each other until the weekend. She called Jerry several times, to let him know that she was thinking about him and that she wanted to see him soon, but just not yet. Not until she'd had a chance to think things through. Jerry had resisted her plan, insisting that they needed to discuss things together.

"We will," she promised. "I'm not going to make any hard and fast decisions without talking to you again. But I need to consolidate where I am, Jerry. I have to get a handle on what I'm feeling."

He had tried not to press her. She could tell how hard he was trying to give her enough "space." And suddenly, too, she believed in space. She thought about how all her life she had not really protected herself quite enough. She'd let Dan have the last word in matters that concerned her intimately. She'd let the girls impose on her at their will. Not that there was anything inherently wrong in generously giving to a husband or to two daughters. But Rachel could see that she had sometimes not respected her own needs quite enough. Instead of her personal needs, she had made sure that her professional needs were met. She had pursued a career, and a successful career, making room for that expression of her personality and creativity. And that was something to be proud of herself for.

As for the rest of it, she would have to forgive herself. And do better next time. And she very much feared that this was the next time.

For several days she threw herself into her work, coming home in the evenings exhausted. She talked to her daughters on the phone and watched television. She picked up several different books and found she couldn't interest herself in them. She had an odd phone call from Nan LeBaron.

"Rachel, I wonder if you'd give me your opinion on something," Nan said.

"Sure."

"You know Roger Janek?"

"Yes. He's a good friend of Jerry's."

"I know. Apparently Jerry suggested that Roger come and live with me."

"I beg your pardon?"

"Exactly. Well, it seems Roger is having trouble sleeping because he doesn't like being in his house since Kerri died. Jerry thought he might sleep better here."

"How very strange. Why you?"

"I gather because I have the room since Angel left, and because I know Roger, slightly, and because since I'm seeing Peter I'm not considered a woman on the prowl."

Rachel laughed. "I don't think Jerry would have put it that way. He does seem to be involving himself in an awful lot of lives these days."

"So I hear," Nan said, somewhat significantly.

Rachel ignored that and asked, "How do you feel about it?"

"Roger living here? Actually, it would make things simpler for me. I wouldn't have to find a new roommate, or at least not right away."

"What if the hospital got gossipy about you two sharing?"

"Like they've gotten gossipy about Jerry and Erika? I hear you put a stop to that real quick."

"See what I mean by gossipy?" Rachel said.

"Doesn't bother me one bit. The guys in my department would probably send me flowers if they thought I were shacking up with someone. A real bunch of chauvinists. Charming, of course. Have you ever noticed that the more chauvinistic a man is, the more charming he is? Or maybe it's vice versa. In any case, I have a department full of them. Not that medicine in general isn't full of them. I think I'll write a paper on the causes of charm in the chauvinistic male. Do you think the *New England Journal of Medicine* would be interested?"

"If they aren't, *Glamour* would be," Rachel assured her. "What about Roger, who is neither chauvinistic nor excessively charming?"

"If you don't think it would be a big mistake, I'm going to say yes."

"I think you'll be a good influence on him. He's very dear but he's a little lost right now."

"That's settled then." Nan sighed. "We had to disconnect Pamela Enderling yesterday. Her husband was jubilant, but he had the wisdom not to say anything. Her sister Beth was distraught. Jerry stopped by to talk to her and seemed to help a lot. Really, Rachel, he's a remarkably gifted man."

"I know."

Though Nan probably expected her to say more, Rachel wasn't prepared to do so. Nan thanked her again for her advice, and her help with Pamela Enderling's husband, and hung up. Rachel sat staring at the phone, shaking her head at the thought of Jerry orchestrating so many lives. What did he have in mind for hers?

Jerry was on his way out of the hospital Saturday morning when he ran into Cliff Lenzini. "You look like your honeymoon suited you," he said, taking in Cliff's tanned face and arms. "Which reminds me, I have a favor to ask."

Cliff, an enormous bear of a man, cocked his head quizzically at the psychiatrist. "From what I hear, you don't need another woman in your life. What can I do for you?"

"Actually, I want you to recommend one of your surgical residents for an experiment I'm conducting. It should be the one who's least competent at dealing with patients, but if that's a woman I'll take the second least competent—who I'm sure is a man."

"Why are you sure of that?"

"Because there aren't that many women in your program and they can't all be duds at interviewing patients. What have you got for me?"

"The perfect candidate. His name is John and he's so awkward with patients we're thinking of asking him to transfer somewhere else, even though he's rather good at the actual surgery. You think you could help him?" he asked curiously.

"Probably. Don't expect miracles but let me get

my hands on him for about twenty minutes a day for a couple weeks. Deal?"

"Hey, what have I got to lose?" There was a speculative gleam in Cliff's eyes. "Would this be a good time for Angel and me to have you and Rachel to dinner? I remember talking about it at the wedding."

"It's too close to Thanksgiving. This all started at your wedding," he added cryptically. "Give me another couple weeks."

Cliff shook his head. "There's no understanding psychiatrists. I'll have John waiting at your office Monday morning right after rounds. Okay?"

"Perfect. Say hi to Angel. I've only seen her in the distance since you've been back. Apparently Angel talked with Rachel."

"Trying to save your ass," Cliff remarked with a grin. "Which she apparently did. Quite a woman, Rachel."

"You don't have to tell me." Jerry drew a hand through his hair. He should never have gotten his hair cut shorter. Longer hair had been symbolic. It had meant he was free, independent, unhampered, uninhibited, and an aging hippie. Maybe he'd have to buy himself a pair of Birkenstocks instead. And he hated those shoes. He glared at Cliff and without another word disappeared down the hall.

Rachel was nervous pretty much all day on Saturday. Jerry had to work during the day, but had insisted that he could be there by five. What good was his coming at five? She would be right in the middle of making dinner for them, caught up in figuring out if she was going to be able to duplicate the pasta dish she'd had at a restaurant a few months ago. Angel hair pasta with artichoke hearts and mushrooms in a delicate lemon-flavored sauce. And for the first time in years, maybe since Dan had died, she'd cultured a sourdough starter and had a loaf of real sourdough bread rising, ready to bake.

Usually, kneading a yeast dough relaxed her, but she had felt a constant state of tension that day. Perhaps, she admitted a bit sheepishly to herself, it was actually sexual tension and not nervousness at all. The knowledge that Jerry was going to be there, and that in the normal progression of things they would make love, was a powerful stimulus to her state of body and mind. But she had to think of the long term. She had to be fair to Jerry. They were not necessarily going to end up in bed. Not if Rachel could keep her head clear.

Who would have thought that would prove such a difficult matter? Rachel wandered into the half bath on the first floor for the third time, and scrutinized herself in the mirror. Maybe she should have dyed her hair. She rather liked the silvery tinges at the ends of her cloud of curls, but they did make her look older. Well, she was older, wasn't she? Jerry's age, and in no position to compete against kids like Erika in any physical beauty competition. Either he could accept her as she was or there was no sense in their seeing each other.

And maybe there wasn't any sense in their seeing each other.

Rachel stared at her reflection, poked her fingers through her hair like a styling comb, and tucked the label of her blouse back inside where it belonged. Maybe she should change her blouse if it was going to keep doing that. But she merely returned to the kitchen, slipped an apron on over the green silk, and began to sauté the mushrooms.

When the doorbell rang she gave a nervous start and simultaneously turned off the burner and untied her apron, realizing as she did so that her hands smelled of garlic and probably now her hair would, too. Well, it was too late to do anything about that.

In one hand Jerry grasped a bottle of champagne by its neck and in the other he had a bunch of flowers that were desperately clinging to life. "I promised one of my patients I'd bring these to you," he explained. "She was going home and she said her husband was allergic to flowers and that I should take them home to my wife. I figure they'll last for the rest of the evening before they completely expire."

Rachel laughed and took them from him, leading the way into the kitchen where she attempted to retrieve a ribbon vase from a high shelf of one of the cabinets. Jerry shoved the champagne into the fridge and came to her assistance, reaching above her and bringing the vase down so that Rachel was enclosed within his arms. "See how well you fit in my arms?" he commented, though he did no more than brush the top of her head with his lips before moving back from her to set the vase on the kitchen cabinet. "I think I have one like that."

"The vase?" Rachel was relieved not to have to comment on how well she fit in his arms. "I think Tricia got it for me at Crate and Barrel."

"I like their stuff. We should go shopping there sometime."

"Whatever for?"

Jerry looked embarrassed. "Oh, I don't know. Just to see what they have. Don't you like window shopping?"

"Not particularly. Oh, sometimes. But I usually only go when I have a real purpose in mind."

"You lawyers. You get too conditioned to billable hours to waste your time doing something frivolous," he teased. Surveying the items set out on the countertop he asked, "Want me to do something?"

"Like what?"

"I can make a salad, after a fashion. You just rinse the lettuce and peel some vegetables and throw them all together with some dressing from a bottle. I do it all the time."

"Okay, I'll risk it, but let's have a glass of wine first."

"Champagne. No reason not to open it now, is there?"

Only what it does to me, Rachel thought ruefully, but she took down two champagne flutes and watched as he expertly opened the bottle. How many times had he done it for Barbara, for family occasions and intimate ones? It didn't matter of course. He was doing it now, with her. His eyes were on her face and his smile was just for her. He looked almost nervous, but that was impossible. No one could find Rachel the least nervous-making.

"To us," he said.

"To us."

He had managed to get it there icy cold. It was

perfectly dry and heady at the same time. "Mmm," she said. "Fantastic. There's one of those cooler things above the fridge."

"Do you want to take it in the other room?" he asked as he deposited the bottle in the marble ice bucket.

Rachel felt the pulse beating in her throat. "I'm not sure where I want to take it."

He nodded, understanding. "We'll take it upstairs, then. And sit up on the bed, propped up with all those pillows of yours. And talk. And enjoy ourselves."

"Yes."

She could not, for the life of her, have suggested it, but it was precisely what she wanted. She followed him up the stairs and tossed extra pillows on the bed from the chairs while he arranged the champagne on the bedside table. It was dark outside and Rachel turned on only the small lamp on her side of the bed, which wasn't even strong enough for reading by. She moved onto the bed and watched as he climbed in beside her. Jerry touched his glass to hers, lightly, and asked, "Do you always keep flowers in your bedroom?"

A bouquet of brightly colored chrysanthemums in a low container rested on the bureau opposite the bed. Rachel shook her head. "I put them there today because I thought we'd be here. I moved them, twice, into the other room. But they were so pretty . . ."

He leaned over to kiss her cheek. "I'm glad you put them there. I'm glad you planned for us to have sex. Then it's your choice; I don't have to worry that I've talked you into doing something you don't want to do."

"It would always be like that, Jerry, you wondering if I wanted to make love. I can't really say it."

"That could change. And I'm really good at listening to what people can't quite say, Rachel."

"You're very good at lots of things. Nan says you were very helpful to Mrs. Enderling's sister. And that you've talked her into letting Roger live in her flat."

"You probably think I've become some kind of yenta," he said with a grin. "I'm not trying to fix him up with her, either. He just needs to live someplace else for a while and I knew she had a room available." He reached across for the champagne bottle and refilled their glasses.

Rachel sipped from her glass, but her mind was on Jerry. She was aware of every movement he made, of how his arm stretched to pour the champagne and return the bottle to the bedside table. Of how his hips shifted to accommodate the motion. How his eyes seemed to linger on her lips. How he raised his glass to drink, and then, miraculously, set his glass down on the bedside table instead of holding it. How his hand then came up to touch her face, his finger stroking along the fullness of her cheek. She was aware of his taking her glass from her and setting it down beside his on the table, of his turning to draw her against him.

"We can take as long as we want, and we can stop if you want." He kissed her nose and then lowered his lips to hers. "We can do whatever you need to feel comfortable."

Her body seemed to have no doubt about what it wanted. His lips on hers called forth a heady response. His hand, straying down to her breast, created havoc with her insides. She cleared her throat and whispered, "Maybe we should get undressed."

"Let me," he suggested as he slowly unbuttoned her blouse.

She had worn her prettiest bra, not that any of them were those lacy, gossamer things she saw in catalogs. As he reached behind her to unfasten it, he nudged the fabric down with his lips, so that they were waiting to capture a nipple when it was exposed. Rachel moaned with the pleasure he gave her. She had slid down on the bed and now reached around him to clasp his buttocks. His chinos were decidedly in the way but for a while she was too engrossed with the excitement in her body to make a further move. Her breast, drawn into his mouth with such urgency, was sending riotous signals to other parts of her body. The ache grew between her legs.

Eventually they stripped off his pants and her skirt, but there was no unseemly rush to consummation. Jerry held her body close against his, rubbing rhythmically against her until the heat felt as though it would cause an explosion. Rachel moaned again with the pleasure of it.

"This," Jerry whispered against her hair, "is almost the perfect moment—when our bodies are at a fever pitch. I love holding you, touching you, pleasing you. I love having you please me. It's ecstasy being joined in expectation. But this," he said, sure of himself, "is also when you leave me, just for a moment, just when the pleasure is so great that there's only you." He touched her, perfectly timing the intensity of his touch to the raggedness of her breathing, sending her spiraling into fulfillment. Joined together, they were indeed one, too enraptured to separate themselves but also momentarily lost in the sensations of their individual bodies. Two, one, linked by a pleasure so great it took their breath away. And left them, afterward, spent and delighted, with themselves and each other.

They lay for a long time in each other's arms, not talking, simply savoring the glow of their joining. For that long Rachel managed to keep her thoughts from intruding, forcing her to confront the significance of the situation. Being held in his arms, his flesh against hers, she felt desirable and cherished. It had been a very long time since she'd felt that way, and she liked the sensation. She could grow, in fact, to need it, if she wasn't careful.

"Maybe we should go down and fix dinner," she said. "I have a loaf of sourdough bread that needs to be put in the oven."

Jerry rolled slightly away so that he could observe her. "Have you let yourself start thinking? Much better to just let yourself feel at this point."

"Too late." Rachel pulled herself up to a sitting position but she didn't make any attempt to cover her nakedness. A faint smile tugged at the corners of her mouth. "Suddenly I don't feel middle-aged."

"You were lovely when you were twenty-five and you're even lovelier now," he said, sitting up beside her. "That's how long we've known each other, since we were twenty-five and you moved next door to us."

"I remember. You were still in your training and Barbara used to tell me that they were after you all the time to dress more formally. But you kept on wearing the kind of clothes that suited you perfectly. I'd see you leave at the crack of dawn and you'd look so excited and eager for every new day. Your hair would be wet from the shower and you wouldn't have finished buttoning your shirt."

"You remember that?" He looked immensely pleased. "Do you know, I'm starting to feel like that again. I mean, excited about each day. The thought of talking with you and seeing you, and the possibilities of working on a new training program for residents in interviewing technique. I've never lost my enthusiasm for psychiatry but . . ."

"But you needed something more in you life. Remember how you were at Angel and Cliff's wedding? You were so restless. I wondered where it would take you, that restlessness."

"Is that what you think brought me here?" he asked, gesturing with amusement toward the bed. "There was certainly something missing in my life, but I think of it more as something an unconscious part of me was trying to make conscious. Like how special you are to me."

Rachel regarded him ruefully. "You practically ignored me that day, Jerry. If your unconscious was talking to you, it must have been in Russian."

"I was a little hard of hearing, it's true. But then you sprang this ethics thing on me. It meant there was a whole part of your life that you weren't sharing with me. That kind of jolted me. I know you've explained but I still don't quite understand why you were so secretive about that."

Rachel had continued to think about it. As she took each course, as she planned her new career, as she negotiated with the medical center, she could have been seeking his advice, his friendly input. But that's not what she'd wanted. It was not so much that she had wanted to make every decision on her own. It was more that the only kind of input she was truly interested in would have been from a partner, and Jerry was not her partner then, or now. Though he was, obviously, now her lover. And that was something that she had to clarify, right now before things got out of hand.

"We need to talk," she said.

"Now why did I know that was coming? Here or in the kitchen?"

"The kitchen, I think."

He nodded but climbed out of bed reluctantly. Rachel quickly slipped on her bra and underpants, her skirt and blouse. She caught a glimpse of herself in the mirror above the bureau and saw that the tag was sticking up from the blouse once again. Before she could move to adjust it, Jerry had efficiently tucked it in and kissed the nape of her neck. In the mirror he said to her, "Maybe it was my longer hair. You probably couldn't take me seriously until I had my hair cut."

"It wasn't your hair, Jerry. I got married on a beach, remember?"

"Still. You probably wouldn't want me to grow my hair longer again."

"Don't be silly. Besides, I don't have anything to say about it."

"Well, of course you do. We're a couple now, Rachel. I don't want you to feel uncomfortable with how I look."

"I liked your hair long, Jerry," she said, avoiding his eyes in the mirror. "I should put the bread in."

Chapter Fifteen

Jerry carried the remaining champagne and their glasses down to the kitchen, where Rachel had already started to busy herself with preparations for dinner. He poured them each a glass and handed Rachel hers with a quizzical smile. He was not trying to avoid a discussion of their relationship; he just had to figure out how to present it in a way that she would find acceptable.

"What are we having?" he asked as he took a sip of the champagne and peered over her shoulder. "Angel hair pasta?"

"Yes. I'm trying to duplicate a dish I had at a restaurant. The sauce was so thin that I'm not sure what was in it, though the menu mentioned lemon." She frowned at the skillet where she had begun to brown the mushrooms such a long time ago. "Maybe some white wine. Maybe some chicken broth. I hope you don't mind my experimenting on you."

His smile widened significantly. "I hope you will. There's nothing I'd enjoy more."

"You know what I mean," she said, almost crossly. "It may not turn out very well."

"But it probably will. There's nothing in it that's going to be inedible. And when you take into consideration a loaf of homemade sourdough bread, how can we miss?"

"That's true." Rachel retrieved a lemon and a bottle of open white wine from the fridge but paused in front of the cooktop. "I don't know why it seemed like such a good idea to try this. It's not something I would have done with company before. I mean, without even a recipe."

"You don't always need a recipe. Sometimes to get the best results you have to experiment. Like you and me, Rachel. There's no recipe that's going to tell us the right way to go about our relationship. We have to test the waters."

Rachel frowned and waved the half-full wine bottle in exasperation. "You don't understand, Jerry. I'm trying to prevent a catastrophe. I don't . . . If you . . . Say we started a relationship."

"We have, Rachel."

"Okay. I know that. But it's just a casual relationship at this point. People sleep together all the time."

"Not you and me. We don't just sleep with someone casually. We wouldn't do it if it weren't important, if we didn't expect the relationship to go somewhere."

"Well, then, you've misunderstood," she insisted, turning away from him. "Because it *can't* go anywhere. For both of our sakes, Jerry. I'm trying to be realistic. I have a problem with sex. You don't need to be involved with a woman who has a problem with sex."

"So what's your problem with sex?" he asked gently. "You haven't exhibited any problems since we've been having it."

"That's just a fluke." Rachel sloshed a goodly

quantity of wine into the skillet with the mushrooms and turned the heat up. "Twenty years of unwanted sex can't be wiped out with a few good sexual encounters. What if at some point I don't want sex and know that you do? I'd be in the same bind all over again."

"That's not really all that unusual, one person wanting sex and the other one not being interested."

"Maybe not, but it's a problem when it's always the same one who doesn't want sex. She starts to feel like a mean-spirited, sexless idiot. Either that or she agrees to participate but feels wretched anyway. Don't you see what I'm saying? How are you going to feel if after a month, or after a year, you want to make love to me and I'm not always interested? I'll tell you how you're going to feel, Jerry. You're going to feel like hell. You're going to feel rejected and hurt and you're going to begin to wonder what's wrong with me. I don't want that. Not for my sake and not for yours."

There was a catch in her voice that made him move close to her, but not so close that she would feel trapped. He picked up the lemon she'd dropped on the counter and sliced it in half. "There's something you should know about me, Rachel."

"What?" she asked, in a tone stiff with the belief that it couldn't possibly be something that would change her mind.

"Intercourse is only a very small part of the things that give me sexual pleasure." He cupped one half of the lemon and rubbed it over the old-fashioned ceramic juicer she had set out beside the cutting board. "When I'm attracted to a

woman, all sorts of movements and vignettes send
a kind of thrill through me. Like when I watched
you swim? You were sending me the most delightful messages. The way your hand stroked through
the water, and the way your body swayed from
side to side. And now, when your head is bent
over the skillet there's that incredible curve to
your neck? I don't have to be in bed with you, Rachel, to have you give me exquisite pleasure."

"It's not the same thing," she said uncertainly.

"It is and it isn't," he said. "I think, for most
men, what happens is that those things make
them want to have sex. But that's not quite the
way I respond to them. They are, in themselves, a
source of complete satisfaction to me. Not that I
can't be tempted into making love." He grinned at
her, reaching out to brush a finger along her
flushed cheek. "Sometimes I think I'm the lucki-
est man on earth."

She gave a hiccup of laughter. "Like having
those ben wah balls inside you all the time. Oh,
Jerry, you're exaggerating, surely. You couldn't be
satisfied by something so simple, so undemand-
ing. Could you?"

"Yep." He bent down to kiss her lightly. "But not
with just anyone. A few times, since Barbara left,
I've been flattered into relationships that I really
knew better than to get into, because I wasn't getting that delightful sensuous feedback from the
women. You see, I'm flawed."

"I should hope so. I don't think I'd last long
around anyone who was perfect."

"Are you planning to last long around me?"

"That's not what I meant, exactly." Rachel
turned down the heat under the mushrooms and

poured in some of the lemon juice he'd squeezed. "This isn't going to be very thick."

"Could we make it a little spicy, too? With some crushed hot red pepper?"

Rachel looked over at him, surprised. "Sure. That sounds good."

"We're a good combination, Rachel, you and I. Just think about it, okay? And remember that I can take care of myself. You just have to worry about you."

She looked at him for a long moment, nodded and said, "How about starting the salad?"

When they returned to Rachel's house after a movie she hesitated at the front door, turning to Jerry with an awkward shrug. "I don't . . . um . . . Maybe we should say good night here."

He kissed the tip of her nose. "You are so adorable, Rachel. Do you remember what I told you earlier? I don't have to make love to feel satisfied. Do you expect me to want to make love every time I spend the night with you?"

"Wouldn't you? I mean, if you didn't want to make love, why would you stay?"

"Just to be close to you, sweetheart. To lie with my body against yours and know that you're beside me all night."

"Yes, and in the morning you'd want to make love."

"Maybe. Maybe you would, too. But we don't have to. You don't have to feel any pressure to make love."

"That's a lot easier said than done." Rachel turned to the door and put her key in the lock. "You can come in."

"Such a gracious hostess," he murmured. But he followed her in with an easy grace, helping her off with her jacket when they stood in the entry hall. The house still smelled of the freshly baked sourdough bread and the spiciness of the pasta dish they'd collaborated on. "Tomorrow I'm finally going to stay for breakfast and if it's okay with you, could we make French toast with some slices of your sourdough?"

Rachel could feel herself relax. There was something about his calm acceptance that made her trust him. They didn't, after all, have the history she'd had with Dan. They were building their own history and she owed it to him, and to herself, to find out what their story was.

And in the morning, when she woke up feeling his body snuggled close to hers, she did indeed find that desire rose quickly in her body. "I think," she whispered when she saw that he was awake and watching her, "that maybe I do want to make love. If you do."

And he did.

Monday morning Jerry discovered that Cliff Lenzini had not been exaggerating about the awkwardness of his second-year surgical resident. John's major problem was not his knowledge but his immaturity. He was also hurt and resentful that he had been sent for this extra training. All in all a real challenge for Jerry's new program. But Jerry had had a long night's sleep, since Rachel had sent him home Sunday night, insisting that she needed a little time to herself.

"Whatever for?" he'd asked, only to be told to go home and soak in his hot tub. Which he'd done.

He would miss his hot tub. That thought had just sprung into his mind minutes before his new trainee arrived and he was still trying to assimilate what it meant. It meant he didn't expect to be living in his condo much longer. Which meant he intended to be living somewhere else. Which in turn meant that he expected to be living in Rachel's house. Not that she'd asked him, or that he'd invited himself. It was just that his condo was too small for two people, and that her house was the perfect size. What if she didn't want to have him there?

"So what is it I'm expected to do here?" John the second-year resident asked, his tone sulky and his eyes narrowed. "Dr. Lenzini said it was for training, not some kind of psychological stuff."

"I'm working on a program to teach residents how to interview patients. Are you aware of any shortcomings in your interviewing technique?"

John slumped in the chair opposite Jerry's desk. "Well, they tell me sometimes I upset the patients. Like once someone refused surgery after I'd explained it to them and my chief resident had to spend two hours changing the woman's mind."

Jerry nodded, careful to restrain his amusement. "Yes, that's the kind of thing that can happen. What I'd like to try doing is teaching you some of the psychological signs to look for in patients that will give you a clue about how to handle them. And the various techniques you can use that will engender patient confidence." Through the window he saw Erika approaching and he waved her into the room. "I'm doing the same thing with Erika, who's a pediatric intern. Erika Amundsen, this is John Lakely, a surgical resident who's going to learn some interviewing techniques with us."

John became decidedly more enthusiastic about the project. Jerry did not assume it was his own clever handling of the situation. Before the twenty-minute session was complete, John had thrown himself with vigor into the project, urging Erika to share her new knowledge with him and to correct him when she felt he was making a mistake. Jerry watched the two of them walk away down the hall, shaking his head. So much for the merits of his plan. Still, whatever worked . . .

His eye fell to a photocopied sheet on his desk that he'd picked up with his mail but had not had a chance to read yet. It was titled "Ethics Consults" and was addressed not to him but to every department head, who in turn must have photocopied it for every doctor under them. Certainly Carl Norridge's initials were at the bottom of the sheet, alongside Rachel Weis's name as the author, and the head of the medical center as approving its distribution. It was dated almost a month earlier, and concerned the issue of nurses being allowed to call for ethics consultations. Jerry's name was featured prominently in the notice. He groaned.

Oh, hell, Carl Norridge must have loved this. It was a wonder he wasn't standing in Jerry's office door glowering (or possibly laughing) at him. Jerry read the relevant sentences again: "I am informed by Dr. Gerald Stoner that this has been the policy at Fielding for as long as he's worked here, and that the reasoning for it is that if a nurse thinks a consult is necessary, the nurse has only to ask a doctor to call one. Dr. Stoner felt this reasoning derived from a time when the supposition was that nurses, being more emotionally involved with their patients than doctors, would be prone to call ethics consults too often." Oh, hell. Rachel went on, in a subtly sarcastic way, to point out the fallacy of this reasoning and to request that the department heads reconsider their stance.

What surprised Jerry most of all was that there wasn't any indication of Norridge's stand on the issue attached to this memorandum. When he looked up from it again, he found the head nurse of the psychiatric unit regarding him curiously. "She doesn't say if you're for us or against us," Ms. Nguyen said.

"Us? You mean the nurses? Oh, God, do we have a rebellion on our hands?"

She grinned sweetly at him. "Something like that, Dr. Stoner. I doubt if there's a nurse in the hospital who wouldn't agree that we should have the right to call an ethics consult. We often know the patients a great deal better than the doctors do. Which is, I'm sure, what you meant when you told Ms. Weis that we were more emotionally involved with them."

He laughed. "Naturally that's what I meant to tell her. Suzie, do you know what Norridge has to say about all this?"

"He looked like the proverbial storm cloud when he descended on the ward after reading it, but he's actually sort of proud of his nurses, and when a few of us told him our reasoning, and that it was a slap at our professionalism, he started to come around. Not that he appreciates your being involved, Jerry."

"I'll bet. As if I weren't in enough trouble."

"I was real glad to see the last rumor die a speedy death. It's kind of a bore all the old men rejuvenating themselves with young chickies." She motioned her head toward the memo with a lopsided smile. "Not that your very own involvement isn't about to cause you a bit of distress."

"How do you people know all these things?" he grumbled.

"So are you with us, kemo sabe?"

"You're not *old* enough to know about the Lone Ranger. And I'm not the Lone Ranger, it just seems that way." He scratched his head and tucked the memo in a drawer. "Yes, of course I'm with you, Ms. Nguyen. I have the utmost respect for the professionalism of our nurses here at Fielding. Just do me a favor and warn me about any more bombshells that are about to burst so I can hide, okay?"

"Hey, you're our hero. We need you right out front, Dr. Stoner." She turned away but swung her head back to say, "And we'll be right there for you, too." She was gone before he could thank her.

It was a long day, which included a talk with Carl Norridge, who managed to convey the impression that he found Jerry's involvement in this matter less than acceptable; with several of the nurses on the floor who seemed to feel they needed to win him over to their cause; with several of the other doctor members of the department who weren't at all sure they believed in nurses having the right to call ethics consults; and a very brief, apologetic talk with Rachel, who said she'd long forgotten that she'd even used his name in the memo she'd sent off in the heat of her irritation about the issue.

"Though the medical director did call to tell me he'd approved it for distribution," she admitted. "He's perfectly willing to see an open debate on the issue. Have I gotten you in trouble?"

"No, no. No more than usual, my dear. Why don't you come over tonight and we'll relax in the hot tub?"

He could hear the hesitation in her voice when she asked, "What time?"

"I'm likely to be here late. How about eight?"

Though she'd agreed, Jerry had wondered if she'd actually show up. When he got home at seven-thirty he half expected to have a message on his answering machine from her, backing out. But the only message was from his older son, who mentioned that he would be spending Thanksgiving with his mother in southern California. Jerry answered the call while he shrugged out of his sport jacket and kicked off his shoes. He was still on the phone when Rachel arrived, a few minutes early, and he opened the door to her still holding the phone to his ear. Holding up one finger, and giving her a quick kiss on the cheek, he said to his son, "Rachel's here, Harris. Have a great Thanksgiving and give my best to your mother."

"We're so civilized," he said as he tossed the portable phone onto a chair. "You look a little down. Is everything okay?"

"Yeah. I got some heavy-duty feedback about the nurses and ethics consults, but I expected that, and it's perfectly all right as long as I do what I know I have to. I'm sorry for your sake, though. It never occurred to me that it wouldn't be a good idea to quote you in my memo." She shrugged out of a down jacket and dropped it into his waiting hands. "It seemed a good idea at the time to give some context to bringing up the issue now. I suppose I could have done that just with the case itself, but not as well."

"Of course not. Don't worry about it, Rachel. How does a good soak in the hot tub sound?"

"Fine."

But she sounded a little uncertain and he cocked his head at her. "Tell me what the problem is. Do you still feel uneasy about being naked in there?"

"Maybe a little. It's nothing. I'll be fine."

Jerry smiled encouragement and led her into his bedroom, where he began disrobing without further comment. "I'll check the temperature. You come out when you're ready."

He thought by leaving her there alone, with a bath sheet on the bed, that she would be able to preserve some modesty if she chose to. Funny, when he lacked all modesty himself, that he would choose such a modest woman. On the other hand he found it an endearing trait in her. Maybe it satisfied his own search for freshness and innocence. Oh, who the hell knew? Who could ever understand why you fell in love with someone? It didn't matter, anyhow. He'd fallen in love with Rachel and that was all there was to it. Jerry did wonder, though, if Rachel didn't feel quite the same way about him.

He was seated in the hot tub when she came out onto the deck. She smiled at him, perfunctorily, and dropped the bath sheet that she'd had wrapped around herself onto the redwood decking. She didn't look at him as she inched her way into the hot water. Jerry knew that she would have preferred his not looking at her, but that seemed impossible. He was intrigued by the lushness of her body: how could she be so trim and so voluptuous at the same time?

"You're lovely," he said.

"Thanks." She peered through the darkness at him. "It's almost too dark to really see anything out here, isn't it?"

"My eyes are accustomed to the light. Doesn't the water feel good?"

"Mmm. It's very soothing. Could we have the bubbles on?"

"Sure." He reached over and turned the dial that made an almost instant cascade of bubbles stream out the four jets in the sides of the tub. As Rachel positioned herself to get the full effect, he stretched his legs to capture the bench on either side of her with his toes. "Have you made reservations for us somewhere for Thanksgiving, or do you want me to?"

Her expression lightened. "Men. If I'd waited until now we wouldn't be able to get in anywhere where they have a decent meal. I've reserved a place for the three of us at three. I thought you could come by about two, if that's okay. Tricia will drive up Wednesday evening after school."

"Sounds fine to me. Are you going to tell me where?"

She laughed. "I'm sorry. Didn't I say? At the Cliff House. They do a special Thanksgiving menu, apparently. I asked a friend and that's what she recommended. Does that sound okay?"

"Fine." He ran a toe along the length of her leg. "It's possible you'll have some success with your attempt to get the nurses the right to call ethics consults, Rachel. Our nurses are adamant about it on the psych wards. And Carl is willing to support them if he doesn't run into too much opposition among his troops. A couple of the older guys can't see it; they think nurses are getting more and more uppity."

Rachel shook her head in disbelief. "Nurses are being asked to do more and more responsible things, is what's happening. Your colleagues ought to be ashamed of themselves."

"Not likely. But what they are likely to find is a lot of pressure. I think they'll come around. Or at least enough of them to change things. Not that it's going to keep Carl from giving me a hard time."

"I really am sorry, Jerry."

"Hey, I didn't mean that. He gives me a hard time all the time, if he can think of a way."

"Well, I didn't mean to give him a way."

Their conversation continued in a desultory fashion. Jerry attempted a casual seduction without much ostensible success. And yet, abruptly, Rachel said, "Let's go to bed."

"Now?"

"Yes." She was already climbing out of the hot tub, wrapping the bath sheet around her. "We haven't ever made love here."

"I know," he said, hopping out after her and rubbing himself down with his own towel. "I've been looking forward to it."

When he took her in his arms to kiss her, she responded a little stiffly, but that might have been because they were still outside. Not that anyone could see them, but still. He wove his fingers with hers and drew her inside. She had left only the corner lamp by his reading chair on. The hair at the nape of her neck was damp and he used his towel to dry it, pressing her against himself so she would feel his enthusiasm. She let her bath sheet fall so that they were touching flesh to flesh.

Jerry rained kisses on her, lost in the exciting texture of her skin and the provocative thrust of her breasts. Rachel returned his kisses; she opened her mouth for his eager tongue. His hands and his tongue explored her obvious and hidden resources. Carried along by his desire, Jerry carried her to the bed and lowered her gracefully to the down comforter. Everything about Rachel was still so new, still so unfamiliar, that he chose to discount the warning signal in his head that was blinking a yellow caution light at him.

Her breast tasted so sweet to his tongue. Her inner thighs felt so silken to his fingertips. It was, at last, her expression that captured his attention. Even in the dim light he could see no passion there. A stillness, a suspension of affect, no real presence at all. Jerry sucked in a sharp breath and drew abruptly away from her.

"What's the matter?" Rachel asked, blinking at him.

Jerry took a moment to sort out his thoughts. His body maintained a level of sexual tension that refused to entirely resolve. "I thought we had an agreement," he said, tugging the comforter out from under them. "We weren't going to make love when you didn't want to."

"I wanted to."

He sighed. "No. You thought you should, maybe, but you didn't want to. You didn't feel like it, your body didn't lead the way. Tell me why you thought you should."

For a moment she looked as though she would dispute him again. Then she leaned her head back against the pillow, and he covered her body with the comforter. A tear slid silently down her cheek. "It's what you wanted. I wanted to give you what you wanted. I owe you that."

"No, you owe yourself to be honest with yourself, Rachel. You've had a lot of trouble with this and you're going to have to pay awfully close attention to what you want. I've told you how easy it is for me to get pleasure. You'll have to learn to trust me around that. Okay?"

She nodded, her eyes closed.

Jerry stroked fingers through her hair, massaging her scalp. "It was because you felt guilty about the memo, too, wasn't it? You wanted to make up for that."

She nodded again and another tear crept out of the corner of her eye. "But I don't know why I didn't want to make love. I should have wanted to make love."

"Ah, Rachel, that's one of the mysteries of life. You don't have to be ready to make love at the drop of a pin, sweetheart. I should have known when I heard how hesitant you were about coming over tonight that it was a mistake to press you."

"But I should have wanted to come, Jerry. And I did want to see you."

"You just felt a little trapped, not knowing if you were going to feel like making love and thinking that you 'should'." He caught the tear on her cheek with his thumb and rubbed it away. "Hey, we don't have to get this all worked out in a week, Rachel. We have a lifetime."

Her eyes fluttered open, alarmed.

"Well, we do," he insisted. "We're a good match. I'm crazy about you. Aren't you a little fond of me?"

"You know I am. I think you're . . ." she smiled almost painfully, "the most incredible man. I was thinking on the way over here how much I adore you. But don't you see, Jerry, that that's part of the problem? I don't want you to be unhappy with me. I want to please you, and then everything gets all distorted and confusing. Why should my needs come before yours? Why should I say no just because I don't happen to be in the mood? If I'm in love with you, then I want to give to you, and that includes sexually. But then I might get upset and resentful. Oh, hell. It seems safer just to keep things the way they are. For now."

"Safer maybe. But not necessarily smarter. You have to learn to trust yourself and to trust me so we can make this work out okay for you."

Rachel gave a tiny snort of disgust. "Obviously I can trust you, but I can't trust me."

He stroked her cheek with his thumb. "All these things take time, Rachel. I want us to work on them together. I want us to be partners. Real partners. Maybe even, eventually, married partners."

She shuddered. "Do you know what that does to me, Jerry? Just hearing the word 'marriage' makes my hackles rise. I'm a lawyer by training, and in marriage there's an expectation of sex. You can get an annulment for an inability to have sexual relations. It's almost like you have to have sex in order to obey the law."

He kissed the tip of her nose. "We can make our own laws, Rachel. What the State of California expects we don't need to worry about."

Her breath came out in a long sigh. "I'm sorry, Jerry. It's not because of how I feel about you. Honestly. It's just that I'm afraid. It would be easier for me if we kept things the way they are."

"Living in different places?" he asked, surprised.

"Well, yes. I mean, it's so much easier for me to stand my ground in my own house. You know, if you lived there, well, it would be like you could do whatever you wanted. Wouldn't it?"

"I feel a little hurt that you can't trust me. I'm trying to understand."

"I know you are!" Rachel took possession of his hand and squeezed it tightly. "It's not you I don't trust. I'm asking too much, aren't I? I want everything my own way."

"You're only asking for what you think you need," he admitted. "I don't know if it will mesh perfectly with what I need, Rachel. We'll see, okay? I've pictured going to bed beside you and waking up with you there. I've thought of us living together and sharing a whole lot more than just sex. Sitting on opposite sides of a room—granted your living room—and reading our own books and looking up to smile at each other. You know, that kind of thing."

Rachel was silent for a long time. "You'd miss your hot tub," was all she finally said.

"Actually, I'd thought we could have one built outside your back door, or off the master suite on a deck."

She smiled, but tentatively. "That would be

okay. In fact, let's do it. It's relaxing, the hot tub. I'd be happy to have one there."

"Oh, Rachel," he said, sighing. "Let's not talk anymore about it tonight. You look exhausted. Did you want to go home or spend the night?"

"I wish you wouldn't keep asking me these hard questions."

Which, Jerry realized, meant she wanted to go home, but couldn't bring herself to say so. "I'll walk you down to your car."

Chapter Sixteen

Rachel received two phone calls on Thanksgiving morning. Tricia had called the previous evening to simply say that she wouldn't be able to come up until the morning. When she called on Thanksgiving, at nine in the morning, Rachel could hear in her voice that something was the matter. "Aren't you well, dear?" she asked.

There was a muffled sob. "I'm not sick."

"Tricia! What's the matter?"

"I heard something last night," Tricia said slowly. "I couldn't believe it. So I had to track down the truth. It ... I ... Oh, Mom, I can't belive this. Steve is engaged. To be married."

Steve, her live-in boyfriend whom she'd given an ultimatum. Who rather than marry Tricia, with whom he'd lived for two years, had walked. Regretfully, insisting that he still loved her but wasn't ready for a commitment.

"Oh, Tricia, I'm so sorry. I don't understand, though. It's not that long since he moved out."

"Less than two months," Tricia wailed. "And, Mom, he didn't even know this woman when he left. Didn't even know she existed! How could he do that?"

How indeed? Steve, a nice enough guy, whom

Rachel would not have been disturbed to see as her son-in-law, had certainly moved quickly for a guy unable to make a commitment. But maybe that was the point. "I suppose," Rachel said thoughtfully, "that he regretted his decision, but couldn't go back. That when he met someone he liked, it seemed like a good idea to sew it up right away. Oh, sweetheart, how awful for you."

"What a slap in my face! It's like saying, oh, she was good enough to live with and screw for a couple of years, but now I've found someone worth marrying. I could just kick him."

What could Rachel say? Only the simple, comforting things that mothers always say, that weren't enough compared with the betrayal of a man one has loved. Because it must have felt like a betrayal. Steve had professed to love Tricia right up to the morning he moved his share of their belongings out of the apartment. Poor Tricia.

"So, Mom," her daughter said, hesitantly, "I don't much feel like coming up. You understand, don't you? You and Jerry will enjoy going out to dinner anyhow, won't you?"

"Of course we will, honey. But are you sure that's what you want—to be alone? It might help to be with other people."

"Not Jerry, though. He's a shrink and he'd probably try to analyze me or something."

Rachel laughed. "Oh, I don't think he'd do that, dear. And he's very understanding. But if you want to be alone . . ."

Tricia sighed. "If it was just you, it would be okay. But I don't know. Not with Jerry, too."

Rachel wondered, fleetingly, if Tricia hoped her mother would offer to cancel their date with Jerry.

She was not willing to find out because she had no intention of doing any such thing. This was not, perhaps, the time to tell her daughter about her new relationship with the psychiatrist, however. "I'll call you later and see how you're doing," Rachel said. "I'm sorry I won't be seeing you today, but maybe later in the weekend."

"Maybe. Thanks, Mom. Happy Thanksgiving."

Sighing, Rachel hung up the phone. It rang again before she removed her hand. This time it was Jennifer, calling from her cousin's house. "Happy Thanksgiving, Mom. What are your plans for the day?"

"Hi, sweetie. Dinner out, fortunately." She explained what the plans had been, and what they would now be.

Jennifer gave a tsk of commiseration with her sister. "What a jerk Steve is. I don't know what it is with men. They don't seem to have figured out how to behave like human beings, do they?"

Oh, boy, Rachel thought, I'm about to hear another problem. Jennifer would never admit to being hurt or devastated by her relationship with a man, which didn't mean she wasn't just as hurt or devastated. "What's the matter, honey? Couldn't Fred come with you to Betty's?"

"Oh, it's not that. I uninvited him after what he did."

"What did he do?"

"He told me to quit my job."

"I beg your pardon?"

"Well, last week someone shot at me. It was no big deal, Mom. The guy wasn't trying to kill me or anything. He was just trying to scare me off."

Oh, God, Rachel thought. But unlike Fred she

was smart enough not to appear to interfere. "And Fred thought you should quit because of the danger?"

"As if he had anything to say to it," her daughter replied indignantly. "It's not like I'm a policewoman or something. It's only in fiction that private detectives get shot at all the time."

"But you did get shot at this time."

"Oh, Mom. It was no big deal. And Fred said he couldn't possibly continue seeing me if I was going to be in danger, that it would be too upsetting for him. It was just an excuse."

"Was it?"

"Sure. He's not some wimp. He's taken lots of chances with his life. So either it's that he won't grant me the same opportunity, or he's just using it as an excuse because he's already tired of me."

"Dear Jennifer. He may not mean it at all. It may just be an instinctive move to get you out of danger."

"Well, I'm sorry, but I can't accept that."

No, Jennifer wouldn't be able to accept that. She had always insisted on being accepted on her own terms, and they were strictly egalitarian terms. Rachel should have been happy, in one way. She hadn't been pleased with the prospect of her daughter marrying a man so much older than she. But there was the fear for her daughter's safety that she felt, too, and couldn't really express because of Jennifer's attitude toward overprotectiveness.

How much easier it had been when they were young! Rachel hated to see her daughters in pain. Long gone were the days, though, when she could in some measure protect them. Now she

could only console them and support them and
make certain they knew she loved them and was
there for them. What more could one human being do for another?

When she had hung up, that question continued to dwell in her mind. Wasn't Jerry offering her
all those things? Unlike Steve, he had no trouble
making a commitment to her, in spite of a beautiful younger woman wandering through his life.
And unlike Fred, he was able to accept that she
had some difficult issues to handle and to offer to
stand by her while she learned to cope with them.
It was she who was having trouble committing
herself to him in a meaningful way.

Rachel continued to mull over this concept as
she tidied the house, wandering from room to
room, picturing Jerry there, trying to get a handle
on how it would feel. When it was finally time to
dress, she chose a fall suit he had once mentioned
that he thought attractive. God, that seemed a
long time ago. And she put on her makeup carefully, constantly checking in the mirror to be sure
she wasn't overdoing it. And just a whiff of per-
fume, walked into the way her mother had taught
her when she was much younger than Tricia. She
felt young, suddenly, excited and full of a prickly
kind of anticipation.

At two o'clock she went to sit in the living
room. At two-ten she picked up a book and read
to distract herself. Jerry was sometimes late, un-
avoidably. Usually he called, but there might have
been an emergency. At two-thirty she dialed his
number and his phone rang and rang. Funny that
his machine wasn't on. But he obviously wasn't
there, which must mean he was on his way.

Only it got to be two-forty-five and Jerry hadn't arrived. Rachel didn't know whether to be concerned or upset. This was so unlike him. She dialed his number again, with the same results. She even tried his pager number, but there was no answering call. Finally, at almost three, she called the hospital.

"He's not on call today, Ms. Weis," the nurse explained. "I haven't seen him around. Want me to ask if anyone has?"

"Please." Rachel held on while she heard conversations in the background. In a while the nurse returned to say, "I'm sorry. No one seems to have heard from him. He didn't even check in about his worst patients. Which he usually does. But then, it's a holiday."

Rachel thanked her and hung up. It was after three by now and she called the restaurant to cancel their reservation. What was happening here? An icy fear was beginning to build under the surface anger she felt at being stood up. Jerry would not do that. He simply wouldn't. If he had changed his mind, if he had decided that he never wanted to see her again, he would have called. So why hadn't he?

Rachel dialed his number once again and listened to the phone ring, and ring and ring. Had he had an accident on the way over? A minor one he would have called about, a major one . . . Rachel could feel her heart start to beat faster as fear gripped her. She paced through the downstairs, trying to calm herself. This was foolish. The chances of his having had a bad accident were really very small. It was a five-minute drive from his condo to her house, with nothing but city neighborhoods in between. No freeways, no major thoroughfares. Besides, he hadn't called the hospital at all that day. If he was going to call to check on patients, he would probably have done it early in the morning so that he could go in to check on them if necessary.

What was going on here?

Rachel strode into the kitchen, where the afternoon sun gleamed into the corners of the open shelving. In a shaft of light an onyx box caught her eye and awoke a memory. Inside were keys to people's houses. Her neighbors on the right, the ones catty-cornered to her. Even a key to Tricia's apartment—for an emergency. Rachel couldn't remember if she still had a key of Jerry's. She lifted the onyx box down from the shelf and poured the contents on the countertop. Most of the keys were marked, in some way, with ribbons or tags. Two of them weren't.

Once, last year, he had gone away for a week to an APA conference and had left her a spare key, just in case. Was one of these it? Or had she given it back when he'd returned? She had never used his key. He had no plants to water or pets to feed. Rachel picked up the two keys and rubbed them anxiously between her fingers. Was it worth going over there to try them? What if he called and she was gone? Well, she thought with a gusty sigh, she'd get his message when she returned. Enough of this hesitation. She was going to act.

As she drove the minivan through the twisting streets of Forest Hills she reminded herself how young he was, really. The chances that he'd had a heart attack or a stroke were very small. Then why hadn't he called? Well, perhaps he'd fallen in the shower and struck his head. Sure, and lay there bleeding to death, she sniped at herself. How long did one stay unconscious from a blow to the head? Maybe he'd surprised a burglar and been shot dead.

Just a minute, she scolded herself. This is ridiculous. He's perfectly all right. Just something has happened that made him unable to come or call. Like what? What could have caused his absence that wasn't perfectly disastrous? Something, she thought. Always it turned out to be something simple, explainable. Try not to panic. You're almost there.

Rachel didn't know whether to be thrilled or distraught when she saw through a window that Jerry's car was parked in his usual parking space under the building. With shaking fingers she tried the first key in the front door of the apartment building. It didn't work. She tried the second key, but it didn't seem to work, either. Relax, she insisted. You could ring a neighbor. Or maybe the superintendent is here, and he'd let you into Jerry's place because you're worried. Rachel found that she was trying each key again, and the second one, jiggled slightly, did seem to slide in, and eventually to release the door.

She rode the elevator up to the third floor. There was no one else around. She almost wanted there to be someone. She could say, "Come in with me. I'm afraid something is wrong." But she found herself, alone, in front of Jerry's door. The same key, she knew, would open it and let her in.

With trembling fingers she inserted the key, turned it, pushed open the door. "Jerry?" she called, softly at first, as though she might be interrupting him, and then louder, "Jerry!" The hallway and the living room beyond were empty, and not very tidy. Rachel hadn't known he was untidy when he wasn't expecting anyone. There were books and papers on several surfaces, an open briefcase on a footstool. Or maybe he'd been interrupted in the midst of his work. "Jerry?"

The door to his bedroom was partially closed and Rachel's heart seemed to be thumping in her throat as she pushed it inward. "Jerry?"

It was dark in the room and she reached to flick on the overhead light. In the sudden brightness she was aware of only two things: A great lump of comforter on the bed and a stainless steel bowl on the floor beside the bed. She took two steps toward the bed and a disagreeable smell assaulted her. Fear rose another notch. "Jerry?"

There was a muffled noise from under the rumpled lump of comforter. As she moved another step closer she could see the top of Jerry's head poking out from under the fabric. She could also see that in the stainless-steel bowl there was vomit. "Jerry, are you sick?"

There was a long pause before his deep voice said, "I must be. Is that you, Rachel?"

"Yes. I've let myself in. I was worried about you."

Another long pause. "I didn't call you, then?"

"No. But it's all right." She was close enough to see his expression now. He looked puzzled.

"I remember trying," he said. "This morning. Is it still morning?"

"No."

"Oh, God. I missed Thanksgiving, didn't I?"

"It doesn't matter, Jerry." She placed the back of

her fingers against his forehead. It was burning. "Let me get a cold towel and some aspirin for you, okay?"

"I tried to get up. A couple times. I must have fallen asleep."

"Do you think it's something we should take you to Fielding for?"

Jerry snorted. "It was that little shit of a surgery resident."

"I'm sorry. You've lost me."

"John What's-his-name. Cliff sent him. He was out yesterday. I should have known."

"Known what?"

"No surgery resident takes the day off unless he's deathly sick. He gave me this, the little jerk."

"You can hardly blame him, Jerry."

"I can if I want to," Jerry retorted sullenly. Then he fell silent.

Thinking he'd fallen asleep again, Rachel picked up the bowl and cleaned it out in the bathroom. Then she soaked a hand towel in cold water and wrung it out. In the medicine cabinet she found a bottle of aspirin and shook two of them into her hand. Together with a glass of water, she carried everything back into Jerry's bedroom. He had rolled over onto his back, and he looked wretched. His face was flushed and a good growth of graying beard powdered his chin and cheeks. His eyes looked sunken and there were bags under them. Rachel wanted very much to kiss him. But she restrained herself, propping him up to offer the aspirin.

"Take these. They'll help get that fever down."

"Who's the doctor here?" he grumbled. Water spilled down one corner of his cheek and Rachel wiped it up with the towel. When he laid back down against the pillow she placed the towel on his forehead. "That feels great," he said.

"I'll change it in a few minutes."

He was sound asleep by the time she did that, and for the next several changes as well. After a few hours his face didn't look as flushed. Rachel would have taken his temperature but she couldn't find a thermometer. Knowing that he'd need some liquids to replenish his fluids, she had a glass of ice water ready when he awoke the next time. "Drink it up," she advised.

"You've been hanging around hospitals too long."

"Probably. I think you'll live."

"But where?" he asked, a quizzical gleam in his fevered eyes. "If I stay here I might die all by myself."

"I doubt it."

"But you wouldn't want to take a chance, would you?"

"No." Rachel ran her fingers through his disheveled hair. "No, I don't want to take any chances of losing you."

"Ah, good." He kissed her wrist with hot, dry lips. And proceeded to fall asleep again, his breathing easier now, his face relaxed into a slight smile.

By late in the evening Jerry had recovered enough to accompany Rachel home so she could keep an eye on him all night. He wasn't well enough to work in the morning, but mostly now he seemed to need only occasional attention. Rachel worked at home Friday morning, and was called in for a brief ethics consult in the afternoon. When she returned she found Jerry sitting up in bed with a mystery she'd left on the night table.

"I like it here," he said.

"Good. You want to stay?"

"How long am I being invited for?"

"I like having you here. I liked knowing you'd be here when I got home."

He patted the bed beside himself. "Does that answer my question?"

"Yes." She bent over to kiss him gently. "Can we compromise, Jerry? I love you and I don't want you to question my commitment to you. I'd like you to live here and have this be your home as much as it is mine. But I'd like us not to get married. Not now. Maybe ever. Could you do that?"

He nodded, and drew her tight against his chest, his chin resting on the top of her head. "As long as you love me, and we agree on a commitment, the rest isn't so important. Your kids won't be shocked, will they?"

"Who knows?" She leaned back to meet his eyes. "We're the ones who decide about this, Jerry. Just you and me. Together. For always."

He traced her lips with a gentle finger. "For always. I feel very lucky, Rachel."

She drew a shaky breath. "Me, too, Jerry. Me, too."

Here's a chapter
from the next novel in
Elizabeth Neff Walker's
Fielding Medical Center quartet,
Fever Pitch,
coming in August 1995.

S teve stopped outside the open door of the office where he could see Nan LeBaron seated at one of two desks. Unfortunately, there was someone seated at the other one as well, and he didn't wish their conversation to be public. He stood in the doorway, knocked on the doorframe and said, "Dr. LeBaron, I wonder if I could speak with you a minute."

"Sure. I tried to return your call yesterday." Nan waved him to a seat but he shook his head.

"Could you walk with me to the lecture hall? I have to give a talk there in a few minutes."

Though she seemed reluctant, the neurology fellow put down her pen and rose. "I only have ten minutes until an appointment," she said.

"Won't take long." When she fell into step beside him, he started for the doors at the end of the hall. "It's about the depositions. I think we should talk about the case before we each have to give our depositions."

"Actually, that's exactly what you're not supposed to do, according to a book I was reading. You want us to coordinate our story?" she asked, her hazel eyes sparkling.

"I don't know how you can take this so casually,

Dr. LeBaron. Our reputations are at stake." He pushed the door open into the stairwell and allowed her to precede him. "And I don't want us to coordinate our stories. I just want to see if we both remember the case the same way. It was some time ago."

"And we've both gone over the records interminably."

"Not interminably. Carefully. Everything is very well documented."

"Yes," she agreed, descending the stairs side by side with him. "The only problem is that we disagreed, and the patient died."

"You think that was my fault."

"Look, Dr. Winstead. I know the mortality figures for stroke as well as anyone: forty-five percent at one month. Not great odds. And the breakdown for strokes, eighty-five percent caused by clots and fifteen percent by bleeds, made it more likely that you were right, since you thought it was a clot. I saw signs that it was a bleed."

"But there was the left-hand and body weakness and right-facial weakness of a classic crossed syndrome. We'd have known a hell of a lot more if the other emergency hadn't coopted the MRI."

"I know." Nan held the door for him this time as they came out on the first floor of the east wing. "I realize the CAT scan showed no bleeding, but you know as well as I do that sometimes they're too small to show up, or that it might have taken longer for a bleed to show."

"And if it was a clot, the heparin might have saved him."

"An autopsy would have shown if there was a further bleed caused by the heparin you gave."

"But they didn't want one, then. It might have saved us all a lot of trouble."

They had reached the door of the lecture hall and Steve glanced at his watch. Still a few minutes. "There's legitimate debate about how to treat stroke. You've probably treated plenty of patients with heparin."

"Of course I have. I wouldn't have in this case."

Steve remembered her urgent insistence that he reconsider his decision. But she'd only been a third-year resident then—knowledgeable, yes, but relatively inexperienced yet. His experience had supported his conviction that it was a clot, and perhaps it had been, already broken down by time. He was trained to respond quickly, aggressively to save lives. There was a heavy toll in that. Human beings were bound to make mistakes, even well-trained and skillful human beings, because medicine was not an exact science, but partly an art. You couldn't always know what was going on in a human body. And in emergency work you had to make constant split-second decisions. If they were wrong, someone could die. Over time those catastrophes mounted.

His companion was watching him, perhaps evaluating the nature of his silence. "Are you worried that I'm going to try to make you look bad in my deposition?"

Steve shook his head in wonder. "I like your directness, Dr. LeBaron. Yes, I suppose that's exactly what I'm worried about."

"You didn't breech the standard of care any more than I would have. It's your emergency room, you had a perfect right to make the final decision."

"They can make any disagreement between doctors look bad."

She shrugged. "So what? We'll have lawyers who know how to defend against that kind of distortion."

"They can argue that we might have waited."

"Waiting could have meant death as well."

A medical student squeezed past Steve through the door into the lecture hall. "I've got to get in there," Steve said, glancing again at his watch. "Just don't let them pressure you into saying things you don't mean, okay?"

Nan bowed her head and said meekly, "Yes, doctor."

Steve could see the glint in her eyes, but couldn't tell whether it was amusement or anger. Who was this woman? Maybe he needed to know her better to protect himself. "Thanks for talking with me. Maybe we can compare notes after our depositions."

"Maybe."

As she walked away from him, he fervently wished that they gave their depositions at the same time, where he could cover for any mistakes she made, fill any holes she left in their defense. Though Steve was challenged by unknown disease in a patient, he felt very uncomfortable with a person as unknown quantity, especially when his reputation might be at stake. Dr. LeBaron, who obviously didn't take this whole matter very seriously, could be a real threat to him. He watched her tall form recede down the hallway, her blond French braid looking as casually constrained as she was herself, and he felt a twinge of dismay.

In the cafeteria Nan carried her tray to the open deck area where only a few braved the mild December day. Nan herself welcomed a breath of fresh air after the antiseptic smell of the clinic she'd just finished. To her delight, her former roommate, Angel Crawford, soon joined her at the gritty table.

"You sure know how to pick your days to sit outside," Angel complained.

"It just feels like fall. Don't you like fall?"

"I love fall." Angel grinned at her and set her own tray with its large salad and whole wheat roll down beside Nan's. "I've got news for you."

Nan raised curious brows. "What? Is Cliff behaving himself?"

"You might say that." Angel tucked herself onto the metal chair and sighed. "I'm pregnant, Nan."

Tears pricked at Nan's eyes. "Oh, Angel, how wonderful! Wouldn't you know you'd be able to get pregnant at the drop of a hat."

"That's not *quite* how it happened, but I do feel very lucky."

Nan reached over to give her friend's hand a warm grip. "I'll bet Cliff is thrilled."

"He is. He grumbles about my having to work so hard to finish the family practice residency, but, hell, this year's so much easier than the last two that it feels like it's going to be manageable."

"And no doubt Cliff will make it easier by waiting on you hand and foot when you're at home," Nan teased.

"He's getting pretty good at meshing his hours with mine, so we eat out a lot." Angel speared a cherry tomato and popped it in her mouth. After a while she said thoughtfully, "We're going to Wisconsin for a few days over Christmas. I hope to hell he likes it."

"Yeah. It could be a problem if he doesn't."

But Cliff had promised that they would go back there to live, because it was what Angel wanted to do, and they both knew he'd keep his promise. Angel sighed and looked out over the view of the Golden Gate Bridge. "Probably we'll both miss it here."

Afraid that her friend was weakening, Nan said, "Now don't forget why you want to go back, Angel. Wisconsin is where you can practice medicine the way you've always dreamed, being the modern version of the old family doc. It's a great dream. Cliff will do fine in his university setting. In fact he should love being a big fish in a smaller pond."

"I hope so." Angel returned her gaze to her friend's face. "Did Roger move in?"

"Last night. He has a lot of nervous energy, but he's a nice guy. He said he slept just fine, so maybe this is what he needs for a while. He's talking about taming the back yard."

"He'll need a machete and a flame thrower," Angel said.

Nan shrugged. "If it'll help him. Angel, do you know an E.R. doc named Steve Winstead?"

"Sure. He was my attending when I did my rotation in the E.R. last year. Super competent, abundant energy, abrupt, standoffish in a social way. I hear he's rich."

"Apparently everyone's heard he's rich. We've both been named in a malpractice suit over a patient who died a couple of years ago."

"Hell, I'd hoped that had been settled. I'm sorry, Nan. That's such a drag."

"I don't mind so much. Rachel has promised to give me some tips. But this guy seems to mind a lot. Well, maybe not that. He seems to be worried that I'll screw things up for him."

"As I recall it wasn't a question of either of you doing anything wrong. Just a judgment call."

"On which we disagreed."

"That happens." Angel regarded her curiously. "He's not putting pressure on you, is he?"

"We've just had a little talk, but I'm not sure I like his attitude. He was polite enough. There was just this undercurrent that he couldn't trust me. Rather annoying."

"Don't let it bother you. That's just the way he is, Nan. He makes everyone feel like they're a little rough around the edges at times. But he was generous with his positive feedback to the residents, too, so they respected him." Angel grinned. "And he's cute."

"You old married women aren't supposed to notice things like that."

"I wasn't married when he was my attending. Neither was he, for that matter. But I never heard of his dating anyone around the hospital."

"There are plenty of other people to date in San Francisco."

"So there are. Tell me about your Christmas plans."

Nan's Christmas plans, as she'd informed Roger, included the invasion of her parents and her two brothers. Periodically during the three and a half years Nan had been in San Francisco her family had come, en masse, to visit her. They never objected to her long hours on duty or her inability to spend massive amounts of time with them. What they did do, rather unnervingly, was storm the hospital to see "where she worked." While any family might have done this, most would have been relatively discreet in their foray, asking for a chance to visit her shared office, to peek at the layout of her clinic, to have a meal in the medical center cafeteria. Not the LeBarons.

The LeBarons were from Oklahoma, and they wanted everyone to know. They took pride in their state, and in their town. Before Nan was born her father had worked in the oil industry, honest hard labor and small-time managerial positions. Through a fluke her parents had inherited a small piece of land complete with mineral rights, which her father insisted on prospecting for the liquid gold. And he'd found it, much to everyone's surprise. Several oil wells now supported the entire family in a style to which the elder LeBarons had grown accustomed, far outstripping their neighbors in wealth.

The money was a two-edged sword for the Lebronskis. Long before Nan was old enough to know her own name, it had been changed to LeBaron, a name her father had taken a fancy to because it spoke to him of foreign elegance. Going from a relatively simple household to one of consumption had carried its obligations. The LeBarons treated the neighborhood to extravagant parties. They hired nephews and nieces to work for their small company. They had wealth that said they were among the richest families in Oklahoma. And yet they had no concept of real elegance. They were what Nan had heard referred to as the nouveau riche, and a prime example of the breed.

And they were wonderful people. A lesser child, entering the sophisticated world of medicine and San Francisco, would have been ashamed of them. Nan held them in real esteem, having a realistic appreciation of both their intrinsic value and the way her new world viewed them. Peter, for instance, had been instantly put off when Nan's father had asked him how much he'd paid for his house. Mr. LeBaron was curious about such things and never hesitated to ask, feeling that one had nothing to hide in answering such a simple, uncomplicated question. He'd been puzzled by Peter's unwillingness to answer. And hurt by Peter's even greater reluctance to allow the LeBarons to visit his architectural firm. Obviously Peter was not looking forward to another visit from the LeBarons. Perhaps, Nan thought, that might explain his sudden pulling back from her life.

During the first week of Roger's stay in her flat she didn't see Peter at all, though she talked to him on the phone twice. Finally he showed up to take her to a movie one evening, but brought her back immediately afterwards. Roger was just arriving home as they drove up in front of the building. Nan climbed out of Peter's Acura Legend and waited for Peter to get out so she could introduce the two men.

Roger shook the younger man's hand. "Nice to meet you. It was good of Nan to let me live here. I'll try to stay out of the way."

"Oh, I'm not coming up," Peter assured him, much to Nan's chagrin. "I have to get some work done before I hit the sack." He gave Nan a peck on the cheek, waved a casual good-bye and drove off.

Nan very much wanted to blame Roger for this defection, but she suspected he'd only proved a good excuse. With a tsk of annoyance she began to climb the three flights of stairs. Roger trailed after her, coming at such a slow pace that Nan turned to observe his reluctance when she had reached the front door. She was surprised to see his troubled expression.

"What's the matter, Roger? Aren't you feeling well?" She slid her key in the lock and pushed open the door. The entry was inky black since neither of them had been home earlier to leave a light on. Nan groped for the switch on the wall, and the light snapped on, catching Roger in a blatant attempt to marshal his expression. "Something *is* the matter. Please tell me. Maybe I can help."

"No, no. It's nothing. I'm fine. It doesn't have anything to do with me."

A curious thing for him to say, Nan thought as she tossed her purse on the hall stand. "Who does it have to do with?"

"That's not what I meant. Really, it was just a stupid thought I had. I'm sure I'm wrong."

Nan remained standing in the entry as Roger edged toward the hall, tugging agitatedly at his left ear. "What are you wrong about?"

"Nothing. Well, I mean, I'm off to my room. A lot of stuff to put away still, you know? See you in the morning."

"Sleep well." But the more Nan thought about it, the more she became convinced that there was something Roger wasn't telling her. There was that edge of guilt to his look, his desperate attempt to disappear. Definitely he was not being frank with her. And Nan very much suspected that it had something to do with Peter. Why else the prodigious frown as Peter had pulled away? Nan had thought at the time that Roger didn't approve of Acura Legends.

His door was already closed and she tapped lightly on it. "Roger? You better tell me. I have a feeling I need to know."

With hesitant steps he returned to the door and inched it open. "I could be wrong," he said. "I'd hate to be wrong and cause you a lot of worry."

"Oh, hell, just tell me. I like things out in the open."

He swung the door the rest of the way open and waved her to the only chair in the room, a wicker basket type with a bright cushion on it that he'd brought from his house. Beside it on a table was one of several pictures of Kerri that he'd also brought. He took a seat on the end of his bed. His expression was pained. "Look, I hate to be the one to tell you this. It seems terribly unfair after what you've done for me."

"It's about Peter."

"Yeah. I've seen him before, but I didn't know who he was, you know?"

Nan could feel her stomach muscles tighten. "When had you seen him?"

"It must have been a week ago, and I happened to see him twice in the space of a few days. That's why I remembered. That and the way he breathes, you know? Patients like that are hard to intubate.

I was just thinking at the time that I hoped he never showed up in my O.R."

"Where did you see him?"

Roger scratched the bridge of his nose. "The first time at the Galleria in Stonestown, standing in front of Victoria's Secret."

"And he wasn't alone."

"No."

"He was with a woman who didn't look like his mother."

Roger smiled briefly. "Right. She could have been his sister, if he has one, of course. But he took her in to buy something."

"And the second time you saw him?"

"He was with the same woman, in line at the Kabuki. They were . . . kissing."

"Oh, hell." Nan leaned back in the chair and rubbed her temples. "I knew he'd been drawing back, but I'm always such a sucker for trusting someone. Why don't people just tell you? It's so much more decent, and less painful in the long run."

"I'm sorry, Nan. Really, I am. But I'm dead certain it was him. You know how someone just catches your attention."

"Yeah, I know. No, I appreciate your telling me. Much better that I know. I was fond of him." She rose tiredly from the chair, which squeaked in protest. For a moment she stood lost in thought, and then she blinked her eyes and said, "But I wasn't in love with him. Maybe that's why he did it. I think Peter wanted to be loved, to be adored. Well, maybe this woman does. Good night, Roger."

"Good night, Nan."

Purposefully she strode up the hall, closed her

bedroom door behind her and picked up the phone. It was a difficult, painful, ten-minute discussion, and when it was over she hung the phone up gently. Funny how a few minutes can change your life, she thought, dry-eyed but tense. She had begun to think of Peter in the long term. Foolish of her, of course. Her attachment to him had been real, but not as strong as she would have expected for their having seen each other for almost a year. Still, he was familiar, he was fun, he was a good lover, and he didn't know a damn thing about medicine. All very fine qualities in a man.

In two months she'd be thirty.

Her family was coming for Christmas.

And Nan was in the midst of a malpractice suit.

Since the Emergency Department at Fielding Medical Center was always chaotic, Steve had decided not to have his deposition taken there. Instead he drove to downtown San Francisco, and parked under the Bank of America building. The attorney hired by his malpractice insurance company had offices high up in the building and the high-speed elevator ascended so rapidly he thought of scuba divers and getting the bends. The offices themselves, he deduced, were an interior decorator's modern interpretation of the sun-baked, earthen-colored simple forms of early Rome. There were mini-columns and glass vistas into offices that looked out over the city and the bay. There were conference rooms with endlessly long marble tables and high-backed, uncompromising chairs. The whole pretentious setting made Steve want to laugh.

The partner who was handling his part of the

suit was Fillmore Rush, an unlikely name that sounded more like it belonged to an actor. Rush was a tall, solidly built man of middle years, graying elegantly at the temples and always dressed impeccably in suits that hinted of foreign tailoring. Steve imagined that he was a very expensive attorney, and probably very good at what he did.

Rush had assured him on their first meeting in the medical center director's office that physicians typically felt betrayed, threatened, and vulnerable when they were sued for malpractice. No lie, Steve had wanted to respond. But he'd kept his thoughts to himself. He remembered the family of the deceased very well indeed, and he thought he had explained everything to them quite clearly at the time of the death. They had seemed to understand. But they'd gone out to hire an attorney to sue him, and Dr. LeBaron, and everyone else in sight. Which, the attorney assured him, was the usual way a medical malpractice case was handled.

Steve didn't care how they were usually handled. He would have felt a lot better if he'd never found out. It was no help that half a dozen of his colleagues had discussed their own malpractice suits with him in an effort to ease his frustration. He could not rid himself of the idea that most malpractice cases were simply an exercise in making fees for lawyers. And his attitude, though not uncommon among physicians, was of no help to him in dealing not only with the opposition lawyer, but his own.

Fillmore Rush escorted him into the conference room with the impossibly long marble table and introduced him to the opposition attorney, Robert

Whiting, and the court stenographer, Pamela Torres. Rush had explained to Steve that this was the discovery portion of the lawsuit, and that the deposition was the main vehicle employed. He would be questioned under oath by the opposing party, which his lawyer assured him was a good thing. Oh, sure, he thought as he set his briefcase on the table and took a chair. But he had learned over a long time to keep his expression impassive and his mind in high gear when faced with unfamiliar situations.

What they would discover, Fillmore Rush had explained, was just what facts the other side knew. What he hadn't said, but Steve obviously understood, was that Rush would also learn how good an impression Steve was likely to make in court. Steve knew he could be persuasive, and he knew he could control his emotions under the intensity of the courtroom cross-examination. But he hated to be caught off guard, and that was exactly what happened a half hour into the deposition.

"Did you tell the family that an autopsy would be useful?" Robert Whiting asked, in his calm yet pointed fashion.

"I did. It's something I always do."

Steve noticed that his attorney almost imperceptibly shook his head. Right. The first rule of testifying, apparently, was that you never volunteered more information than you were asked for, even if it sounded like you were saving your own butt. He made eye contact with Fillmore to show that he'd understood.

"Even though the family was visibly upset, you suggested an autopsy?" the opposing counsel asked.

"Yes."

Fillmore smiled beneficently at him.

"Tell me, Dr. Winstead, why did you think an autopsy would be useful?"

"It's always helpful to know the exact nature of a disease that kills someone. Also, we're a teaching hospital and autopsies are teaching tools for medical students, residents, and clinicians."

"So you had no personal interest in the results?"

"I'm not sure I understand what you're asking."

"Didn't you want to find out if you had made a mistake?" Whiting asked.

Steve could think of several answers to that particular question. The one that sprang first to mind was that it bore a striking resemblance to the age-old When did you stop beating your wife? But Fillmore Rush had explained quite patiently the preceding day on the phone that in giving evidence the rule was to clarify the question if necessary, not to stall but to get on with answering the question. "No, my purpose in suggesting an autopsy was not to find out if I'd made a mistake."

"Would an autopsy have identified whether the stroke was caused by a bleed or a clot?"

"Probably. If the clot was older, it might have already broken down and been harder to identify."

"But the family refused to agree to an autopsy, didn't they?" the opposing attorney asked.

"Yes. They were adamant."

"And there was no doubt in your mind that death was caused by a cerebrovascular accident?"

"None."

"But you were not the physician who signed the death certificate, were you?"

"No. I believe Dr. LeBaron signed the death certificate."

"Why would that have been?"

"We both consulted on the case and were familiar with its details. I had other emergencies to attend to and Dr. LeBaron agreed to handle the paperwork." Steve felt certain that had been the progression, since it was the ordinary way things happened in the emergency room.

"But it was you who spoke with the family first?"

First? What did he mean by first? Steve frowned slightly. "I spoke with the family, yes."

"Why was that, if Dr. LeBaron handled the paperwork and was familiar with the details of the 'case'?"

Steve knew that people outside the medical field detested the way physicians referred to cases and illnesses without seeming to assign humanity to them. Very deliberately he said, "I had met Mr. Murphy's wife when he was brought in. She answered a number of questions about the circumstances of his illness before going to wait outside the Emergency Department."

"Did you and Dr. LeBaron disagree about how to handle Mr. Murphy's case?" Whiting asked.

Don't hurry your answer, Fillmore Rush had told him. So Steve let a moment pass as he thought how best to respond. A simple yes was obviously not enough in this instance. "We disagreed about the cause of Mr. Murphy's stroke. The CAT scan showed no bleeding, and we were unable to check that finding on the MRI because the equipment wasn't available."

That should cover it, he thought. But the opposing attorney came back quickly with, "What would an MRI have shown?"

"That would be speculation," Fillmore Rush interceded. "Dr. Winstead can't know what a scan would have shown."

And for a while they quibbled about how to phrase the question so that Steve could answer it. He followed their discussion with only half his mind. There was something here that hadn't been clarified, something he needed to know. If he'd been the first one to speak with the family, who had been the second? Is that what Whiting had meant? When the two attorneys had decided on a proper course of examination, Steve filled in all the technical detail requested, but his curiosity was aroused. At the completion of the deposition he waited impatiently for the other attorney and the court reporter to leave so that he could speak alone with Fillmore Rush.

The senior partner took him into an office with a panoramic view over the north and east of San Francisco. Clouds scudded across the sky making bands of shadow race over the buildings below. It would be nice, Steve thought, to work in such a setting instead of a windowless, oppressively sterile white suite of rooms. But he wouldn't have been an attorney, like his father, for all the money on earth.

"You handled that exceptionally well," Fillmore complimented him. "You'll make a good witness, as long as you maintain that air of frankness you had just now. It's very hard for the other side to batter down that kind of impression."

Steve thanked him but asked, "What did he

mean, asking if I was the first to speak with the family? Did someone else speak with them?"

The older man pursed his lips. "I don't have the transcript of Dr. LeBaron's deposition yet. Is it possible she spoke with them?"

"I can't see why. I had already done it."

"Hmm." Fillmore made a note on his legal pad, where he'd jotted a number of things during the deposition. "I'll be sure to check it. Do you want me to give you a call when I find out?"

"I'll speak with her myself."

"That might not be wise."

Restlessly Steve rose to his feet and picked up his briefcase. "Oh, I'm sure it won't be a problem, Fillmore. Dr. LeBaron is a very easygoing sort of person. She won't mind my curiosity."

His attorney looked skeptical, but rose along with him and offered his hand. "Still, I'll give you a call when I've read her transcript."

"Good idea."

Steve checked his watch as he left the ersatz sunbaked Rome offices. Almost noon. Dr. LeBaron might be free. He picked up his car phone and had her paged.